don't
ever tell

BOOKS BY LUCY DAWSON

don't ever tell

LUCY DAWSON

bookouture

Published by Bookouture in 2019

An imprint of StoryFire Ltd.

Carmelite House
50 Victoria Embankment
London EC4Y 0DZ

www.bookouture.com

ISBN: 978-1-78681-965-9
eBook ISBN: 978-1-78681-964-2

For James, for everything.

PROLOGUE

As I open the front door, the birds are chattering, the shrubs and trees in my parents' garden are glowing honey-gold in the sunrise, but while the air smells invitingly fresh and crisp, I scan The Close anxiously. The neighbours' curtains are still shut, everything looks normal, dewdrops are *sparkling* on my father's neatly cut lawn – it's all calm, but… there. I stop suddenly. I can feel it. They're already coming for me. A shiver of panic whispers over my skin and small hairs lift on my arms. I take a barefoot step over the threshold and glance across at the parked-up cars; windscreens covered in condensation, the little boy's bike left out on its side in the drive next door – wheels motionless in the air, handlebar bell silent. My glance shifts through the gap between the houses down towards the distant sea and the silver slice of water glinting brightly. I'd never make it there in time. They are already on their way. This quiet corner of town will soon be swarming. There will be nowhere to hide, no shadow to creep into – the light is going to reach everywhere. They WILL find me.

Breath leaves my body in a short exclamation of fear and I begin desperately to pick my way over the sharp gravel path to my father's car, ignoring the dig of stones in the soft soles of my feet. I have to try and escape. I have to do *something*, however futile it seems. I reach the bonnet and extend a hand to pull off the cover Dad has carefully placed across the windscreen to prevent frost forming. But as I lift the shiny corner of the foil-like material, it buzzes and comes to life in my hands; the wing of a fly. The car is completely covered in a dense layer of bluebottles that I have now disturbed. They rise into the air and start to swarm about me. Within seconds, I can feel them crawling over my legs, in my hair, on my ears – I scream, but quickly close my mouth when I sense one on my lips. I flap about wildly and move backwards, but it makes no difference. They follow. I fold my hands in over my head to protect myself and drop to the ground, huddling into a little ball. The noise of a thousand beating wings grows louder and louder still. It will not stop…

I gasp and jolt awake, scratching at my skin and raking my hands through my hair – but there are no flies. For a brief second the relief is enormous. I put my hand out and feel something spiky beneath my palm. I realise it's the doormat and I'm lying on the floor. What am I doing out in the hall? Sitting up stiffly I look around me in confusion. It's freezing, barely light and my mouth is dry. I blink and my head throbs in response. Oh God… the contents of my stomach begin to churn and a bubble of gas pops at the back of my throat as I haul myself to the wall and lean heavily on it. I drank so much last night, too fast. Why do I do this to myself? I close my eyes to get the energy together and wobble to a stand, but yelp aloud as the buzzer goes off right above my head again. Someone is leaning on the bell, *demanding* to be let in. Who can that be, at… whatever time it is right now? I reach my hands out, patting the ground for my phone. Thankfully, I find it – there have been plenty of nights when I haven't been so lucky – and pressing the home button it lights up and informs me it's half past eight in the morning. Saturday, the tenth of November.

The buzzing starts again and I groan, covering my ears and closing my eyes. I lay my cheek against the wall but the vibration of the bell goes right through me. I put my hands on my head to stop it throbbing. Just go away, whoever you are. I'm cold and I'm going to be sick. I cover my mouth with my hand instead – but urgh, what is that smell? It's like someone has spilt a jar of pennies. The air is full of metal. I blink again and look down the dark hallway through into the sitting room. There is a large lump on the floor.

Everything else falls away as I stare at the lifeless body. I lift my head slowly and as it comes into sharper focus, I cover my hand with my mouth and gag again.

That smell is blood.

CHAPTER ONE

CHARLOTTE

The first time I met her was at the Edinburgh book festival last year, in August 2017. I'd been asked to fill a spot on a panel as someone else had dropped out at the last minute. I'd not wanted to go, but Tris persuaded me that it was the sort of opportunity I ought to be grabbing with both hands.

'You don't network enough.' He didn't look up, frowning at his laptop as he worked at the kitchen table while I cooked supper. 'You need to be doing more of this stuff, treating your books like a business – getting yourself out there and meeting other writers, editors, influencers. You're never going to raise your profile until you start being proactive.'

'It's all right for you, you're good at it. You *like* presentations and public speaking.' I opened a jar of pasta sauce and slung it in the saucepan. 'The entire wedding party told me on Saturday that yours was the funniest best-man speech they'd ever heard.'

Tris looked delighted. 'It *was* good. But I didn't just wing it. I prepared – and we'll prepare you too. You'll be great.'

'No, I won't. I'll say something accidentally inappropriate or offensive that will get plastered all over Twitter – or I'll just be dull. No one ever wants the understudy.' I sighed, put my head back in despair, and then reached for my glass of wine. 'I hate this. I wish they'd just not asked me.'

'No, you don't,' Tris said. 'I'll come too, it'll be fun, we'll go and see some of the other festival stuff while we're there. When was the last time we had a weekend away just the two of us?' He looked up pointedly.

'It'll be a load of book people.'

He shrugged. 'So? I like books. It'll be fine. Don't worry, I won't trail you around everywhere like a sad act. I'll amuse myself and just be there in the background if you need someone to talk to. I'll ask Mum and Dad to come and stay a couple of nights with the kids. They'll be thrilled. They've offered enough—'

'*Two* nights?' I said anxiously.

'It'll be fine,' he replied. 'Fly late on Friday, come back Sunday. I'm not going all that way for one morning. I'll book the flights now.'

He'd not taken no for an answer. In the end, the panel itself went OK. I remember the room laughing at something I said – and I sat up tall and smiled like I did this sort of thing all the time, when rather humiliatingly it was only the second time in ten years that I'd been asked to speak at an event.

Afterwards though, the three other authors I'd shared a stage with, and I, were ushered into a side room to take a seat at a table stacked with three neat piles of hardbacks and one of paperbacks; copies of each of our latest book, in case any of the audience wanted to buy a signed edition. My heart sank as I took my place at the far end, the door opened and everyone began to file in and drift towards the others. I kept a fascinated smile on my face, silently begging someone, anyone, to come to me. A sweet little old lady wandered over, picked up one of my paperbacks and asked me what it was about. I gave her my best one-line pitch, she frowned, fixed me with a stern eye and demanded to be told if it contained profanities. I confessed it did. She placed it back on the pile with a firm 'thank you', and moved immediately to the author on my left. I swallowed and turned back to find a very blonde girl, dressed in a floaty cream gypsy dress, looking down at me, smiling and clutching my book. I actually jolted and my mouth fell unattractively open because she looked like… me. Me twenty years ago and a couple of dress sizes smaller but nonetheless I saw the similarities instantly; the shape of our eyes, mouth and colouring. I was so astonished, I even blurted 'you look—' but before I could finish, she bit her lip, lowered her gaze shyly and said 'familiar? I'm an actress'. She spoke very proudly. 'I was in something on BBC Two last week. That might be where you've seen me.'

'That'll be it,' I said generously, not wanting to prick her balloon and admit that wasn't it at all, but still I stared.

'I loved what you said in the talk about how we need to stop describing female leads as "strong". I totally agree. It happens way too much.' She offered me her hand. 'I'm Mia Justice.' Then she held out the book she was clasping. 'Would you sign this for my sister? I think she'd like it. If you could put, "to Kirsty"? Thank you so much!'

'You're very welcome.' I signed with a flourish.

'Is Charlotte Graves a pen name? It's a very good one for a thriller writer.'

'No. It's my actual name, funnily enough!' I laughed. There was no one stood behind her, so I continued. 'Are you acting in something at the festival? Is that what brings you… here?' I was a little confused at how she'd wound up at an author's talk.

She rubbed her nose, and I sat back in shock, again seeing myself in the mannerism. It was starting to feel a little unnerving.

'I'm in a show my boyfriend, Hugo, is directing, but my best friend, Ava, is also a children's author. Ava Timney? She wrote *A Dragon's Wish*? No?'

I shook my head apologetically.

'Well anyway,' Mia laughed. 'She's here today doing a masterclass thingy on illustration techniques, which isn't really my bag.

They've gone to that, and I saw this talk on the programme and fancied it – so here I am!'

'Well I'm glad you enjoyed it and thank you for taking a book. I hope your sister likes it.'

'I'm sure she will!' She smiled and gave me a little wave before spinning on the spot and drifting off towards the door.

Someone else wandered up at that point and I had to talk to them instead, but while they fumbled for their reading glasses and their own pen at the bottom of their bag, I peered back through the small throng – still distracted – searching for another glimpse of her.

She was about to walk through the door, just as Tris came in. She stood back to let him pass and, as he turned to thank her, I saw him do a double-take too. I just about heard her laugh carry across the busy noise in the rest of the room as he said something, but by then, my last signing had found their pen and I realised they'd been talking to me and I'd not heard a word. I forced myself to concentrate on what I was being asked to write and when I looked up again Mia had gone. Tris was sitting on a chair over by the window, waiting patiently for me while checking his phone and tapping away on the small screen, but I knew he'd seen the resemblance too.

Despite it being a warm August day, even for Edinburgh, I shivered and reached down into my bag for my new and carefully chosen cardigan, slipping it around my bare shoulders. Tris looked up and mouthed 'ready?' I nodded, and once we were back outside among the tables and milling crowds, I looked for Mia again, but she had disappeared.

*

I was still thinking about her on the plane home as the twist of the Thames came back into view and we snaked down it, towards London City.

'What's up?' Tris removed his headphones and shut his laptop, before checking his watch. 'You look anxious. We'll be back by three. The kids will be fine. Don't worry.'

I didn't answer and watched Canary Wharf loom closer. Both the plane and my mood had begun a descent. I was already irritated with myself for wasting some good opportunities during the weekend. Tris had taken himself off to watch a play after we'd had lunch the day before, leaving me with strict instructions to mingle and network, but although I hadn't admitted it to him, I'd lasted five minutes before slinking back to the hotel, smoking an illicit cigarette en route. I'd been unable to find the jollity required to go up to people I only vaguely knew and join their conversations. Mia had spoken to me with such a natural ease and confidence, but then perhaps I would be that relaxed if I still looked like her. How old would she be? No more than twenty, surely?

I wasn't even aware I'd placed my hand on my stomach until Tris poked my arm, nodded at it and said: 'Tummy ache? You're not the only one by the smell of it.' He grimaced. 'The door to this plane is going to fly open with the noise of a giant whoopee cushion; it'll probably blow the landing crew off their feet.'

I stared at him. 'Tris!'

He grinned and zipped his laptop into its protective cover before sliding the whole thing into the backpack at his feet. 'Everyone farts, Charlotte. Even you. You think you don't, but when you turn over at night…'

Embarrassed, I glanced at the man to my left who, thankfully, still had his headphones in. 'Can you shut up, please?'

'Sorry.' He picked up my hand and kissed it. 'Ignore me. I had a lovely weekend with you.' He rubbed my thumb with his, 'a *very* lovely weekend indeed.' He raised an eyebrow suggestively.

'Tris!' I felt myself flush scarlet which made him laugh. 'There might be people I know on this plane listening to everything you're saying,' I added unnecessarily, sounding prissy when I hadn't intended to.

Tris sighed and let go of me. 'I was only trying to be nice.'

'I know, but—'

He held his hands up. 'It's fine. I don't want to ruin what was genuinely a good weekend with you. Let's pretend I didn't just mess up, as usual.'

'It wasn't that you—'

'Honestly – I don't want to talk about it anymore.' He got his phone out. 'And before you say anything, it's still in flight mode. I'm just checking an email. That's all.'

*

The closer to home we got, the faster the novelty of having stepped out of our normal routine began to fall away. As the train pulled past Lidl on the approach to the station, I started to think about tea for the children and clean school uniforms. By the time we were in the back of the taxi, it had dawned on me that Clara needed full PE kit for the morning – which I'd meant to put on to wash on Thursday night, and hadn't – when Tris said loudly: 'CHARLOTTE!'

I jumped and turned to face him. 'What?'

He smiled briefly. 'It's OK. Don't worry. I've already lost you, haven't I? Back into the cogs of the machine.'

That cheerful thought rendered us both silent, although as we pulled up outside the house, I felt my heart lift at the thought of the two happy little faces waiting for us on the other side of the front door. Unfortunately, when I opened it I found a note saying they'd all gone to the park – which I just about managed to read through watering eyes while being nasally assaulted by the smell of bleach. My mother-in-law had not only made the downstairs loo and upstairs bathroom smell like a municipal swimming pool, she'd ironed Tris's shirts, all of the bedclothes and every single item belonging to the kids, dusted and hoovered everywhere and lovingly left clean, folded pyjamas *on my husband's pillow*. Had I been in the right mood, I would have found it funny. As it was, I stared at them in disbelief, deliberately messed them up and stalked off back downstairs to find the PE kit smugly drying on the airing rack.

When they finally returned from the park, breathless, huggy and hungry, I put the kettle on, while Moira reached for a Tupperware box on the table.

'The children baked shortbread,' she said, as I opened the cupboard to get some mugs out, only to find it full of gleaming glasses instead, 'and I swapped a few things over while I was giving the shelves a wipe through. It makes so much more sense to have cups and teabags right above the kettle, I think. Would you pass me a plate for these? They're in the bottom left now. I hope you don't mind?'

'Not at all.' I gave her a tight smile as I turned round, and she looked away, quietly satisfied.

'Mummy, when can we do more cooking?' asked Clara disloyally, grabbing a biscuit. 'It was really fun!'

'Wow! They're *so* good, guys!' said Tris through a mouthful, pulling Teddy onto his lap for a cuddle as he gazed around him in amazement. 'Thanks a million, Mum. The house looks incredible.'

Moira beamed pinkly and patted his knee. 'It was an absolute pleasure. You work so hard, it's nice to be able to help. I made some casserole and a chicken pie for the freezer too. It's always good to have something fresh you can take out in a rush.'

It was such a thinly veiled dig at me – my not adequately caring for or supporting her best boy – I had to leave the room, feigning to need the loo. Standing in front of the mirror in our bedroom – which had been polished, I couldn't help noticing – I lifted the skin above my eyebrows, watching as they arched and my eyes became more feline. Then I pulled up my top and looked at the spare skin spilling over my trouser waistband. I tucked it back in, sat heavily on the edge of the bed and thought again about Mia. Reaching into my back pocket, I googled her and found a couple of images. She didn't look quite so much like me in the photographs after all and I began to wonder if I'd imagined it, felt a connection or seen something there that simply – wasn't. Just a pretty girl who had asked me to sign a book. Nothing more, nothing less.

I think I was called back downstairs after that. Donald and Moira were ready to go; their car neatly packed, a blanket carefully spread over the back seat for their Border Terrier, Pip, to recline on. I forgot about Mia and gave her no further thought whatsoever.

*

Almost exactly a year passed until she reappeared. I wouldn't have chosen the middle of August to go to Mallorca – the heat was blisteringly intense – but it was either that or nothing since term-time holidays had been officially outlawed. On the plus side, one end of the villa pool was shaded and the kids were more than happy to spend hours simply jumping in and out.

'Quick, Aunty Flo!' Clara wrapped her arms round her tiny shoulders, shivering on the white paving stones. 'Pass me my towel! I'm freezing!'

'Please!' laughed my younger sister, grabbing for one from the pile on the sun lounger and making a tent with it so that Clara could shimmy out of her wet costume under cover. 'And you can't possibly be cold. It's 29 degrees!'

'I'm thirsty,' announced Teddy as I whipped his trunks off, wrapped him in an enormous towel and lifted him up so that I could cover him in kisses. He giggled, but with a four-year-old boy's impatience, admonished, 'Hey! I said I need a drink.'

'Politely please, Teddy,' frowned Tris, from under the umbrella in the shade where he had his laptop balanced on his knees, legs stretched out in front of him. 'That's not how a gentleman speaks to his mummy.' He didn't look up and carried on tapping away as I released our son, who promptly legged it – his towel falling off completely – over to the table next to Tris, grabbing his cup of water, gulping noisily and then slamming it back down perilously close to the screen.

'Careful!' Tris snatched the computer away in alarm. 'You're spilling it!'

'Sorry, Daddy!' Teddy said cheerfully and ran off over the grass to the left off the villa. 'Clara! Catch me!'

She eyed him, then suddenly bolted off in pursuit, both of them giggling madly and shouting, 'we're bare bears!' as they skipped around in the nude.

'You've got one minute and then come back here for more sun cream and your hats,' I called after them. 'No one wants a bare bear burnt bottom.'

They collapsed with laughter at the thought, before shrieking as the automatic sprinklers came on, dousing them and fanning out over the lush green lawns.

'Quick, Teddy!' shouted Clara, 'let's run under them!'

'Good,' muttered Tris, 'that ought to keep them quiet for at least the next ten minutes.' He pulled a face at the screen, groaned and put his head back. 'This bloody thing.'

'What are you doing?' I asked, flopping down onto a lounger to dry off. 'I don't know how you can work in heat like this.' I yawned. 'Plus the screen glare. Anyway, can't you just put it away? You're on holiday.'

He closed it. 'Sorry. I just had a bit of something to finish off. I'm done now.' He got to his feet. 'Do either of you want a drink while I'm up?'

'I'm OK, thanks.' I got up again and moved my lounger into the sun.

'I'm fine too, thanks, Tris,' said Flo. 'I'm going to go and get showered and changed in a minute.'

He shrugged and made his way back to the villa, disappearing into the cool of the house as I grabbed my phone and did a time check. 'It's only quarter past four, you've got ages before you need to start beautifying. We won't go for another hour at least. I thought we could eat at the same place as last night. That fit restaurant owner likes you.'

She blushed. 'Shut up. No, he doesn't. He's like that with every woman that walks into the place.'

'He's not like it with me,' I pointed out truthfully. 'I could see you running an upmarket eatery. You'd have to learn to speak Spanish though.'

'You're just saying that to cheer me up,' she grumbled, but looked pleased.

I smiled, glancing at the children, who were still leaping around under the arc of water, closing my eyes and sighing happily. 'A minute's peace.'

'Charlotte!' yelled Tris almost immediately, having reappeared on the terrace.

I opened one eye and squinted at him. 'Yes, what?'

'I'm going to go for a bike ride, all right?'

'What now?' I sat up astonished. 'No! Of course it's not. We're going out for dinner in a bit. There's not enough time.'

'But,' he gestured widely with his arms, 'I've not done any exercise all day!'

'Have a swim!' I pointed at the pool. 'And try to remember you're *on holiday*. It's too hot for cycling anyway; I've never heard anything so ridiculous.' I leant back and closed my eyes again. 'You don't even have a bike here.'

'I'll go to the hire shop.'

'No!' I repeated firmly and gave him a pointed look.

He sighed crossly and disappeared back inside.

'What's rattled his cage?' Flo asked, her own eyes closed as she smoothed her wet hair back. 'Oh, this is lovely. Thanks so much for inviting me.'

'You're very welcome and I've no idea.' I lowered my voice discreetly. 'He's on that computer non-stop at the moment. He's worse than me. He seems to have completely forgotten how to relax. I woke up at five a.m. the other morning and all I could hear was this tap-tapping. He was working in the spare room "getting a head start" on the day, apparently.' I sighed.

'Has he got a new big project on, or something?' Flo frowned.

'No idea,' I replied. 'Probably. You know what he's like... Flo was just asking if you've got a big project on.' I smiled at him as he re-emerged clutching his book in one hand and a bottle of sun cream in the other.

'Sort of.' He sat down on the edge of my lounger. 'Can you do my back, please? Anyway, you're right, I need a break. It's doing my head in. You know this bloke?' He lifted his book up and showed me the back cover author photo.

'Not personally. I know of him, why?'

'It's complete rubbish, and yet it's *everywhere*. I just don't understand.'

I shrugged and splurged some cream on his skin, making him inhale sharply. 'Big marketing budgets, that's all. You shove something in enough places, people will eventually pick it up and buy it.'

'But it's so badly written,' he complained. 'Like, really basic grammar errors.'

'Spoken like a true English graduate,' I teased and started to rub it in.

'You're not much better,' he remarked. 'You still don't know the difference between it's, its' and its. Ten books published.' He shook his head. 'It's a bloody disgrace. And you're appallingly badly read.'

'Hey!' I exclaimed. 'I'm just not a literary snob, that's all. I'd rather read something entertaining than a completely unintelligible snore-fest. That creative writing course I taught recently was *full* of efforts like that. The students' manuscripts were just awful: self-conscious, wordy twaddle. I actually felt bad for some of them, paying good money to learn how to be a better writer when it's just never going to happen. It's a fallacy that everyone has one book in them. Or at least in most cases, that's where it ought to stay.'

Tris pursed his lips and said nothing, glancing over instead at the children who had quietly started picking flowers, correctly thinking that they weren't being watched.

'HEY!' he bellowed, and they jumped guiltily, dropping them instantly and putting their hands behind their backs. 'What did I tell you about that yesterday? *They are not our plants!* Leave them alone!'

'Tris,' I chided. 'Gentle. You can make the point without shouting.'

'Can you just back me up, please?' He spun round and glared at me. 'If you want to criticise my parenting, don't do it in front of them. That's why they always come to you when I've already said they can't do something. In fact, you know what? Let them pick all the flowers, whatever. I don't even care anymore. And don't think I haven't noticed you've only done half of my back, because I have.'

'She's drawn a massive cock and balls while you were busy ranting. It's going to look really good when you get home to the gym,' Flo said, and I burst out laughing.

Unfortunately, Tris chose not to see the funny side, got up and stomped off into the house, despite us calling after him that we were only teasing, and to come back.

'Sorry.' Flo looked worried as we heard a door slam from within the villa. 'I shouldn't have wound him up.'

I snorted. 'Don't be silly. He's being completely oversensitive.'

'You're right to tell him to ease off with the shouting though. I've noticed that Teddy, in particular, gets really agitated when Tris loses it. Look.' She nodded over at Teddy, who was now kicking and karate chopping one of the plants, while Clara wandered back to us, the game ruined, to find her towel.

I picked up the sun cream again, holding my hand out to Clara. 'I'll have another word with Tris later.'

'Oh no, don't,' Flo said. 'He'll think I'm interfering. I shouldn't have said anything. Ignore me.'

In the event, Tris perked up by the time we went to dinner and the temperature had dropped a bit. After a couple of drinks he was better still, fondly watching the children play in the square as we finished our food, joking about with us like nothing had happened, so I decided to leave it.

It was only when we were getting ready for bed that he began to niggle again.

'It's actually really important that the kids respect me as much as they do you.' He watched me take my earrings off.

'They do,' I said firmly. 'I'm just around them more than you are, that's all. That's why they look to me first.'

'Because I'm at *work*,' he said.

'I'm at work too!'

'Oh don't start,' he said. 'I meant I'm physically absent from the house more than you. It just pisses me off that everything I do is judged as "wrong". I bet you and Flo had a right old bitch about me after I went back in.' He got into bed under the blanket and lay down, facing away from me.

'Of course we didn't.' I unzipped my dress. 'Although she did quite rightly point out that Teddy became *more* destructive after you lost it.'

He turned back indignantly. 'I did not lose it! Look, I'm very happy for her to be here on *our* holiday with us, but I can do without her shoving her professional opinions my way, thanks very much. Why is it that therapists always seem to know how to fix everyone but themselves?'

'Shhhh!' I hissed. 'She'll hear you. She's not here to analyse you, she's on holiday getting over her boyfriend. Don't be mean.'

'Yeah, well you know why her blokes only last for six months max, don't you?' He looked at me pointedly. 'It's because she either goes for the twats who are *never* going to commit and gives them this "independent woman" bullshit when in fact that's the *last* thing she is… so that's on a hiding to nothing. OR she dumps the normal ones before it even has a chance to get going. She's the queen of self-sabotage.'

'That's not fair, Tris, she knows she finds it hard to hold down a relationship. It's something she's working on, OK? Not everyone has parents who think the sun shines out of their children's arses and gives them the kind of nuclear confidence you got when you were growing up, all right?'

'You're kidding me?' His mouth fell open in apparent astonishment. 'I know you think most things are my mother's fault, but that's a stretch, isn't it?'

'I don't like you criticising my sister.' I folded my dress, putting it over the chair and reaching for my T-shirt. 'Is it any wonder Flo has self-esteem issues when it comes to men? We didn't exactly have a cracking role model.'

Tris sighed tightly. 'She's having an "about to turn forty" midlife crisis – that's all. She just needs to calm down and take a step back from it all. Can you come to bed now, please?'

'I'm not tired all of a sudden.'

'That's OK, neither am I.' He grinned at me.

I snorted. 'You *are* joking?'

'Um no, I'm really not.' He sat up. 'You *promised* me that if she came with us, we'd still have some time together. In fact, wasn't she meant to babysit so we could go out just the two of us? When's that going to happen, then?'

'I don't actually want to spend time with you when you're being like this, funnily enough. Just go to sleep, wake up tomorrow in a better mood and don't take whatever's got your goat out on the rest of us. Good night.'

I made my way irritably to go and have a cigarette – now the kids were finally asleep – quietly slipping through the door, only to find Flo on the other side, sat on the sofa with silent tears streaming down her face, having heard every word.

*

Tris was appalled when I told him and offered to apologise to Flo. I said truthfully I thought that would make it even worse, so instead he seemed to have a word with himself, because the rest of the holiday was blissful. He played with the kids, joked around with us and didn't touch the laptop again for the rest of the week. We actually did go out to dinner, just the two of us, on the Thursday night. We drove to the coast. It was warm enough to undo the car windows and the cool breeze blew through my hair as we listened to the radio while picking our way along the shoreline looking for somewhere to park. We ate outside, watching the sea sparkle in the moonlight as strings of twinkling fairy lights bobbed in the branches of the restaurant trees. We even chatted about something other than the children for a bit before returning to laughing about something Teddy had said, while idly wandering hand in hand past elaborate sand sculptures and night-time market stalls. Tris insisted we stop for one final drink at an exclusive hotel, deciding that we should come back and stay for a weekend, just the two of us, as soon as possible.

'I love you,' I said on the way back in the car, sleepy-tipsy and happy.

'I love you too. I'm sorry I've been a bit of a twat this week. All that stuff with Flo.'

I looked across at him. 'You're just stressed out. You're working too hard. We both are.'

He sighed. 'Yeah, we really need to do more stuff like this.'

'Fly to other countries?' I teased.

'No, spend time together, you and me.'

'Agreed. Let's actually stick to it when we get home though, not just pay it lip service. I'll find us a regular babysitter. We should get back in the habit of going out for a date night every week.'

'That's a good idea. We'll do that.'

For the last couple of days we slipped back into a groove we'd not found for a long time. We kissed and held hands, cuddled and laughed on the sun loungers. It made me sad when Clara spied us having a hug by the pool and remarked aloud, 'Daddy's hugging Mummy!', as if it was unusual enough to comment on, and rushed over to join us, hotly followed by Teddy. I privately resolved to pack our happiness in the suitcases and ensure it came home with us.

Even Flo was a million per cent more relaxed. She assured me again and again that she wasn't still upset about what she'd heard Tris say. 'In fact,' she said, bravely, on the last evening, as we sat on the terrace watching the pool lights attracting moths in the dark while I quietly smoked, 'he's right. I do become too clingy with a certain type of man. I do self-sabotage. It needed to be said. It hurt, I can't lie, but it did me good. He's done me a favour. When I get back, I'm going to have a complete break from men and just throw myself into work. There are a couple of new clients I've been offered that I wasn't going to take, but I will now.'

'Good for you,' I said, delighted. 'Anything interesting?' I always liked to hear about Flo and her counselling network's particularly juicy cases. 'All names changed to protect their identities, of course.'

'No bin-bag shaggers at the moment, I'm afraid. Just lots of anxiety cases.' She sighed. 'Keep Clara and Teddy off phones as long as possible. Kids have it so tough now. You know that poor boy who killed himself because he learnt how to do it by watching self-harming sites? He was seeing someone I trained with.'

I fell silent. 'I don't know how you do your job,' I said truthfully. '*Why* do you do it?'

She shrugged. 'All the clichés like wanting to make a difference, helping people help themselves, but it's a genuine privilege that people trust me with stuff that they might have been keeping locked up inside for years, sometimes not having told a single soul.'

I listened carefully, looking down at the ground and absently watching an ant searching methodically for food.

'They're so brave. I love that bit when I open the door for the first time, they walk in and it all begins…' She smiled. 'I've had a really lovely week, thank you, but I'm excited to get back now. Bring on the new clients! I'm ready for them.'

*

We were so genuinely optimistic, but within forty-eight hours of returning home all that remained from Mallorca were our already fading tans and the echo of good intentions. A mountain of holiday washing for me, a deluge of emails on Sunday night for Tris when he switched his work phone on and two dull, grey last weeks of the holidays to fill before back to school saw to that. It was almost as if we'd never been away, save the tantalizing taste of a different, better life still lingering in our mouths.

Everyone was unsettled.

The stage was set for Mia to walk back into my life and for the true significance of that first meeting in Edinburgh to become shockingly apparent.

CHAPTER TWO

MIA

'I'm not abandoning you, Mia. I need to end our sessions because I have personal physical health issues.' Maureen watched me blow my nose. 'But I hope you will decide to continue with the colleague of mine I've recommended.' She placed a neatly folded square of paper on the side table between us, next to the box of tissues. 'Florence would really like to start working with you. These are her contact details. She's based in Bromley; it would be just as easy for you to get to as here.'

I nodded, looking around the small room with its familiar two floral chairs, small antique writing desk with the white orchid in the top left corner and pretty, chintzy curtains at the window; my safe space. I felt my eyes well up. 'I'm sorry,' I breathed, 'of course you are entitled to look after yourself – it would also be really selfish of me to say: "just keep me on and ditch your other clients".' I looked at her hopefully.

Maureen smiled. 'You're right, I'm not going to be able to work to the best of my ability and I have to be realistic about that.'

'I just can't help feeling that everyone ends up leaving me!'

Maureen clasped her hands in her lap and looked at me steadily.

'I'm not comparing you to Hugo and Ava, or my biological parents, but it still *feels* like I lose everyone who is important to me.'

Maureen opened her mouth.

'I *know* what you're going to say,' I continued quickly, before she could speak. 'I have a mother and father who love me and wanted me so much they *chose* me to join their family. I have a big sister and brother who love me too. I lead a very privileged life, *over*privileged in my huge luxury flat in Blackheath that Mum and Dad let me live in for pennies. I know ALL of that. Lots of good things… blah blah blah. But I don't like change.' I stopped, aware suddenly of how childlike I sounded.

Maureen put her head on one side and raised her eyebrows patiently.

'Yeah, OK, so no one does. It's not only me.' I looked down at the balled-up tissue in my hands. 'You've just helped me so much,' I whispered. 'I feel scared to think about not being able to come here once a week. I'll miss you – that's all. Are you going to be OK?' I looked up at her anxiously. 'With this illness, I mean.'

She smiled gently. 'Thank you. Yes, I'm going to be OK. You have made so much progress, Mia. You still have the unmet goals we've discussed today but I'm confident that you and Florence, or whomever else you decide is a good fit for you, will continue to facilitate the excellent work you are doing. I don't want to have to end this therapeutic relationship prematurely, and it's understandable that my needing to is causing you a very real sense of anxiety and loss. We have four more sessions together, however, and we can explore those feelings next time, if that would be something you'd like to look at, but we need to leave it there for today.'

She smiled, and at my cue that our time was up, I picked up the folded-over piece of paper and my bag from the floor, then let myself out into the sectioned off part of Maureen's back garden and through the gate onto the street. What a crap start to the week.

Increasingly twitchy, as the quiet overland train carried me into London Bridge, I stared out of the window listening to Sam Smith and started thinking about Hugo and Ava, out there somewhere, together… *No!* I was not that gullible girl anymore. I immediately reached into my bag and pulled out the piece of paper Maureen had given me, determinedly dialling the number.

Florence sounded nice in her answerphone message – young, which I thought might make a change. I left her my number asking her to call me back and felt proud of myself. I had taken control of my anxiety. Maureen would be pleased.

I took a deep breath, pushed Ava and Hugo away, and instead flipped onto an ancient Dizzee Rascal track that made me smile. They had no more power over me. It was time to focus on the day of rehearsals ahead. One week in, everyone was still at the polite stage, tiptoeing round each other, but that would change pretty quickly if I didn't get my shit together. A WhatsApp pinged in from Mark asking if he could see me later, and I instinctively shuddered at the memory of his puckered, wet lips looming towards me two nights before. I'd *said* to everyone it was still too soon… or maybe it was just that he was completely gross? I instinctively wiped my mouth on the back of my hand and resolved either way to message him back that I'd… died, or something. Urgh. But then I brightened. At least I'd gone on the date in the first place. I was back – and there was nothing crazy about me… Not anymore.

We began to slow. I stood up, automatically slinging my bag over my shoulder, tapping my fingers on the strap to the beat, and put my head down as the doors opened. I stepped onto the platform and joined the slipstream of people walking purposefully towards the main concourse. It wasn't even like Hugo made me happy when we were together, he didn't. If I had just ended it *before* finding out that he and Ava had started fu—

Someone deliberately touched my arm and, frightened at the unexpected contact, I spun round, simultaneously yanking my headphones out.

'I'm sorry, I'm sorry!' A businessman was standing there, hands up. 'I didn't mean to scare you!'

I stared at him, shocked into silence, and he hesitated, running his fingers through his hair, awkwardly. 'Um. I'm Seth. Hi.'

Did I know him? I scanned his face and looked at his suit. He wasn't an actor. He wasn't familiar at all.

'So – this all sounded a lot better in my head,' he swallowed nervously, 'less mental and stalker-y, but I noticed you here on Friday too and I wondered if you might like to have coffee with me?'

My gaze automatically flitted to his hand. No wedding ring, but I hesitated anyway. He was good-looking but…

'Hang on.' He held up a hand suddenly. 'Excuse me!' he called out after a mother pushing a buggy past us. 'You've dropped something…' He darted forward, picking up a toy dog from the floor, dusting it off and passing it to her with a grin.

'Oh, thank you so much!' she said, her eyes widening. 'That would have been trouble later!'

'No worries!' He turned back to me as she disappeared off on her way. 'When I was about five I left my bear by the sink in a service station toilet. My parents wouldn't go back for him and it pretty much broke my heart.'

'That's a sad little story.'

'Yeah. I'm over it now, obviously, but…' He shrugged and smiled. He had nice laughter lines. 'Anyway – I was about to explain my stopping you doesn't mean I'm insane, or a serial killer. In fact, we've—'

'I might be though,' I interrupted, and he looked surprised.

'I actually hadn't thought of that and now I'm a bit worried. Should I be worried?'

'You haven't seen *Killing Eve* yet then?' I said lightly. 'It launches here in a couple of weeks. You should watch it. You'll never walk up to a strange woman again.'

'I think I've seen a trailer for that.' He frowned. 'I've definitely read the book it was based on. I liked it a lot. Very classy – she's an assassin, right?'

I nodded slowly, and he laughed.

'I actually went for that part,' I confessed. 'Didn't get it, obviously, but…' I shrugged and made myself smile.

He suddenly reached out and put his hand on my arm again, moving me in towards the wall as some bloke barged past us with a huge rucksack, actually catching Seth and forcing him to step back. He rolled his eyes but didn't say anything.

I, however, instinctively yelled after the retreating backpack. 'Look where you're going, why don't you?' I earnt myself a raised middle finger in response.

'Arsehole.' I shook my head and looked back at Seth who was pulling an 'okkaayyy…' face.

'Seriously,' I said. 'You should just say, "nice to meet you, Mia. Have a great day", turn around and go while you still have chance.'

He blushed. 'So Mia, do I play it cool and pretend I don't know who you are, even though I think you're an amazing actress because I've seen you in a couple of things now?'

I laughed. 'If it makes you feel any better, actors *say* they love it when people don't recognise them – it's bullshit; they hate it.' I offered him my hand, my turn to suddenly feel shy. 'Nice to meet you, Seth.'

His skin was warm on mine. We stared at each other.

We went for coffee.

CHAPTER THREE

CHARLOTTE

'I'd just like to have a go at something more creative, that's all I'm saying,' Tris announced as we drove into East Molesey. 'It was a given when I left university that I'd go off to the city and get a proper job, but I never intended to do it for the rest of my life. I'd *love* to be the one at home all day.'

'No, you wouldn't.' I put my phone back in my bag. 'You'd go off your head without anyone to talk to.'

'Well it's pretty academic anyway, you're never going to get an office job, are you? You're basically unemployable now. Plus, you hate people telling you what to do. In fact, you hate people.'

'I do not "hate people".' I widened my eyes and nodded my head in the direction of the kids in the back.

'They're not listening.'

'Yes I am,' said Clara, not looking up from her colouring.

I looked at him pointedly.

'Well anyway, *I'd* like to stay at home making up stories all day,' Tris grumbled. 'How hard can it be?'

I leant forward and changed the radio station, refusing to rise.

'Do you mind?' he said indignantly, leaning forward and flipping it back. 'I was listening to that! It's like I simply don't exist! God!'

'You can't say "God" only "Goodness",' said Teddy immediately, from the back seat.

'Excuse me, *you* don't tell Daddy what to do. That's very rude.' Tris looked in the mirror at Teddy crossly.

'Tris!' I said sharply. 'He's only repeating what he's been told at school. You're quite right, Teddy, we shouldn't say God like that. Thank you.' I glanced at Tris and rolled my eyes before looking back out of the window.

'Will you please not address me like I'm also one of the children?' He wasn't finished.

'OK, *enough*, thanks,' I said warningly, not prepared to have a scene in front of Teddy and Clara. 'We're nearly there now anyway.' To lighten the mood, I added cheerfully, 'perhaps, if you think you'd like to write stories, you could help me with a plot niggle I've got?'

'Oh yes, please. I'd *love* to,' he said sarcastically.

I turned away. 'OK. No problem. Forget I asked.'

We lapsed into silence. Once the children had started chattering away to each other again, I said, quietly, while still looking out of the window, 'I'm not sure what's wrong, but could you please park it until later? Today's going to be stressful enough as it is. I could really use some support rather than a row.'

He didn't respond, just stared out of the windscreen before saying moments later, as I opened my mouth to ask if he'd heard me, 'Yes. OK. I'm sorry. It's just work stuff at the moment, that's all. I'm going to need to be in Sheffield again for most of next week.'

I patted his leg briskly as we pulled onto my parents' road. 'Bad luck. But this contract won't last forever, and you're not there now. Try to put it at the back of your mind and let's just get through today.' We drew up outside the house and I took a deep breath. 'OK. Happy party faces! Happy anniversary, Grandpa and Nona!'

'Why does your mother insist on being called that?' Tris undid his seatbelt. 'She's not Italian or Greek. It's such an absurd middle-class thing… like getting your grandchildren to call you Gangi or Oompa – or some other wanky version of their actual name blended with Granny. It's ridiculous. I mean, why Nona?'

'Feel free to lead with that question,' I suggested politely, opening the car door. 'See how far it gets you. Smiles everyone!'

*

'You're a darling to have come! Thank you so much! *And* a present! You're so naughty!'

I watched my mother lean in to embrace an equally glamorous, gym-sinewy sixty-something woman I didn't recognise. It was an uncomfortable-looking hug: clashing cheekbones, sharp shoulders and oversized-scratchy jewellery on their nut-brown tanned hands, before Mum drew back and took the proffered gift box, passing it smoothly to me.

'This is my daughter, Charlotte; Charlotte, this is Pam. Pam has recently joined our aerobics class. Oooh!' Mum looked surprised as Pam suddenly performed a dynamic star jump on the spot. 'So anyway, Pam used to be…' Mum lowered her voice as if about to confide something top secret, 'an air hostess. You *must* get her to tell you some of her stories for one of your books. They're a scream. Charlotte's the *author* daughter I was telling you about, Pam. Don't frown, darling, you'll get lines.'

I blinked, realising she was talking to me again. 'Sorry,' I apologised automatically. 'I left my sunglasses in the kitchen. I'll go and get them and pop this somewhere safe.' I held the gift box up. 'Nice to meet you, Pam.' I quickly made my escape and retreated gratefully into the house, to find Flo in the kitchen chopping fruit.

'So this is where you're hiding!' I shoved the champagne on the table with the other bottles and presents. 'Jane Fonda's just rocked up, by the way – aka Dynamic Pam. Thank goodness they've been lucky with the weather today, she'd have knocked someone out doing star jumps in the living room. Phew!' I fanned myself.

'You wouldn't think it was *October* though, it's a bit odd, isn't it? Too hot really. Unless this is just me? Oh, please don't let me be early menopausal. I can't bear it.' I turned as Flo stepped to one side to rinse her hands, revealing a small mountain of strawberries and apple. 'Wow. Are you making fruit salad or is that just for the Pimm's?'

'The Pimm's.' Flo returned to chopping.

'OK. Do you think we really need to bother with more fresh stuff?' I said carefully. 'Maybe just chuck more booze over what's already in the jugs. That's the bit they're all interested in anyway.' I looked at my watch. 'I can't believe we're two hours in and she's still got more people arriving.'

'I can,' Flo said tersely. 'It's ridiculous. Heaven help us if the emergency services need to get up the street. They'll have to ram about a hundred Jaguars out of the way just to get through.'

'Are you thinking about setting fire to the house to get them all to bugger off then?' I reached over to grab a strawberry.

Flo snorted. 'Don't tempt me. I'm more worried about one of them having a heart attack or something. I mean, look at that.' She pointed the knife at the window; Pam was bouncily demonstrating a grapevine followed by alternate knee lifts to our slightly bemused but fascinated father. Her fake boobs were impressive.

'I think he's OK. You meant Dad rather than her, right? Are you sure you want avocado in the Pimm's, Flo?'

Flo stopped and looked down at what she was holding in her hands, having just reached into the fruit bowl. 'What the hell am I doing?'

'Are *you* OK?' I looked at her more closely. She was flushed and had stopped to wipe her brow.

'Not really,' she said. 'This whole thing is… beyond messed-up.'

I looked out into the garden again, at approximately sixty of our parents' friends, milling around eating finger food, drinking and guffawing in the late autumn sun. 'Yeah, I know. We're all on edge, aren't we? Tris just asked me how I'm going to tackle the toast.' I leant on the side and crossed my arms. 'Let's just pretend for a minute we actually are glossing over the fact Dad disappeared overnight and didn't come back for *eight years*—'

As ever when I said it out loud, I immediately pictured the day I arrived home, walked back into the sitting room as an almost eighteen-year-old, chatting to my then boyfriend, Daniel, only to stop dead because my father was sitting in his chair – after the best part of a decade of absence – just like normal. Mum walked in to find me staring at him speechlessly and said calmly: 'Shoes off, darling. Daddy and I are having steak for tea. Do you and Daniel want to join us? Flo is out at a friend's tonight, I think.'

'It's still not their ruby wedding anniversary,' I continued. 'I'm forty-three. They got married two years before I was born. If you subtract the eight years he wasn't here, it's their thirty-seventh anniversary. If you ignore that – which clearly we are – it's the forty-fifth. Either way there's nothing ruby about it.' I sighed.

Flo opened her mouth to say something else, just as Mum appeared in the doorway. 'Well done you two, thank you!' She nodded at the empty jugs. 'You'll bring them out in a minute once you've topped them up, won't you? Isn't this such fun?' She beamed at us. 'Oh Florrie, I do wish you'd brought your new chap with you. Harry, isn't it?'

'What new chap?' I looked at Flo who went pink again, but angrily.

'No one important. We're just dating. I only told Mum so she wouldn't try and relentlessly fix me up with everyone's single sons all afternoon. I didn't think this was quite the right occasion to introduce him to the family, funnily enough.'

'Oh dear. He doesn't sound much fun.' Mum pulled a face. 'Who doesn't like a party? Anyway, I need to get back out there.' She peered out of the window. 'Martha is winding up Lesley, which will end in tears if I don't nip it in the bud! Darling,' she placed an immaculately nailed hand on my arm, 'has Tris noticed Teddy climbing the tree, do you think?'

I spun round, and clocked Teddy perilously balanced on much too high and thin a branch. Clara was tugging on Tris's jacket – who was deep in conversation with the cleavage of a woman I didn't recognise – trying hard to get her father's attention.

I rapped on the window furiously and everyone within earshot looked round as I gestured frantically to Teddy. Tris frowned, walked over to the tree, lifted Teddy down and returned to his conversation with barely a pause.

I shook my head. 'I better go back out too, before he scales the fence and winds up in the river.'

'Yes, you do that,' Flo said tightly. 'I'll carry on in here. Next time, Mum, will you just get some caterers in if you're going to have this many people?' She paused chopping and put her knife down.

Mum laughed and looked at her pityingly. 'Dearest, do calm down. Everyone is *fine*. They've all got plenty to eat and drink. Just relax and try to have some fun for once. You do make such a *drama* out of everything.'

I raised my eyebrows and looked down at the floor silently as she grabbed two bottles from the side and wafted from the room. I heard her announce gaily to the congregation: 'Who needs a top-up of fizz?'

Flo looked at the ceiling, near to tears, then wiped her eyes and started cutting again.

'Just leave it for a moment.' I put a gentle hand over hers.

'You understand why she's like this,' she practically exploded, nodding at the window. 'All the parties, endless streams of people here all the bloody time while we were growing up? It was so she didn't actually have time to think about it all, or have to talk to us. The hostess just keeps smiling, flitting around filling glasses up, never revealing herself, and then when everyone goes home, there's only time to sleep. You and I did all of the washing-up the morning afterwards. You can have that metaphor, by the way, stick it in one of your books about mentally messed-up people.'

'Flo – has something else happened?' I looked at her worriedly. 'I appreciate today is challenging for lots of complicated reasons, but—'

'It's not challenging, Charlotte.' She swung round to face me. 'It's completely abnormal.'

'Will you put that knife down, *please*!' I reached out and took it away from her.

'It is *not normal* to have one parent literally disappear for eight years and no one, NO ONE tells us where he is, just that he's not ever coming back, only then – whaddya know – he DOES!' she hissed at me. 'No explanation, no discussion – just literally like someone hit the pause button for eight years and now here we are, twenty-five years later and it's like the whole thing never happened. Sometimes I wonder if I dreamt it and it *didn't* happen, like my actual life was a Bobby-Ewing-in-the-shower scene.'

I folded my arms. 'No, it happened. You didn't imagine it.'

'But how does it not bother you?' she said incredulously. 'I don't understand. Why is it just me that goes mental about this and no one else does? *Is* it me? *Am* I the crazy one?'

'Of course you're not crazy.' I looked down again, starting to feel anxiety tightening my stomach. She was right. I didn't want to talk about it.

'But I *feel* mad.' She got up close to me, tears in her eyes again. 'Don't you understand? If I were my therapist, I'd be encouraging me to try and work out why none of my family want to discuss this, but how can I? On the handful of occasions I've tried to raise it with Mum she literally gets up and leaves the room. Dad does too – then it's back to jollysmile-ville and "would you like a drink, darling?" You're the only one who acknowledges it's not my imagination, but if it's real, *why* did it happen? Was he in prison? Was he ill? Did he go off and join a cult? Was it something Mum did, or we did?'

'It wasn't your fault,' I told her truthfully.

'But you don't know that! It could be!' She laughed and put her hands on her head. 'Anyway, yes,' she wiped her eyes, 'let's go and toast their not even real ruby wedding; forty pretend happy years together. Yay them.'

'I know it wasn't your fault, because it was mine.' I blurted it out just like that, after three decades of silence, in our mother's strawberry-scented kitchen.

Flo went very still.

'What do you mean?'

I shook my head, already regretting it. 'Ignore me. I'm talking crap. I just hate to see you upset like this, that's all.'

Flo stared at me then grabbed my hand, leading me out into the hall and upstairs to my old bedroom, now Mum's odds and bobs room. My single bed was still against the wall, my chest of drawers under the window where it had been when I used to hurriedly pull vests, then bras, then secret packets of fags out of it – now filled with prettily wrapped soaps, assorted occasion cards in cellophane waiting to be written, baby blankets for friends' grandchildren, scarfs and other random gifts. A framed picture of me and Flo sat on top of it, next to a china ballerina that I used to love with all my heart. I tried not to look at us smiling for the camera, aged about thirteen and nine, arms around each other. We'd been snapped at the back of the same garden now spreading out below us. I glanced through the dense lace curtain, starting to feel light-headed, and could just make out the river flowing beyond the fence.

Flo shut the door firmly and turned to look at me. 'What do you mean, it's your fault?'

'I honestly don't mean anything! I just don't want you to blame yourself. You were only six when he left.'

'You have never, ever referred to Dad's disappearance as being your fault. Why would you suddenly choose to do that today, for no apparent reason? It doesn't make any sense.'

'Try not to read into this, Flo. You're not going to find anything by digging deeper.'

Flo sat down on the edge of my bed and crossed her arms. 'Do you know it is almost completely impossible for a human being to keep a secret forever? That's why there is such a thing as deathbed confessions. It's why people like me have jobs. It's simply too much to bear, because when you can't release the truth, the secret keeper's anguish begins to turn inward and causes genuine pain, sometimes it actually becomes physical... *that's* how powerful the mind is. I've always thought that's why you write the kind of books you do. It's your way of releasing some of the pressure you keep built up within. Alternatively, in situations where someone has repressed something for a very long time, it can just randomly escape out.'

'Oh please!' I laughed, crossing my arms and looking out of the window again. 'Don't try and counsel me, Flo. I know you don't mean to, but you end up sounding really patronising.'

'Look at your body language right now.' Flo ignored me. 'Defensive, shut down. I'm your *sister*. If you can't trust me, who can you trust? Dad was missing for eight years – a huge chunk of the most formative parts of our lives. I want to know what happened. I *deserve* to know what happened.'

I closed my eyes and wavered on the spot.

'Please, tell me,' she begged. 'How am I supposed to move on otherwise? I need you to help me. I know that you were about to sa—'

'When I was ten, I went on some car journey with Dad,' I blurted. 'I don't remember why and I have no idea where you and Mum were. I had my Walkman on – I had that thing for Wham's 'Make It Big'. Anyway, it was hot in the back – no air conditioning then, obviously – and I fell asleep. I woke up to find we'd stopped and some woman was sitting in the passenger seat. I honestly don't know who she was. My batteries had run out so I could hear everything. I think they thought I was still asleep. She told Dad she loved him and they kissed on the lips.'

Flo gasped.

'Then she just got out and we drove home. When we got back, I wrote about what I'd seen in my diary. I was big into diaries then, as you'll remember.' I swallowed and sat down next to her, feeling unsteady on my feet. 'Twenty-four hours later, Dad was gone.' I turned to her, frightened. 'Mum must have read it, challenged him and thrown him out – or he left. I mean, obviously she forgave him eventually, or he came back or something… but it was my fault she found out in the first place.'

'You wrote it down *in your diary*?'

'Yes.'

Flo simply stood up and left the room. I closed my eyes. I felt sick.

'Charlotte? You up there?' I heard Tris calling and then he appeared in the doorway. 'What are you doing? Everyone's looking for you to do the speech?'

'I can't,' I whispered. 'Can you do it for me, please?'

'Of course.' He came right into the room. 'Are you crying? What's going on?'

I wiped my eyes. 'I'll tell you later.'

'OK.' He watched me, concerned. 'I think I better take the kids home after they've done the cut the cake bit though. Teddy's getting a bit much. They need to calm down. You're still good to come back with Flo?'

'I think so, yes.' I looked up at him. 'Try not to let Teddy fall asleep in the car, will you?'

He rolled his eyes. 'Obviously. You say these things like I don't know.'

'Sorry. I'm just tired now, that's all.' I stood up. 'I'd like a quiet evening later, rather than him up until who knows when. It's been a challenging day.'

'I'll do my best. You stay as long as you want though, you don't need to rush back. I've got a fair bit of work to do tonight once the kids are down, so you might as well enjoy yourself. Come on then, let's do this speech.' He took my hand and led me firmly downstairs.

He hit exactly the right tone once everyone was gathered around the cake in the garden, clutching filled flutes. He avoided talking about my parents personally, but reflected wittily on marriage in general. Holding everyone in the palm of his hand, he spoke confidently while the lazy afternoon sun shone down on all of us. I was both proud of him and enormously grateful.

'So please raise your glasses to the happy couple. We wish you love, happiness and plenty more fabulous parties. To Joan and David.'

I watched as my father kissed my mother on the lips and everyone cheered. I glanced at Flo who was looking down at the ground, clutching the stem of her glass so fiercely I have no idea how the whole thing didn't just shatter in her hands.

*

Once everyone had gone home and we were silently washing up, Mum appeared in the kitchen and announced brightly she fancied a walk to the pub as it was such a beautiful evening, did anyone want to join her? Flo shook her head. 'You and Dad go. We'll finish up here.'

'You're sure?' Mum said, gathering up her wrap. 'You're good girls, thank you.'

'We probably won't be here when you get back though.' Flo didn't look up from the sink. 'I'm going to drop Charlotte off on my way.'

'You'll go M25 then A20?' Dad said.

'Of course. I wouldn't go cross-country even if I was going straight home to Chislehurst. It'd take hours,' Flo said shortly.

There was a pause. 'I'll say goodbye then.' I moved to kiss my parents. 'I'm going to grab the rest of the dirties from the garden. Thanks for a nice afternoon and congratulations.'

'Thank you, darling.' Mum hugged me. 'Take some cake back with you, won't you? I can't possibly eat it all. I'll get fat as a pig. And we'll see you at yours for lunch next Sunday? What would you like me to—'

'Mum, Dad. I want to ask you both something.' Flo whipped round suddenly, her wet hands dripping all over the floor.

I turned as cold as if she'd poured the washing-up water down the back of my dress. I stared at my sister in horror. *Oh God no. Not now. Please.*

Flo glanced at me and I begged her silently not to say a thing… *not* to ask them what I'd written about all those years ago.

'How do you think it makes me feel when…' She paused and breathed out, as if she was psyching herself up.

I braced myself.

'How do you think it makes me feel when,' she repeated again, her voice trembling, before stopping and turning her head away, her eyes full of tears. She bit her lip. 'How do you think it makes me feel when we always have lunch at Charlotte's if we're not here? It's just assumed. None of you ever come to my house…'

I began to breath out, very, very slowly.

'It's like I don't exist.'

Mum raised her eyebrows. 'You want us to come to you for lunch next weekend?'

'Yes,' Flo mumbled. 'I know it's not the easy option for everyone, but yes, I do.'

'Of course we'll come,' Dad said quietly. 'That would be very nice, thank you, Flo.'

She nodded, swallowed and turned back to the washing-up. 'Great. It's in the diary.'

*

I walked around collecting glasses from the patio at the end of the garden, wondering how best to tackle everything with Flo again.

My stomach was a tight knot of anxiety and I didn't feel tired anymore, but rather alert and focused. Should I wait until we were in the car – some neutral space? I didn't want her getting upset while driving though. I simply shouldn't have blurted it out like that. Perhaps she was right, the 'celebrations' had distressed me too, far more than I'd allowed myself to realise. I stopped for a moment to look at the water and the late afternoon sun dappling the surface. A breeze had picked up and it was starting to feel cooler. Autumn was in the air. Mum was going to need her wrap on the way back. Without warning, as I looked upriver, the years rolled back in a flash and suddenly I could *feel* myself in my ten-year-old body, lifting the stone with the stupid diary page tied to it, sobbing as I struggled not to drop it, but finding the strength from somewhere to fling it as far away from me as possible, exclaiming aloud as I let it go… watching the water where it sank without trace, horrified and frightened by the power it had possessed.

I felt a hand on my back and turned to find Flo there, her eyes red from crying.

'I'm so sorry!' My voice gave way and I hugged her to me tightly.

We clung to each other for a moment before she pulled back. 'You should have told me, for lots of reasons… but you've honestly *never* talked to either of them about what you saw?'

'No,' I said truthfully. 'I didn't want to ask Mum at the time. I was frightened that if she hadn't read it after all, I'd make everything that was already awful a million times worse. Remember how often we were told "he's not coming back"? I was really scared by what I'd done.'

Flo shook her head.

'Then when he did just… walk back into our lives… I definitely wasn't going to rake it all up again *then*. I kept quiet.' I paused. 'You're right though, I'm assuming this is what happened, that it *was* my diary. It might not be, but I think it probably is. Anyway,

I love you so much.' My eyes filled with tears. 'I didn't want you to hate me more than I hated myself.'

'That's so stupid. We're sisters.' She held a hand out, and I took it. 'Dad's absence was acutely painful for both of us. You've just dealt with it differently to me. I'm so sad that you've kept this secret for so long though. What a burden for you to have carried alone.'

'Well, Tris knows.'

She let go of my hand. 'You told *him*?'

I gestured helplessly. 'He's my husband.'

She shivered; at first I thought she was cold, but her cheeks and neck began to prick violently red, and I realised she was angry as she looked out over the water.

'Charlotte, there's something *I* need to tell *you*. All of this has just made up my mind. Secrets are destructive and you mean more to me than anyone and anything.'

'What are you talking about now?' I laughed nervously. 'Are you in some sort of trouble or something?'

'Do you know a woman called Amy Hendricks?' She turned to face me.

I shrugged, blankly. 'No. Why?'

'She's an actress, her stage name is Mia Justice.'

Immediately, a bell rang. I'd never forget a name like that. I scrolled back through my mind and arrived at the book signing in Edinburgh, the year before. I saw her standing in front of me, smiling.

'She looks a lot like you.' Flo took a deep breath. 'She was, until last week, one of my new clients. There's something you need to know about her…'

TWO AND A HALF
WEEKS LATER

CHAPTER FOUR

MIA

I have to shove to get past them. They've crowded round Matthew in a hungry, breathless crush, shoving programmes and pens in his face, phones held aloft as they film and selfie themselves stupid. Someone steps back and squashes my rucksack against the wall, trapping me. I yelp and yank at it a couple of times to free myself, but they don't even notice.

I wipe the tearstains from my face, pull my hood up and shove my hands deeper in my pockets. I just want to go home. My bottom lip trembles. I want to climb into my bed, pull the covers over my head and cry myself to sleep.

'Excuse me? Mia?'

A forceful voice calls my name and, obediently, I turn back.

The bright lights shining from the stage door have also illuminated the wall across the street. A woman is leaning against it. The tip of her cigarette glows before she pulls it away from her mouth, exhales deeply and the smoke clouds around her. She's got her arms tightly crossed over her chest against the cold, and I can see why. Her dress is long-sleeved but she's not wearing a coat. The days might still *just* be warm enough to get away with that, but not at this time of night – it's practically November – she must be freezing. It *was* her that said my name, wasn't it?

I take a hesitant step towards her as she straightens up and smiles.

'Mia' she repeats, only this time she speaks like she's sure of it.

I pause, pulling my own parka more tightly around my body, scanning her up and down. She looks familiar. I know her, I'm sure of it – but from where? She raises an amused eyebrow, steps forward and twirls around slowly on the spot to make it easier for me to assess her.

I blush. I didn't mean to be rude, I'm just confused, but the only way out of being called on my bad manners is to hold my head up high… and coolly continue, which is exactly what I do. She's mid-forties. Very slim, clearly eats like a sparrow. Brunette hair piled up on her head in an artfully messy way, but with a heavy, blunt fringe that covers her eyebrows; she's almost peeping out from under it. Not had any work done, but good skin about to go over. She has very round, high cheekbones that are as red as the very tip of her small nose. How long has she been out here waiting for *me*?

She crosses the street, and my attention immediately shifts to her dress and the full skirt swishing with every step. Up close it's stunning: midnight blue velvet with a lush pattern of green foliage fronds and peony-red, exotic flowers in full bloom. They weave around a slender bodice and tiny waist, before cascading down to her ankles. I want to reach out and stroke it, it's so beautiful.

She offers me her hand and as I take it, her skin feels cool.

'We met briefly last year in Edinburgh. I'm Charlotte Graves. You came to my book signing?'

My mouth falls open. *Now* I remember. 'Of course! Wow! Good to see you again. You look – er, a bit different.'

She reaches her fingers up and touches her hair – 'not blonde anymore.'

That and you've lost a couple of stone. 'No,' I agree politely. 'But now you're talking, I completely remember your voice too.'

'My voice?' she repeats, surprised.

'Yeah, it's really…' I'm about to say 'posh' but manage to settle on 'grand' instead.

'Years of elocution lessons,' she says drily.

That and a lot of cigarettes. Suddenly I hear my most intimidating tutor from drama school in my head: *You must command the stage, Mia! Your voice is an instrument. At present you have a voice for film, and film is for people who cannot act.* Then I hear the director, telling me pretty much the same thing in my dressing room ten minutes earlier, only much more angrily. My eyes fill with humiliated tears again; I swallow and have to look away, rummaging around in my pockets for some old tissue.

'You were outstanding tonight.' A fresh, folded Kleenex appears under my nose. 'I couldn't take my gaze from your every move. I saw no one on that stage but you.'

I look up, surprised and pathetically grateful. Does she really mean that? I stare into her violently black eyes. Unafraid, she smiles again. I take the tissue, whispering 'thank you', before sneaking another glance. I can't imagine someone like her allowing either of those two arseholes to denigrate *her* and pin her down like a butterfly to a board. She's both delicate and terrifying all at once.

Charlotte reaches back into her Mulberry handbag – my mum has one exactly the same – and drops the tissue packet into the depths. 'You look like you need a drink.' She twists suddenly on the spot and glances to the far end of the street at the pub on the corner.

I hesitate, knowing most of the stage crew will already be in there. I can't face them. Everyone heard Theo yelling at me. I know they did.

She is already looking at me again, not missing a trick. 'It's OK, we can go somewhere else.' Before I can comment, she's turned and is walking away from me, calling over her shoulder: 'I'm heading back in the direction of Charing Cross. I need to be on a train no later than eleven. Let's find somewhere on the way, shall we?'

I find myself hastening after her and falling into step. I can hear her heels clicking on the pavement. It's a bit like being accosted by a sexy Mary Poppins.

'Your dress is very nice,' I say breathlessly, like I actually am Jane.

'Thank you. It's The Vampire's Wife.'

I nod like that's what I thought – even though it's a label I've never heard of and am taking note.

'So Mia,' she moves us on, 'I'm no authority on Chekov – my tastes are more pedestrian, if I'm honest – but I thought your Nina tonight was utterly convincing.' She steps briskly round a group of noisy, sweaty-suited drunk blokes mucking about in the middle of the pavement. A couple of them look at her; she ignores them and marches on. 'I completely bought into your ravening ambition and determined passion.'

'Thank you.' I'm delighted, but confused. What exactly does she want with me?

'I have a role that I'd like to discuss with you,' she says calmly, reading my mind and I don't even care that she probably hears me catch my breath.

YES! I internally air punch. *This* is why you always give your best performance – you never know who is in the audience. Oh, thank you, God! I feel faint with relief. Thank you! Thank you! With only a week left to go of the run, you've cut it a bit fine – but thank you. *And ha ha, Theo*; I picture the disgusting white tidemark of saliva drying around the director's thin lips as he repeatedly licked them, while shouting at me earlier. *You have horrendous breath by the way... like The Seagull actually died in your mouth.* That's what I should have said.

'Mia?' Charlotte has stopped and is holding open the door to a glitzy hotel.

I blink and force myself to concentrate. I don't want to screw this up. I take a deep breath and smile confidently like I come here all the time, although during my most indulgent phase, I *never* drank at the bar here on account of it being outrageously expensive, even by London standards. Charlotte pulls the door a little wider; a beautiful, fierce fairy Godmother inviting me into a world I've always wanted to be part of. I nonchalantly cross the threshold but, in my head, The Jam is playing and my insides have begun to leap and dance about like Billy Elliot.

'This is very exciting!' I beam. 'So one of your books is being made into something on TV or a film then? Congratulations!'

'You grab a seat and I'll get a waiter.' She gestures at a small table in the corner.

I settle myself on a small mushroom-like stool, leaving the comfy armchair for her. When she returns, she sinks onto it elegantly – and a waiter appears, silently placing down two heavyset, cut-glass tumblers containing an inch of amber liquid and lumps of ice. Neat whisky? Urgh. I smile politely as she reaches forward and raises one up.

'Cheers.'

'Cheers.'

We clink glasses and they scratch against each other, which makes my teeth go funny. She sits back and takes a mouthful as I pretend to take a kitten sip.

'I hope you don't mind me ordering for you? It looked like you needed something a little stronger than Prosecco. Had a rough night?'

I set the drink down, carefully, next to my mobile phone, on the mirrored table top. I now need to explain my tears but I'm obviously not going to tell her about Theo letting rip about how crap I am, what a disappointment I've turned out to be and how he should have actually cast someone who was nineteen, not twenty-five. And definitely not that I shouldn't rely on looking young to get me any more jobs, rather than talent. Bastard. My eyes well up again.

'I had a row with my boyfriend,' I lie, instead, feeling instantly bad about blaming poor Seth, who I bet would actually give me the biggest hug if he were here now, and probably offer to punch Theo's stupid weasel face in. 'He hasn't apologised yet.'

'Oh!' She puts her head sympathetically on one side. 'I'm sorry to hear that.' She waits for me to continue.

'Seth struggles a bit with me being an actress sometimes.' I get into the part, feeding the roots easily as the lie sprouts leaves.

Don't tell fibs! I hear my mother scolding in the back of my head. I can't help that it makes life more interesting. It makes *me* more interesting. And now I'm paid to pretend, so it all worked out in the end. In any case, sometimes – like now – it's necessary to lie.

'So what exactly doesn't he like about your job?' Charlotte frowns. 'Isn't he in the business then?'

I laugh. 'No! Been there, got the T-shirt. I'd rather be in a relationship with someone who isn't mad, gay or married, thanks very much.'

She doesn't laugh back, just stares at me as it dawns on me *she* might be with an actor for all I know. I look quickly at her hand and spy a wedding band and several large diamonds sitting on her finger above it.

'No offence,' I stammer.

'You're all right, my husband works in an office.'

I feel so relieved I could practically neck that whisky. 'Like I said, my boyfriend gets a bit jealous, that's all,' I plough on quickly. 'We've not been together long.' I blend in a bit of truth. The best lies are always anchored in reality. 'He's still getting used to the idea that I'm only acting up there.'

'But doing it very well,' she says smoothly, hauling us back on track, as I remember she's got a train to catch.

'Thank you,' I say quietly, and then unable to help myself, I blurt: 'so tell me about this job I might be able to help you with?' I can practically hear the desperation in my own voice and I want to punch myself in the face. I need to shut up and let her talk.

She drains her drink and sets the glass down. 'How old are you, Mia? I mean really.'

OK, here we go. I swallow and step into my professional persona. Not easy in a manky old jumper and no make-up, but I do at least manage not to say, 'how old do you want me to be?' like I'm Julia Roberts in *Pretty Woman*, or something. I will always love that movie so much, even if it wouldn't stand a hope in hell of being made today. I read that, originally, it had a much darker, more serious script – which still lurks in there somewhere – but they changed it because Julia Roberts and Richard Gere had such amazing chemistry, how could they not end up together? It would have been a travesty. Everyone wants the dream, right? No matter the circumstances you overcome to get you there. We all want a happy ending.

'I'm twenty-five,' I admit. 'But as you saw tonight, I can play late teens… right through to mid-thirties.'

She nods. 'Did you always want to be an actress?'

'No. I wanted to be a singer. Well, a songwriter mostly. I was the kid up in my bedroom filling notebooks with crappy lyrics about boys who had broken my heart. I hope none of them have survived. The notebooks that is, not the boys.'

She smiles faintly. I politely pick up the glass and let the ice bash against my teeth as I mime the whisky disappearing into my mouth. 'I wasn't a strong enough singer though,' I continue. 'I can hold a tune, obviously, but I was never going to stand out in a crowd. It's a shame, really, because I love singing, but I'd have been nothing but a disappointment to myself and I'd never have made it.'

'And is that what it's all about?' Charlotte asks casually. 'Making it?'

I hesitate and put the glass back. 'Being the best I can, as opposed to just wanting to be famous? Yeah, that's what it's all about.'

'Who is your inspiration?'

'Glenn Close.' I don't miss a beat.

Charlotte laughs. 'You weren't even born when *Fatal Attraction* came out!'

I stare at her blankly. So what? '*Dangerous Liaisons* is my favourite. That bit where they all hoot and hiss at her in the theatre because they've discovered what she's done? Her revenge has ruined them all. She's humiliated but she won't show it. She holds her head high even when she stumbles – until that last scene where she takes her make-up off and you see she's actually totally broken. It's incredible. A masterclass.'

'Is Mia Justice your real name?'

She completely ignores what I've just said. I obviously sounded pretentious. 'Strictly speaking it's my stage name,' I say, quickly, 'but I pretty much use it all the time now. Even with my family.'

'It's great. Sounds like an action hero.'

I shrug and smile. 'I'm fully stage combat trained, so maybe one day!'

She nods briskly. I get the feeling my initial interview is over and we're moving on. Sure enough she shifts position.

'So – let me tell you a little bit about this job.'

But before she can continue, my phone lights up next to the glass with a WhatsApp from Seth. I see his name immediately and snatch it up, paranoid that she might notice the cheery message from him that won't support my earlier lie. 'Sorry about that,' I say quickly, scanning it anxiously, before shoving the phone in my hoodie pocket.

'Seth has apologised, I hope?'

I nod and blush. 'He wants to meet me in a bit.'

'Well, there we go.' She smiles. 'All's well that ends well. Now – as you know, I'm a writer.'

I brace myself, already seeing the future. Me sat in my own hotel suite. PR people milling around as I do the press interviews: *Charlotte was in town researching her latest book adaptation for Netflix, she came to see the production of The Seagull I was in and we ended up having a drink afterwards that changed everything! And here we are now – about to start the second season with all of these Emmys and Golden Globes! It's been one crazy ride!*

'I've actually been writing for – hang on a minute.' Charlotte stops and checks in her bag, pulling out a mobile phone. 'Sorry – my turn. It keeps vibrating. Do you mind if I take this quickly?'

I shake my head. I've been waiting five years and counting – I can hang on another minute or two.

'Hello, darling,' she sounds impatient as she presses the phone up to her ear. 'No, I'm not at home yet – that's why. I'm sorry to hear that. Ask reception if they've got some earplugs maybe? I've got to go – let's chat in the morning. You too. Night.' She hangs up and turns back to me. 'Sorry – that was my husband. He's away on business, in a noisy hotel, apparently. Anyway, my books. In case you don't remember, I write thrillers. My first was a bestseller back in 2008 – funnily enough about a girl called Mia. I think it's fate.' Charlotte smiles at me, then beckons to a waiter, who glides over. 'I'll have the same again, please,' she tells him, then looks at me.

I shake my head. 'Just water for me, thanks.' It's genuinely what I want and, moreover, this might be a test. Stay professional. 'Tap is fine,' I add, gunning for 'down to earth' bonus points.

'Anyway,' Charlotte continues, 'the book did pretty well. It's about a girl who finds out her boyfriend is cheating on her, and the lengths she goes to, to keep him. She does things like break into the other woman's flat and pulls all sorts of stunts to make her rival look crazy… but I'm getting distracted, That's not what I want to talk to you about now. You look relieved?' she says sharply.

I re-arrange my features quickly. 'No, no – not at all. It's just…' I hesitate. 'No one really wants to play just the wife or girlfriend anymore – the love interest/victim – you know?'

She doesn't react at all, just stares at me again – and for a horrible moment I think I've overstepped the mark completely, blown this and she's just going to get up and leave.

'Sorry, what I mean is…' I try to explain myself. 'I'd rather do something more interesting than that.'

She laughs. 'Says the girl who played the victim earlier this evening. Isn't the part of Nina all about a perfectly happy girl destroyed by a man out of sheer boredom?'

'Yes, but its Chekov, isn't it?' I explain. 'That's different.'

Her smile fades, she gives me a long steady look and sighs again. 'Sadly, Mia – yes, it is. I take your point though. I've written a lot of women-in-peril stories and I want to do something different now. I'm bored of them. If I was writing my first book today, I probably wouldn't do it the same way.'

'Yes, because wouldn't someone just leave a boyfriend if he was cheating on her?' I think aloud. 'I would. Does she?'

'No. She stays with him.'

'Really?' I reply before I can stop myself, adding quickly, 'but maybe stuff was different back then. I mean, things feel different now. Post #MeToo. Women are standing up for themselves.' Then I remember Theo shouting at me, me saying nothing – just taking it – and shut the hell up.

'The book was more complicated than that, but I take your point.' Her second whisky arrives and she drinks some immediately. 'Anyway. The story I want to talk to you about is different. My next one is about an extraordinary woman and it's a *very* good book.'

I manage not to raise my eyebrows. We'd all like to write our own reviews.

'It's going to be a bestseller and almost certainly a major film,' she continues, without a hint of embarrassment, 'as long as certain measures are put in place first.' She puts down the whisky. 'That's where you come in.'

This is where I need to stay calm. I've been here before and messed things up. I'm not going to again. But I'm already an over-excited puppy. 'You want me to audition for you?' I blurt eagerly.

She laughs properly and her face is transformed as it lights up. She's very beautiful when she looks happy. 'No! You've already got the part. I think you'd be perfect.'

Huh? *Now* a bell rings. A great big, fat warning one. If she were a bloke, I'd assume she was talking crap and trying to sleep with me. As it is…

'You're going to have *the* starring role, Mia. Everyone is going to know who you are.' If she's noticed my hesitation, she's ignoring it. 'You're going to make a lot of money and this is going to launch you so high, so fast, you're not going to be able to see the ground as it falls away from you.'

'I'm confused,' I say slowly. 'You're telling me I've *already* been cast in a screen adaptation of your new book?'

'No. You're going to pretend to be me.'

I must look as lost as I feel because she puts her drink down quickly.

'Stay with me. I'll explain. Let's go back to Glenn Close for a moment. She's amazing, you're right. She has undeniable raw talent but she's also spent years learning, practising and perfecting her craft. Experience has made her one of the best, right?'

I nod.

'She's deservedly at the top of her game. But for every Glenn Close, Judi Dench or Meryl Streep there are hundreds more very experienced, very good actresses clinging on lower down the ladder, going nowhere fast… no one's looking at them. Everybody is too busy watching the pretty, young newbies climbing on right at the bottom, ready to work their way up, because no one wants to miss the *new* Glenn Close. It's just the way the system works… the way *life* works.' Charlotte shrugs and takes another sip of her drink. 'It's no different for female authors. I've been hanging onto the middle of the ladder for such a long time now I'm stuck… and it's so frustrating because I'm a million times better a writer than I was when I first started, yet it's all going to waste. And that's when it occurred to me… it doesn't have to be this way!' She lowers her voice and leans forward. I feel myself instinctively lean in too. 'This very good book that I've written?' she whispers, 'we're going to pretend *you* wrote it. Beautiful, new, shiny, exciting, you. An almost-famous young actress who can write too… they're going to fall over themselves to snap you up.'

'But,' I begin.

She holds up a hand to silence me. 'A debut author that *everyone* wants to publish could be offered as much as a million pounds for her first book.' She laughs as my mouth falls open. 'That's just in this country. A worldwide smash, one that's translated into dozens of different languages, could easily earn you double, triple that… and that's before you've even *thought* about the *film* of the book. Not that it's all about the money, of course. If you "write" a book that successful, people are going to know who *you* are, Mia Justice. You're going to get called for acting jobs that once upon a time you could have only dreamt of being seen for – and you'll get them, because you're genuinely good. I saw that tonight. You're *really* good. You just need a much bigger stage to shine on, that's all.' Her eyes glitter with energy, and I almost feel breathless myself. 'Think about it, Mia. We combine my experience with your beauty and youth. We'll be unstoppable. Let's use the system to our advantage! You'll be the next big thing and it'll change both of our lives forever.'

She stops talking suddenly, sits back and crosses her arms. 'And all you have to do is pretend you wrote a book.' She falls silent and picks up her drink again, while I begin to entertain the very real possibility that she might be completely insane.

'It sounds crazy, I know.' She doesn't take her gaze from my face. 'But it'll work… I promise you that. The only thing is we get *one* shot at this. You never get another chance to be a debut.' She drains her drink and looks at her watch. 'I need to go. You literally can't tell a soul about this – not your agent, your best friend, your boyfriend. Everyone always tells someone else and then boom, the secret is out. If that happens, we'll have torn up our golden ticket.' She gets to her feet.

'Hang on a minute. You can't just… I mean – how come this didn't happen to *you* with your first book then? Why didn't you get a million quid for that?' I'm babbling.

She shrugs. 'It wasn't a very good book. It was all right, but it wasn't *brilliant*. I told you – I'm a much better writer now than I was ten years ago.'

'So why don't people pull this trick all the time then, if it's so easy?'

She laughs again. 'They do! You honestly think all of those celebrities who suddenly turn their hand to writing a book sit down and do it themselves? Of course they don't! Someone like me writes it, the celeb is coached on how to talk about it as if *they* wrote it, the readers buy it in droves – everyone's happy… well, almost everyone. The big difference in that scenario is the writer gets a usually very shitty one-off fee for their efforts. You and I will be splitting the profits from our adventure 50/50.'

She's talking as if we're definitely doing it. I watch her reach for her bag and put it over her shoulder. 'I appreciate you're going to want to think about this and that's fine but I really hope you'll say yes. When the idea came to me, I thought of you straight away. I remembered *you*.' She points at me sweetly. 'I'll come and find you again in a couple of days when you've had a chance to let everything sink in. You can give me your answer then. In the meantime, remember the rules – tell no one, or the deal's off.'

'Wait.' I grab her arm as she passes the table, about to leave. She glances coolly down at my hand and I let go of her quickly, embarrassed. 'All I have to do is pretend I wrote it?'

'Yes. You have to act the part of a talented actress who wrote a book that went on to open a million doors for her…'

I immediately picture my Oscar moment – I can't help it – I'm walking up onto the stage, clutching my chest in shock, everyone is clapping and cheering. I inhale sharply.

Charlotte watches me. 'I know. It really could be wonderful, couldn't it?' She looks at her watch again. 'I'll be in touch.'

'Wait! You haven't even told me what the book is about!' I call after her as she reaches the door.

She stops and looks back at me over her shoulder. I'm not sure, but I think I briefly see pity, or is it irritation, in her eyes?

'It hardly matters, does it?' She smiles again. 'It'll hold your attention, I promise. You'll be hooked until the very last page.'

CHAPTER FIVE

CHARLOTTE

The last train home is predictably horrible: bright, shouty, packed and pissed. Phones are going off left, right and centre, there's a nauseating fug of sweaty bodies, burgers in takeout boxes and paper bags full of greasy fries. The final panting passengers flop into their seats with relief, having run through cold streets in their coats to make it on time. The heating is faulty and maintaining the carriage at a steady subtropical level, but not only have I left it too late to move further down the heaving train, my random choice of whisky in the bar is having a dire effect on my otherwise empty and now churning tummy. I'm concentrating on staring ahead to quell the nausea and the creeping arc of bright colours appearing in my left field of vision. I do not want a migraine. I want to be in bed, now.

My throbbing head is not being helped by the young couple squashed into the seats to my left, the other side of the narrow aisle, who are playing back a noisy recording of some comedy gig they've just been to, without a thought for anyone around them. I imagine reaching out and snatching the phone from them before flinging it down the carriage. Except it would hit someone. Maybe I should crush it under my heel instead? The girl has the sort of 'common and lazy' accent my mother warned me and Flo would stop us getting into grammar school unless we finished our words properly, as we'd been exhaustively taught. I think about Mia implying I'm posh and smile grimly. Mum would be delighted to hear that. I do, however, have a little more gratitude for her efforts as I listen to this girl say over and over again: 'E's so *funni*! Inni? Inni funni, Mycool? E's sooooo funni! Lissen!' Her boyfriend – Michael, I assume – turns it up even louder, presumably to drown her commentary out.

I sympathise, only my ears are about to start bleeding, the colours are getting brighter and the waves undulating more rapidly in front of my eyes. I blink and slowly turn to look at them. 'Excuse me, do you mind? It's a bit noisy.' I point at the screen.

They both look at me, at each other, laugh and then without a word, the bloke turns his back on me, blocking them from sight, but not sound. They don't turn it down.

I imagine reaching into my bag – calmly pulling out a knife, sinking it through his buttery soft black leather jacket until it finds jelly-like back fat. Or maybe simply stabbing it into the blue jeans that are straining over his trussed ham thighs. I gingerly turn away, lean back on the headrest, close my eyes and wonder when I became such a bitch. The simmering rage is a new thing, I know that – but when did this sheer intolerance for the existence of other people kick in? At the same time, two and a half weeks ago, when *everything* changed?

But I must not think about that right now. Tears are a breath away from flooding into my eyes and I will not lose it. I will *not* be The Emotionally Unstable Middle-aged Woman On The Train.

I reach down into my bag and pull out my water bottle, take a sip, screw the lid tightly back on, put it back and carefully twist the clasp of the bag shut. Hesitating, I also try to fold the curling corners of the front leather flap back under on themselves. It's aged well, this bag – as it should have given how much it cost – but it's starting to look battered now. I've spilt the kids' school water bottles in it so often, the base is now permanently darkly stained and the leather has hardened. Tough luck though, because when I googled a new 'Heritage Oak Bayswater' recently, I discovered it would now cost the best part of a grand and a half. I imagine Tris asking incredulously '*how* much? What's wrong with your old one?' We're past the extravagant presents stage now. I would have quite liked an eternity ring after Teddy was born – but I don't think that's ever occurred to him either. Still, only seven and a half weeks until Christmas. I wonder what this year will bring? I open my now-clear eyes and stare past the woman to my right, out of the window at the trees and blocks of flats rushing past us in the dark, and picture the John Lewis coat he got me last year. Nothing says desire like an anorak.

'It's got a lined hood,' he said helpfully, as I held it aloft and stared at it. I'd not been specific enough. I'd meant I needed a going out winter coat – one to wear out to dinner, or maybe even the odd black tie do. 'And it's fully waterproof. You said you wanted one, didn't you? I thought this would be good for the school run? It's got lots of pockets.'

I didn't even try it on, just thanked him with a kiss on the cheek and had it refunded. When I checked the receipt I noticed he'd paid for it on the joint account in any case, so there we are. Ultimately it was as if it had never happened. I intended to buy myself some expensive underwear instead, but I didn't get round to that either. Although I must. I used to have so many matching, pretty pairs of bras and knickers. Now I am a woman who has two bras: one black, one skin-coloured with a wire that keeps popping out. I shift uncomfortably and close my eyes again as the train begins to slow – we must be approaching Orpington. I force my hands to uncurl from their tight fists and spread the fingers in my lap instead, resting them on my knees as I focus on my breathing. I hear the Canadian voice of my yoga teacher from this morning's class in my head: '*I invite you to let the negativity drain from your fingers and toes. Breathe the gunk from your lungs. Don't let your thoughts pollute and weigh down your opportunities… be the best version of you.*' She always does a funny little laugh at the end of statements like this, as if her own wisdom has taken her by surprise. She gets away with it though, *because* of her accent. It makes everything feel authentic. I don't think it would have the same conviction if she was from Liverpool. I'm no more flexible for going two hours a week during term time, but just while I'm there, I don't think about anything. I hear her voice and switch off from my life… although I found it a bit much at the end of today's class when she started talking about how what we celebrate as Halloween used to be a pagan ritual to mark the end of summer and the arrival of darker days.

'*While the leaves fall and the new moon arrives, see this as a time to cleanse and rejuvenate. We welcome the phase of the year when what we no longer need dies away – but we must also remember to nurture and care for ourselves.*'

I laid on the mat and thought back to Mallorca. All of us laughing and splashing in and out of the pool. Spritzers in the square before dinner as the children played together in front of us. When I was happy.

I had to leave the class; I knew I would break down then and there if I stayed. The teacher gave me a quizzical look but didn't say anything. Hopefully she'll have the sense not to ask me if I'm OK at the start of next class either and let it go. On the up side, I'm slightly calmer for going today, which is good. I almost lost it completely last night.

'I'm going to Waitrose.' Tris had appeared in the kitchen doorway and hovered until I couldn't ignore him anymore and had to take my headphones out. 'Tell me what you need and I'll get it – but I want to go now.'

'Could you please just give me a moment?' I begged, closing my eyes as the sentence I'd been struggling with, and just grasped, slipped through my fingers and vanished forever into the ether.

'C'mon. I want to go *now*. I've got a really early start in the morning.'

'It's OK, thanks. I'll do it tomorrow.' I stared desperately at the screen, hoping to, somehow, magically see the words form in front of me, or will my brain to hear an echo of their order at least – but it was too late. 'Shit! It's gone.'

'Don't swear at me, please.'

'I'm not swearing at you!'

Tris frowned. 'But because of me? There's not really a difference, I don't think? I'm trying to help. I know it's tough for you having to do everything when I'm away, but there's not even enough milk for me to have some cereal. Obviously I don't expect you to have cooked for me when I get back from the gym, but I need to eat *something*. So I'm going to go now. Text me a list.'

'Tris, I'm working!' I rubbed my eyes, tiredly. 'If I turned up at *your* work – halfway through a meeting – and told *you* I was going to do a food shop and could you text me a list immediately, what would you say?'

He threw his hands up. 'Exactly! I get it, OK? I'm never around to do a shop. You're making a point that I should go more by letting us practically run out of everything – so now I'm going. Congratulations.'

I looked at him confused. 'What are you on about? We're low on food, I know, but I'll go tomorrow. I'm not making a point about anything?'

'Can you please not be deliberately difficult and just *text me a list*.'

I stopped what I was doing and stared at him. 'Deliberately difficult? Seriously, what?'

'I'll be gone tomorrow – all right? I know I drive you mad, that my even being in the same room annoys you.'

'Tris, why are you picking a fight with me?' My voice had become emotionless.

'I thought you said you weren't going to do evenings anymore. I thought your deadline wasn't until after Christmas?'

'I write when the kids are at school, which usually works fine. It does not work when one of them is ill for a week and then it's half term, which puts me two weeks behind schedule, so I have to work all the hours God sent in the evening instead.'

'Then just tell them. Tell your publisher the book is going to be late. This is such bullshit!'

'The point is, I can do it, if I don't have to stop all the time to do lists. I told you, I can go shopping tomorrow.'

'Fucking hell!' He put his hands on his head. 'I am TRYING to help you, so you don't HAVE to go tomorrow. Look, just stop writing, OK? We don't need the money. I make enough. You don't *have* to do this.'

My whole career neatly dismissed. Just like that.

'I want to make this work,' I said quietly. 'You know that. It's important to me. It's my job and it's actually a good one to have when you have kids.'

'You make less from your writing, annually, than your agent's assistant makes. You realise *that*?'

I ignored him. 'I've worked really hard to keep it going and still be around for them before and after school. We've had no childcare costs at all. I've done it all, and you know what? Our kids have *inspired* me. They've driven me. I have made the time to write when I couldn't buy or borrow it.'

'That's really great,' he sighed. 'You go, girl!' He mimed a fake little fist bump, and I wanted to use mine to punch him in the face.

'I'm working on something I have to get finished sooner rather than later. It's important.'

'Aren't *we* important too, though? You and I? Our marriage? There has to be some time for that too, doesn't there?'

That was what did it. Wow. Just… wow. I went cold and then hot all over. I had to bite the inside of my lip to stop me from saying something I would regret and opening the box that it would then be impossible to shut.

'You know what? I actually think I will go and do the shopping now.' I put my computer to one side. 'I need to get out of the house. Perhaps you're right. I'm going slightly crazy. I've had the build for next door's extension going all day – the drilling has been hard to concentrate through and – you won't know this because you've been at the gym – for the last hour someone a few streets away has been having a party. Listen.' I stood up and walked to the window, throwing it open. A cold gust blew over me carrying with it the shrieks of overexcited teenage girls and the bellows of equally hyped up boys over a relentless bass. 'It took forever to get the kids to sleep.'

He listened. "But they're asleep now, and you've got headphones you can plug in, haven't you?'

The same ones I'd pulled out when he'd appeared in the doorway to complain about there not being any milk, in fact? I kept silent.

He came right up close to me and I looked away.

'Is there anything else wrong? Something you're not telling me?'

I shivered and shook my head as he reached past me to close the window again.

'I'm just very, very tired.'

'Neither you nor I are saving lives for a living. I think we need to remember that.' He placed a hand on my shoulder. 'Fucking hell, Charlotte, I'm just touching you. You don't have to flinch like I actually repulse you.'

I closed my eyes. I couldn't look at him.

He let go and when I opened them, he was sat on the sofa in his sweaty gym gear, peeling his socks off, glowering. 'Well as I said, I'm off tomorrow to Sheffield. I'll be back late on Friday night, so I can take over then. I'll take the kids out on Saturday. You can have the *whole day* to yourself to write. And before you say *anything*, I'm about to pick those socks up off the floor and put them in the washing basket, OK? They're not staying there.'

'You've got new gym stuff?' I noticed suddenly.

He stopped dead and glared at me. 'Do I need your permission before buying something?'

'Of course not. I just—'

'So then, yes, I've got a new top and shorts.' He spoke over me. 'If I can't buy myself a t-shirt from time to time, I'm not sure what the point is, to be honest?'

'Your case of wine arrived earlier today as well. The signature collection apparently.'

'*Our* case of wine.' He looked up at the ceiling. 'OK. You know what? Message received loud and clear. You *can* go to Waitrose. I'll only mess that up too. You know me – I'll just come back with foie gras and truffles. I'm such a cunt.'

'Tris! Please! That's revolting language.'

'It's just a word.' He shook his head and muttered something I didn't quite catch.

'What do you want to eat tonight then?'

'Nothing now actually,' he said simply, to which I inwardly screamed loud enough to pierce souls. 'It's obviously too much trouble. You sort yourself out. I'm going to bed.' He stood up but suddenly bent at the knee. 'Ow What the—!' He crouched down and peered at the rug, picking up the small piece of Teddy's Lego that he'd just trodden on, before flinging it violently at the log burner. I jumped as it hit the glass, and he marched from the room – leaving his socks in the middle of the carpet.

I didn't drive to Waitrose once I was in the car. Heart thumping, I pulled out of our space and drove the other way, to the end of the road, where I undid my window and listened. The party noise was coming from up the hill, several houses behind ours – one of the big ones on a private road. I hesitated and impulsively put my foot down, swinging right, into the lane at the top, ignoring the pompous sign that told me I had no right of way. Typical Sevenoaks – almost entirely constructed of discreet lanes leading to huge detached houses owned by CEOs. I crawled slowly past several multimillion pound homes, listening carefully through my open windows before arriving at a set of open, electric gates. I drove through, as three young girls, probably no more than sixteen, came out of the vast front door holding cans – I couldn't see in the dark if they were alcohol or not – seemingly about to walk around the side of the house where the noise was coming from.

'Excuse me!' I called through the passenger window as I pulled up alongside them. 'Girls?'

They turned and looked at me smiling at them. 'This is the house that the party's at, right?'

One of the three nodded cautiously.

'Can you do something for me?' My voice was friendly – and trustingly, they came closer. 'Could you tell the boys who are shouting that unless they keep it down, I'm going to call the police and tell them I've heard screaming here? And then I'm going to tell them I think there are illegal drugs on the premises.'

'Oh but there aren't,' one of the other girls stepped forward earnestly. She was right alongside the window. 'We're not like that, we—'

'It doesn't matter if there are or not,' I said. 'That's what I'll tell the police, and then I'll tell them you're all underage drinking too.' I smiled. 'So tell your friends *to shut the fuck up*, and let MY kids get some fucking sleep.'

They all drew back and stared at me. 'I think you need to calm down?' said one of the girls. She wasn't being rude, just truthful.

Her responsible bravery drew me up short, but I wouldn't allow myself to admit she was right. Instead, I merely glared at them, did up the window, reversed sharply backwards and roared off back down the lane – in my sensible Volvo estate, complete with kids' car seats in the back. Quite the slick getaway car. I looked down at my hand when I reached the main road, gripping the gearstick so tightly my fingers were white. I was shaking. I'd just sworn at and threatened three teenage girls when it wasn't them I was furious with.

I burst into tears and sobbed in the car. I had to pull over until I was able to drive away again. I could feel the tightly bound pain and anger bleeding out within me: old scar tissue barely holding together, in danger of ripping wide open. I felt bitterly ashamed of what I'd said to those poor girls and disgusted with myself.

*

And it's not even as if the occasional misdirected lancing over the last couple of weeks has relieved anything. It hasn't. This is eating me up from within. The nice, kind bits are almost all gone. I am not myself.

I take a deep breath and open my eyes as I feel the train slowing again and look around me. Inni Funni and her boyfriend have gone. We're pulling into Sevenoaks. I carefully lean forward, pick up my bag and make my way to the doors.

There is a massive queue for the taxis, so although I know I shouldn't, I start to walk home. I'm too tired to wait, the fresh air will clear my head – that train was unbearably hot – and there are plenty of other people around. A lot of them are male commuters late home from the office. I walk briskly and with my head up high, to make it clear I am not drunk – should any of them be thinking of attacking me. My stance makes it clear I will put up a fight. In my current state I would probably kill them.

I begin to feel less confident as the further we walk, the more people drop away... until it's only two men walking behind me. I can hear the sharp tack of my heeled boots striking the ground and echoing up the still, residential street. The temperature has significantly dropped – the Indian summer has well and truly ended – and even though I'm walking fast, I'm now cold. It's also hard to march and keep up any pace when I'm worried about slipping on the carpet of damp leaves. Lots of the houses still have last nights' pumpkins on display, no longer lit. When I put the kids' efforts in the garden waste bin this morning, one of them was already covered with creeping green fur inside, escaping through the mouth and dotted with small flies. We carved them too early. Peaked too soon.

I glance behind me and find that it's now just one man. I speed up as I walk right under a streetlight – exposing me completely – and wonder if he's aware of the effect of his presence. Or do men just walk home, oblivious? It's not that Sevenoaks is a particularly dangerous area, it isn't, but I am now moving so fast I have to pick the skirts of the dress up, as if I'm in a costume drama. That reminds me of Mia's comment about *Dangerous Liaisons* earlier, and I pant round the corner of our street as if I am being pursued by John Malkovich himself, smirking in his periwig, gaze fixed upon me. Except of course, I am no longer that young, attractive girl. He wouldn't bother. I clatter up the steps and our path, before rapping on the curtained sitting room window, my breath coming in short gasps until a shadow appears in the lit-up hallway, behind the fleur-de-lys etched glass panels of our front door. I hear the lock turn and it opens to reveal Flo's tired but smiling face.

I push past her and shiver as the warmth hits me, while she closes the door and shuts the rest of the world out. She frowns. 'You're freezing.' Her expression changes to one of disbelief. 'You didn't walk from the station?'

I sit down on the stairs and start to take off my boots. 'There were no cabs. I didn't have a choice.'

'You always have a choice. What you mean is, you couldn't be arsed to wait. That's really dangerous, please don't do it again – it's almost midnight. Anyway, how did you get on?'

I stand up and kick the boots away. 'I need a wee. Two seconds and I'll be right back.'

I pad upstairs and, en route to my bedroom, pause and stick my head around Teddy's door. The stars are still swirling on his ceiling, so I tiptoe in, turn off the nightlight and they vanish as quickly as if they were never there in the first place. I move over to the bed. My small son is squashed right against the wall – Clara taking up the rest of the space as she snores. They are both fast asleep. I'll move Clara back when I come up – or put her in with me. Heaven forbid we should all spend a night in our own beds. I cover them both and hold my breath as they stir slightly, escaping back out before either of them wakes.

In my room, I peel off the dress, glancing at my reflection in the wardrobe door with morbid fascination. If anyone had told me that I would drop several dress sizes effortlessly in a mere two and half weeks, I would have hugged them, but it's true. The weight has fallen off me. Incredibly, I'm in danger of starting to look too skinny. I really *must* buy a new bra. This one doesn't fit me anymore, which is a shame because my boobs were one of my best features. Now, I look like a little girl dressing up in her mother's underwear.

I turn away from myself, unhook the back and let it drop to the floor. You can't have it all. A thigh gap or boobs, but not both. I pick up a creased sweatshirt and shove it on before stepping back into my yoga pants from earlier. Folding up the dress carefully, I carry it back downstairs and, having collected my mobile from my bag on the way, go into the sitting room to find Flo curled up on the sofa watching Saturday's *Strictly* on catch-up.

'Here you are.' I pass the dress over to her as she sits up. 'Thank you for lending it to me. You were right – it made a difference. I felt a little less the woman who works home alone in sweatpants and a little more the old me.'

'You're very welcome. When everything settles down a bit, we'll get you some new clothes. You've just got out of the habit of shopping for yourself. You'll get your mojo back – don't worry.' She looks at me steadily. 'So how was it?'

I shake my head. 'We don't need to do this now. I can tell you everything in the morning. I've got a bit of a headache, to be honest, and you must be knackered. I feel really bad that you've waited up. Can I get you a glass of water? Did the kids wake, by the way? I see Clara got in with Teddy as usual.'

She pretends to narrow her eyes at me. 'Don't be ridiculous. I was hardly going to go to bed, was I? The kids were fine. I didn't hear a thing. I'm also going to need to be out of here by 7 a.m. tomorrow, so come on – let's do this. Did you see her?'

She is not going to be dissuaded. I take a deep breath and cross the room to sit down on the sofa opposite her, putting my mobile down next to me. 'Yes. I did.'

'You watched the play?'

I nod, and then everything goes. The control I've kept in check all evening since I kissed the children goodbye, smiling brightly to skip out of the door as if everything was normal – just breaks. I crumple from inside out – tears flood my eyes, snot pours from my nose, I close in on myself and start to sob.

Almost simultaneously I feel Flo's arms wrapping around me. She's already jumped up and is pulling me into a hug. I lean my head on her shoulder and moan with such pain that I hear her voice waver as she says: 'You are so brave! You are so, so brave!' She kisses my hair fiercely and I can tell without even looking at her face that she's crying too, because she wishes more than anything in the world that she could make all of this go away for me. She can't bear to see me hurting like this, when all she can do is hold me. She rocks me gently as I do big, ugly, noisy gulps and try to get a grip – but instead start shaking violently.

'I should never have told you,' she says after a moment more. 'I'm so, so sorry. I made the wrong decision. She definitely *is* the girl from Edinburgh then?'

'Yes,' I admit, my voice cracking again, and Flo groans, hugging me tighter.

'I'd forgotten how *young* she is,' I gasp 'and...' I draw back from my sister and meet her gaze head on, 'you're right. She looks exactly like me. More so than I remembered.'

Flo hesitates and then nods slowly. 'I told you, it was the first thing that struck me when she walked into my room and sat down. I was blown away. It could have been you. Well, you when you were still blonde and before you cut the fringe in.'

I swallow. 'I spoke to her, Flo.'

My sister's eyes widen and she shrinks back away from me, horrified. 'But you promised me. You swore that you wouldn't. Charlotte! What did you say? I could lose my job over this! You know that!'

I hold my hands up. 'Don't panic. I didn't say anything that could link her to you. I would never do that.'

'Not intentionally, no – but the brain works very differently in high stress situations, you don't recall things in the same way. You can let slip details you don't think are that significant but are a dead giveaway. I can't believe you did this!' She jumps up off the sofa and puts her hands on her head in panic as she looks at me. 'Even the fact that I told you about her and where to find her would see me struck off for breach of patient confidentiality. You get that, right?'

'Of course I do, but you're not her therapist anymore. You said you stopped seeing her?'

'I have, it was complete conflict of interest, but that's not the point. She'd already told me more than enough sensitive stuff about herself by the time I'd realised who she was. What did you say to her? Tell me exactly what you discussed. I need to be certain you haven't said anything that might compromise me.'

'How could I? You haven't told me any *details* at all!'

'What did you discuss?' She's starting to look angry as well as worried.

'I went to the stage door afterwards and asked her if she remembered me from Edinburgh; I don't think she did really. I wasn't going to say anything at all but she came out and she'd obviously been crying.' I clear my throat and look around for a box of tissues. I can't meet Flo's eye. 'I wanted to know what had made her upset.' I find them under the sofa and blow my nose.

Flo starts to pace up and down in front of the fireplace. 'This is exactly what I was afraid of. I explicitly told you *not* to talk to her. It's dangerous and it's not going to bring you the answers you want. You must see that?'

'She said she'd had a row with her boyfriend, Seth. They haven't been seeing each other long and he gets jealous of her being on stage because he's not an actor himself, apparently. She doesn't date actors because they're all gay, mad or married.'

Flo sighs heavily and flops down onto the sofa, opposite me, staring up at the ceiling.

'It's OK though,' I whisper. 'He texted and they arranged to meet up later tonight.'

Flo doesn't say anything for a minute, then jerks her head back and looks at me challengingly. 'Can we just stop for a minute before we go any further into that and discuss how that's an awful lot of information to get from just asking someone if they're OK? Lots of people would just say "fine thanks". At most they might say "I've had a row with my boyfriend". What you're describing sounds like a full-on conversation.'

I shake my head. 'She was very upset, that's all. She just blurted it out on the street in a rush. She was holding her phone as we were talking. I saw the message from him come in.'

Flo looks at me silently. 'OK – then what happened?'

I shrug. 'Nothing. I offered her a cigarette; she declined. She left.' I clear my throat and wipe my eyes with another tissue. 'That was it.'

'Bullshit,' Flo replies without a pause. 'I don't believe you. I thought we weren't doing secrets anymore? You wouldn't offer her a cigarette! Moreover, you forget I know *her*. Mia would have come after you – she'd have been curious about the woman who looks just like her, waiting by the stage door to ask her if she's OK before walking off into the night.'

'It wasn't like that. It was dark. You said yourself my hair is very different now. She barely recognised me, if at all – she was upset. I don't actually think she noticed for one second what I looked like. She was more interested in the dress.'

'Then you *did* discuss something else.' Flo pounces on that. 'She said she liked your dress?'

'So what? You didn't wear it in one of your counselling sessions, did you? No – so I think we're OK.' It's my turn to get up, arms crossed defensively and move to the door, pretending to listen for Clara and Teddy, so I can get off the hot seat under my sister's unfaltering gaze. 'Plus I'm pretty sure the designer made more than one.'

Flo points a warning finger at me again. 'Don't you dare get arsey when you broke every single promise you made to me. We agreed; just look, nothing else. I understand why you wanted to go and make sure it was her. I totally get that. I'd want to as well – but you did NOT need to speak to her, when you promised me you wouldn't. I shouldn't have told you.' She puts her head in her hands. 'I absolutely shouldn't have told you. No good is going to come of this. Please tell me what else you discussed with her, because I know you're not being honest with me.' She looks back up at me and waits.

'I made out like I was there to get Mathew Goode's autograph along with the rest of the female audience. He was very "good", by the way. A younger, sexed-up version of a self-obsessed, middle-aged, manipulative and amoral writer.'

'Great. I'm really pleased for him,' Flo says flatly. 'I still don't believe you.'

I don't say anything, just stand by the door, arms still folded. 'I want to go to bed now. Please. I'm so tired.'

'I know you are. You're exhausted. You're not eating properly. This is all you can think about. I understand that totally, but tonight was supposed to be about getting closure. Satisfying yourself that it's her but then moving on with *your* life, because you decided two weeks ago that's what you wanted to do. You told me that you had no intention of letting this change anything, or your family set-up. You know I'm not sure I agree that's the right path to go down, but I'm not going to influence you either way, other than to remind you that you were *adamant* you didn't want to say anything.'

'Tris rang me while I was with her,' I blurt. 'To let me know that he was in a noisy hotel in Sheffield.' I pause. 'I could have just told him then and there. It would have been so easy. "Guess who I'm looking at right now." He asked me outright yesterday if there was something I wasn't telling him.' I come back into the room and sit back down on the sofa, arms now hugging around my drawn-up knees. 'Mia has no clue who I am. She's just living her life, totally unaware of me, Clara, Teddy… it was like looking in a mirror and seeing myself from twenty years ago. She told me she was twenty-five – but that she can play younger.' I bite my lip and shake my head in disbelief. 'She's still just a baby. Just starting out.' I exhale again and look up at the ceiling to try and stop more tears from spilling over. 'I'm so angry, Flo. I don't know what to do with this *anger*.'

'I know. All of this is very complicated for you. It's shining a light on *lots* of feelings you've not had to confront for years.' She begins to drum her fingers on the side of the sofa. 'Look, I'm sorry to keep on about this, but you very obviously had a conversation with her. Why would she randomly tell you she can play younger, that she's twenty-five? You're not telling me the real context here and that's not fair. I took a huge professional risk in talking to you about her at all – but that's not actually the worst thing about this. You haven't thought this through. I told you not to talk to her for lots of very good reasons. Why do you think she's in therapy in the first place?' She sits forward, energetically. 'Suppose I was to tell you that she's dangerous?'

'She can't be, because you would have told me that straight away. You wouldn't have risked her hurting me.'

'But what about if she's a risk to *herself*? Did you think of that? She's vulnerable – by the very definition of being in therapy. Forget the impact of her finding out who you are, it would be enough for most patients to discover their therapist has divulged information they were trusted with to *anyone* else, full stop. That's the whole point of having a counsellor. You tell them your innermost thoughts and fears. The deep dark stuff no one else knows. So suppose Mia finds out I've betrayed that trust, has a massive setback, kills herself and then it all comes out why. Now how do you feel? Still OK with talking to her?'

I don't reply.

'Charlotte?' Flo presses me for an answer, but all I can do is look away.

'I don't want to hurt her.'

'Then leave her alone.' Flo is emphatic.

'Why was she in therapy?'

'I can't tell you.'

'But there's nothing seriously wrong with her?'

'All I can say is I'm not working with her now. You've got to step back from this. You have a life with Tris, Clara and Teddy that you want to keep exactly as it is, for the children's sake. Remember? Remember telling me that?'

'Yes,' I admit.

'If you *do* want to confront this by getting it all out in the open and telling Tris, you can – there are ways we could think of that would achieve it without compromising me, but that isn't what you want. You want your life to stay as it is.' She sighs and retrieves her phone from the floor by the sofa. 'Why don't I babysit for you and Tris next week so you can go out together?'

'Maybe. We'll see. Go to bed,' I say. 'And thank you for tonight, in every which way.'

'But you'll stay away from her now? Promise?' She stands up.
'Yes. I promise.'

She walks over to me, bends down and kisses my forehead. 'You should go to bed too. Even if you don't sleep, your body needs to rest. You don't wish I *hadn't* told you, do you?' She looks down at me, suddenly troubled.

I shake my head. 'I wish she'd found someone else to be her counsellor and not you, though.'

'Me too.' She sighs. 'I just imagined how you would have felt if it had somehow come out that I knew all along. You'd have forgiven me, obviously, but you'd have been heartbroken.' She reaches out and squeezes my hand. 'I love you. We're going to get you through this. I promise.'

I blow her a kiss as she disappears off upstairs, and lean back on the sofa, retrieving my mobile from where it's slipped under a cushion. No new messages.

I think about Mia, out there somewhere in Blackheath. I close my eyes and see the confusion on her face when I made my offer: half a million pounds – her share – to pretend to be me.

I slip out into the side passage to smoke a last cigarette before bed.

It's not as if it *couldn't* happen. I've heard of mega deals being done and read about them in the news. I *really* want Mia to do this and to do this for Mia. I breathe a cloud of smoke out and begin to settle back down, but there are, of course, a thousand reasons why it might not work and then what? I shiver. I have already lied to my sister, which makes me feel dreadful, but I had no choice. Flo would make it her mission to talk me out of my plan if she knew what I'd actually said to Mia tonight… It's not as if I'm going to let any of this compromise Flo; not for a second. This is *my* risk. I stub out the fag on the wall. There is still time to stop this, of course. It's barely begun.

'Mia Justice.' I whisper her name under my breath like a promise. I'll sleep on it.

CHAPTER SIX

MIA

'Get off your phone!' Seth teases as he comes back into the bedroom. His hair is still damp from the shower and as his elbows open wider to force a stubborn top button, his shirt lifts, briefly exposing his chest and flat tummy. Such a shame he has to go to work. 'It's a really unhealthy way to start the day,' he nods at my mobile, 'binging on a load of other people's anger.'

'All right, Dad,' I tease, and his face falls. 'Sorry,' I say immediately, propping myself up on my forearms.

'It's OK,' he says bravely, but I see him glance at himself worriedly in the wardrobe mirror and I feel bad for making such a stupid throwaway remark.

'To be fair, it *was* a Dad thing to say.' He tucks his shirt into his suit trousers and turns his attention to his cuffs.

I watch him, fascinated. 'Why don't you just have buttons there too, wouldn't it be easier?'

'My father always told me that a gentleman is someone who can play the accordion, but doesn't—'

I laugh, having not heard that before.

'And he also never wears button cuffs.' He turns to face me. 'I think that probably gets cancelled out if you're putting links into last night's shirt though.' He gestures down at his creased sleeves.

I smile lazily back at him. 'Will everyone at work think you're a dirty stop out?'

'I'll sneak in via the back door.' He winks at me. 'I have a fresh suit and shirt hanging in my office – they'll be none the wiser… it's sensible to keep a clean uniform handy in case you have to pull an all-nighter,' he explains; I must have looked confused. 'Although that usually involves a mountain of very dull client work, several colleagues and a lot of coffee. This was a lot more fun. What are you listening to?' He nods at the phone. 'I like it. It's very chilled, bit sensual for 7 a.m. though.'

Sensual… Yessss! My careful selection has had just the effect I was looking for. 'Jamie Woon. The track's called "Sharpness",' I say nonchalantly. I roll over onto my tummy, but no one ever pulled off seductive while looking like a giant sausage roll, all wrapped up in a duvet, so I deliberately push it down to reveal my bare back. 'It's hot in here,' I yawn. I can feel his eyes on my skin.

Sure enough, he climbs on the bed behind me and kisses first the base of my back, then moves up to my neck, softly sliding his hands round onto my breasts. 'I don't want to go to work.'

I twist onto my back and look up at him innocently. 'Then don't. Stay and play with me instead.'

He groans and lets his head drop. 'You have no idea how much I want to do that, but I have to go.' He studies my face and moves a stray bit of hair out of the way before gently kissing my lips. A new track comes on: Eliza's 'Wasn't Looking'. It's a blatant sex song. Slow, persistent beat, dreamy, husky vocals.

Seth looks at me and raises an eyebrow. 'What are you trying to do to me? This isn't on random shuffle at all, is it? This is a playlist. A deliberate, seduction playlist.'

'Of course not!' I protest, embarrassed at being caught out.

'Where's your phone, let's see what else you've got lined up to lure me.' He tries to grab it, but I get there first, rolling right onto it, hiding it under my body, my hair falling over my shoulders.

'Noooo! Don't,' I insist, my voice muffled – as, laughing, he tries to reach it – 'You'll break it!'

'OK, OK.' I feel him get up and release me. 'But honestly – you don't need to try and persuade me. There's nothing I want to do more than stay.'

I turn onto my back again and blow him a kiss.

He looks at me, lying in front of him, half-naked and his smile fades. 'You're so beautiful.'

His sudden serious tone makes me stop playing games and blush bright red. In the beat of silence that follows, where we look at each other, something shifts in the atmosphere. I know I don't imagine it and sure enough he hesitates, before saying casually: 'suppose I were to leave a couple of things *here*. A clean shirt, a toothbrush – that sort of thing. Would that be OK?'

I bite my lip, unable to hide my delight. 'I think that would OK, yeah.'

'Not too soon?' He looks suddenly uncertain and shy. Basically completely adorable. I have always had a thing for men in sharp suits, working that competent, professional vibe. Probably because it's the total opposite of what I'm usually surrounded by? If most actors were an item of clothing, they'd be slightly grubby jeans.

'Not too soon at all,' I tell him truthfully.

His face splits into a huge, spontaneous smile. He darts forward and, putting his hands on the bed either side of me, he kisses my mouth as I sit up, almost knocking me off balance in his enthusiasm.

'Shit – sorry!' he says, as I giggle, and gently put *my* hands either side of his face to steady myself.

'It's OK,' I whisper, feeling happiness beginning to suffuse through me. I can feel his stubble beneath my fingertips. I don't want to let him go.

'Could I see you tonight?' he asks. 'I mean, you've probably already got plans, but…'

I pull a face. 'Yeah – I do. I'm sorry. I'm meant to be going out to a friend's birthday drinks after work.' I hesitate, about to say I could cancel them, but I've not totally abandoned my senses yet, or my principles. It's still early days and I'm not making the same mistakes again this time and ditching my whole life, much as I like him. And I really like him.

'No problem, I understand.' He grins when I don't even offer to meet him somewhere afterwards. 'It's my turn to have my kids this weekend, but can I take you to dinner on Monday night?' He straightens up, swings round and grabs his jacket from the bedroom chair in one smooth movement.

'I'm not free then either,' I say regretfully. 'Gotta show to put on!' I do half-hearted jazz hands, then let them fall to the bed. 'I really need to try and get a fun job next. Something sparkly and silly. But in answer to your question, I wish I could. I'm sorry.'

He sighs. 'Is this why most actors date each other, because you're the only ones lying around in bed all day while everyone else has to get up and go to work?'

I give a mock, outraged gasp and fling a pillow at him, which he dodges, adding: 'And then all you do is go and faff around for a couple of hours.'

I flick him the vs but confess, 'Yeah, pretty much. It's just easier for most people in the biz to date each other, I guess. That's not to say dating a civilian can't work,' I add quickly. 'It just takes a bit of effort.'

'"A civilian"?' He picks me up on it immediately, amused.

'What Liz Hurley once called non-acting folk.'

'What a fabulously derogatory term.' He checks his pockets for his phone, then moves over to pick up his laptop bag, resting it on the bed and unzipping it to check he's got everything.

'I know someone else who calls you Muggles.' I consider. 'That's worse, I think. Still – only a week to go and I'll be officially unemployed. I'll have all the evenings free you want then. You'll be sick of the sight of me.'

'No, I won't – and something is going to come up. You'll see.'

I open my mouth to tell him about Charlotte's offer, but stop at the last minute. She specifically told me not to.

'No one as talented as you gets to rest up for long,' he continues. 'We should enjoy it while it lasts though. We'll actually be able to go out to dinner together at a normal time in the evening. That would be nice.'

I can't help noticing he's really starting to talk like we're a proper couple. Things are definitely getting more serious. 'Silver linings to every cloud,' I agree calmly, determined not to betray my excitement. 'Yes, it will be very nice.'

Before he can answer, the music changes again, only this time it's Robin Thicke's 'Lost Without U'. I forgot this was on there and hastily scramble to the phone, to change it, but it's too late, Seth is already pulling a face. 'Not sure about that one. It's a bit Man from Del Monte, isn't it?'

'Huh?' I look at him, confused. I have no idea what he's talking about.

'Never mind.' He picks up his laptop bag. 'Right. I really must go.' He bends and kisses me briefly this time. 'I'll call you. Have a great day.'

'You too.' I listen for the front door to the flat slamming shut behind him and once it has, sigh and collapse back onto the pillows, still holding my phone. I lie there for a minute staring at the ceiling, already bored in the silence and now nervy too, thinking about this time next week, when the run will be finished and I'll have nothing I need to get up for. No commitments bar one weekly counselling session with yet *another* new therapist. That's not at all depressing.

I should just go back to sleep and not start to squirrel about this. I'll be shit-tired tonight otherwise, but my brain is *so* wired now… plus even if I were to doze off again, I'd get make-up all over my pillow. I'm looking forward to the bit where I feel relaxed enough not to have to sneak out of bed before his alarm goes off, to put on some slap, so I look 'naturally beautiful' when he wakes up next to me. The trouble is, I spend so much time in heavy stage make-up, I really do feel naked without it, and I'm not ready to reveal myself completely – yet.

I turn onto my side decisively and select a new playlist. The sound of Glen Campbell fills the room and I start to sing along as I return to Charlotte Graves's Instagram page and the information-gathering sesh I was conducting while Seth was in the shower.

It's not that it's a *bad* account. She's got some reasonably funny posts on there, but I can see what she meant last night about her career having flatlined. I'm not surprised – she's definitely not getting her social media right. There's nothing to mark it out as special or interesting – which will be why she only has four hundred followers, most of whom seem to be other writers I've never heard of either. Her feed is all cappuccinos and glasses of gin, random book covers and the stupid 'arty' shots everyone chucks in – the last of which was a blue sky seen through the branches of an autumn tree… yawn… She also doesn't know how to use hashtags, doing that really irritating thing of thinking they're meant to be funny add-on comments rather than understanding they're actual search terms. Someone needs to tell her there is no point whatsoever to putting #anyoneseenmybraintoday? Weirdly, there's hardly anything personal at all. No pics of her, or other people and only a handful that show the inside of her house – a Victorian terrace, from what I can make out. I scroll over one and realise there's a toy kitchen in the corner of the room. She's got little kids? I peer at it more closely. Most parents I know – my sister for example – have their kids in pretty much *every, single* picture they post. I guess Charlotte is just very private. Maybe *that's* her problem and why this page has no identity whatsoever but, given how striking she is in real life, it's also a strange decision. Who wouldn't want to look at her? She's fabulous.

I turn over in bed again and switch to her Twitter, which is even worse. Just a pinned tweet saying she hardly ever tweets and redirecting potential followers to her Facebook page, which in turn is much of the same as her Insta. Fifty Shades of Beige. Wow.

Well, I get why she wants a new public persona, that's for sure, but approaching me to *be* her is a pretty extreme way of going about it. In fact, it feels even more outlandish the morning after the night before. What makes someone proposition a virtual stranger like that? She's either completely convinced that this new book she's written is SO good she's not messing, and bringing in the big guns from the outset to do whatever it takes to make it work… or she's completely mad.

I hesitate – but she didn't seem mental. I've both been one, and had my share of, crazies… mostly at the stage door. Everyone has. The super-keen fan who is convinced you should be best friends. The dodgy bloke following you on Twitter; the pushy mum who pretends to want to ask your advice about how to get her daughter into stage school, but is really hoping you know the producer and will introduce her. Charlotte was none of those. She was very – poised.

She spoke about life-changing sums of money so calmly, like it was normal. I chew my lip. I mean, it happens. People make a *lot* of money from films, books and music. Millions and *millions* of pounds. Obscene amounts of money… and she's obviously an established writer, that's not in doubt. I completely remember speaking to her at the Edinburgh book festival. She looked *so* different then – and getting to ten books doesn't happen overnight. If it *were* to all work out as she promised… I jump up suddenly, throwing back the covers. Did I keep the book she signed or actually give it to Kirsty? I scan the extensive shelves in the sitting room, mostly full of my parent's books – but there's nothing. Instead, I look her up on Amazon. It turns out she's got quite a few decent reader reviews… although one of the top ones for her first book, about the crazy lady, is a one star total takedown that baldly states: 'The writer has either never been in a relationship or has only been in dysfunctional ones.' Ouch… But it's a novel, right? So fair to assume Charlotte made the story up and didn't, in fact, base it on real life, as this person is obviously suggesting? I buy it with one click. And just like that, it's on the way to me, all set for delivery in the morning.

*

I actually forget all about it after that – until the doorbell goes off like machine-gun fire in my head at 10 a.m. the next day, jolting me awake with several shocked expletives because I randomly had a setback last night. I was only going to have one drink after work – but went badly off-piste after that – so if I'm going to get up and do anything, it'll be to puke, violently – not for some non-essential action like answering the door. I ignore the buzzer and go back to sleep; only realising what it was when I practically brain myself tripping over the packet on the doorstep when leaving the flat a couple of hours later for the Saturday matinee. It's not just because it's been left in a stupid place – although it has – but mostly because I'm wearing shades in an inadequate defence against the aggressively bright November morning and so simply don't see it.

I clutch the book to my chest, eyes down, as I walk to the train station, stepping round people on weekend time. It seems like I'm the only one not in love with London today. Everyone has gone all bright-eyed and bushy-tailed in the cold winter sunshine.

There's a palpable sense of 'leading up to Christmas' excitement in the air as I walk through Covent Garden at the other end of my journey, and in the queue at Starbucks – this gingerbread latte is either going to kill or cure me – I hear two girls talking about how they need to have their annual watching of *Love Actually* when they've finished their shopping later. I have to restrain myself from butting in and asking them exactly what they find so cute about

Andrew Lincoln telling his best mate's new wife that he's in love with her, *behind his pal's back, mere days after their wedding.* I don't really want to get started on the subversive subtext of *Love Actually.* I am the Grinch: taking out on other people my disappointment in myself for getting trashed last night.

My mood has crashed dramatically and I find myself wishing I were with Seth. The fact that he always has a smile on his face is one of the things I like best about him. I pull my phone out of my bag, but change my mind at the last minute. He's with his kids. It's not fair. It's their time with him now. I don't want to disturb them.

So for want of something better to do – I take my drink, sit down at a table and start to read Charlotte's book. I'm pretty proud of myself as I'm the *only* person not on their phone, but it's not long before I'm genuinely engrossed. Charlotte's précis was bang on: the woman in the book – coincidentally called Mia, which is a bit freaky – is batshit mental, but like a car crash; I can't tear my eyes away. I want to find out what's going to happen next. Having found out her boyfriend is cheating on her, she does indeed go after the other woman, stopping at nothing to protect her happy ever after with the man she believes is 'the one'. It's pretty chilling. And very sad, because how could a man like that ever be worth fighting for? Emotional rawness pours off the page and I wonder if that one star reviewer might not be right after all. The way Charlotte describes the discovery of betrayal feels very authentic indeed. She's been there too – I can tell.

*

I'm hooked… but have to put the book down to do two shows… so, I'm only just getting to the bit where they are blatantly going to have a dramatic love-triangle-three-way-showdown, on the bus to my parents' for lunch the following morning. I wander up their road slowly, turning the pages eagerly and stop outside the gate to read the final chapter.

My sister opens the front door and calls: 'Are you actually coming in, or are you just going to stand there all day?'

I hold up a hand absently, read the last few lines, shake my head in disbelief and walk up the path, still holding it.

'What's that you've got there?' Kirsty grabs my hand and inspects the cover, before taking it and flicking through. 'You got me one of hers last year, didn't you? I've read this one too – it's really old, isn't it? A sort of *Fatal Attraction* set-up?'

I consider that. 'Not really. Nothing happens, to be honest. No one dies or anything. A woman finds out her bloke is cheating on her.'

'It's a revenge thing then? I can't remember.'

'No. She just wants to keep him at any cost.'

Kirsty shrugs, pulls a face as I walk past her into the house and shuts the door behind me. 'Honestly no recollection of it at all. How are you anyway?' She leans in to kiss me.

'Tired,' I sigh, and Kirst narrows her eyes.

'Sorry. Not in your league tired,' I say hastily. 'It's just been a bit of a full-on week. That's all. Where are the boys?' I kick off my shoes before slipping my bag from my shoulder, which Kirsty catches, placing the book back in it and hanging it up on the end of the bannister. I take my coat off, shivering luxuriantly as the cosy warmth begins to spread through my body.

'They're upstairs. Let's go through though, because lunch has been ready for a bit and I'm not sure they can hang on much longer. EVERYONE!' she bellows suddenly, inches from my face, making me wince and step back a bit. 'Auntie Amy's here! We can eat now!'

'Mia! It's Mia now, remember?' I correct her and, flustered, she waves her arms around before taking my coat, too.

'Sorry. Genuine mistake. DOWNSTAIRS, PLEASE!'

The ceiling creaks in response to three small boys scrambling to attention above us. Seconds later they appear and thunder down the stairs in a pushy crush, breathlessly shouting 'hi Auntie Amy!' as they shove past me on their way to the kitchen. I throw my arms wide in frustration, and Kirsty shhhes me, hanging my coat over my bag.

'They're so hungry they've gone light-headed – that's all. They don't know what they're saying. Come on, or there might not be anything left.'

She needn't worry. My poor mum has obviously worked very hard all morning and there is a veritable mountain of food to go round. As everyone starts to load up plates, she trots backwards and forwards from the kitchen to the dining room, re-appearing with yet another dish of vegetables, or Yorkshire puddings, her glasses steaming up as she carefully places down a brimming gravy jug before wiping her hands on her apron. 'Has everyone got what they need?' She looks around us anxiously, then glances at the clock. 'Well there we are – it's only just gone one o'clock.' She sinks down onto a chair in relief. Kirsty obviously set a specific time to eat and Mum has bust a gut to get there. Time trial roast cooking. Lucky her.

'Thanks, Mum,' Kirsty says, patting her arm. 'It's just they go beyond hunger if it gets too late, then no one eats anything properly and it's just a *nightmare*.'

I look doubtfully at my three nephews. They don't look like they're having any problems to me. They've gone completely silent and have their noses in their plates, troughing away like piglets. I'm reminded suddenly of the scene in *Snatch* where Brick Top does his monologue about pigs being the best way to dispose of a human body as they eat *every last scrap* of skin and bone – but keep my mouth shut. Firstly Kirst would not be amused by the comparison, although I have to say, much as I love my nephews – and they are the cutest ever – it's a pretty spot-on likeness right now.

Secondly, although I know the boys would *love* to hear all about pigs' more hardcore characteristics, my sister would not. It would not be deemed 'suitable' information. She has only just let them watch the *Peter Rabbit* movie, because Mr McGregor dies graphically on-screen of a heart attack. She told them he trips over a rake you can't see and just passes out. Bad things don't happen in my sister's kids' world.

I take a mouthful of roast potato and silently thank God that I never have to watch *Snatch* again as long as I live. Hugo must have made me sit through *hundreds* of viewings of his starring role: Angry Gypsy #2 – as he appears in the credits, alongside Brad Pitt and Jason Flemyng. Part of me secretly hopes he's out there right now, inflicting it on Ava instead. That might just be a fitting punishment for her being such a disloyal best friend; a lifetime of being forced to watch Angry Gypsy #2 – the role that was going to launch Hugo's career into the A-list but never did. Anyway… water under the bridge. Make like Elsa and 'Let It Go'… Good luck to them both; I mean that sincerely, but I also hope neither of them ever dares contact me again as long as I live. Particularly Ava. Not that she ever would after what I did.

'You all right, darling?'

I look up quickly to see Mum watching me keenly. She does not miss a trick, my mother – not a single trick. I nod, and she looks relieved.

'How's work been this week?' Dad asks, smiling at me.

'Oh, you know.' I decide not to tell them about Theo's ranty, unkind outburst. They'll only become outraged on my behalf, and this time next week he'll be out of my life for good. 'It's always a bit weird when you get to the end of a run.'

'We wondered if you'd let us take you to a late dinner after your final show on Saturday?' Dad enquires, adding hastily 'or not?' as I hesitate. 'You've probably got after-show parties and that sort of thing though,' he continues, waving a hand. 'We didn't think of that, did we?' He turns to Mum. 'No – don't you worry. You see your friends instead. We've got all the time in the world to take you out. You should put the run to bed properly.'

In truth, I'm only dithering because I suspect Seth is going to ask to see me afterwards and, much as I feel bad about it, I'd rather see him than Mum and Dad. I couldn't give a toss about giving this play a proper send-off. It can get its coat and sling its hook for all I care. 'But you don't really want to come into town on Saturday night, anyway, do you?' I wrinkle my nose. 'Plus you've seen me in it a million times already. Honestly, I don't mind.'

Mum looks doubtful. 'But you need *some* family there on the last night. We're so proud of what you've achieved and we want to be there to support you.' She reaches across the table and gives my hand a squeeze. 'You've come such a long way, sweetheart.'

There's a moment of pause and I wonder if they're also picturing me lying listlessly on their sofa in pyjamas this time last year, catatonic with grief, unable to do anything but watch *Strictly Come Dancing*, those constant tears streaming down my face. I clear my throat. 'I'm very lucky to have you all. I couldn't have got everything back on track without you. My er…' I glance at my seemingly oblivious nephews but nonetheless try to think of another word for breakdown, 'perfect storm moment,' I pause to let my meaning sink in, 'was really challenging all round. You were brilliant and I love you all.'

'What's a perfect storm?' Max, the youngest, asks.

'A really big whirlwind, thunder and lightning, all at once,' says my brother-in-law, and my sister smiles at him gratefully, but then he burns his brownie points by asking me: 'So have you got anything lined up for when you finish, then?'

My sister scowls at him, and he looks confused. 'What? What's wrong with asking that?'

'Everyone knows actors rarely go from job to job these days,' Kirst says quickly. 'Even the household names.'

'It's OK,' I step in. 'I don't mind. I haven't had any castings yet, but something will come up.'

'So do you call your agent and have to hassle them for stuff or do they call you?' Bill persists, and Kirsty looks at him incredulously.

'What?' he says again, genuinely confused. 'I'm just interested. What you want to do,' he looks at me thoughtfully, 'is get a part in *EastEnders*.'

'That's what *everyone* says to actors,' Kirsty snaps. 'You should get a part in one of the soaps.'

'Oh. Sorry,' Bill shrugs and returns to his food, 'I'm obviously way behind the curve.'

'Something *will* come up though, darling,' Mum adds reassuringly. 'I can feel it in my bones.'

'Absolutely!' beams Dad. 'It's just a question of time! That's all, and—'

'Actually,' I cut in, having been made more than aware that they are all genuinely anxious about me; obviously terrified that I'm going to crash and burn in seven days' time, once I've got no focus anymore. 'Something is already in the pipeline.'

I can't bear it – I want to make it better for them and take some of their worry away… it makes me feel so guilty that I've been such a burden to them.

'Oh?' My mother instantly looks proud and excited, putting down her napkin.

They all look at me and my mouth just says it. I don't even know what messed-up part of my brain it comes from, except it's probably the same bit that *always* gets me into trouble: the act first, think later lobe.

'I've written a book.' Oh god, I've said it out loud…

Kirsty gives a surprised half-laugh, mouth falling open, and Bill's eyebrows rise up before he shrugs and helps himself to more potatoes. Mum just stares at me, and Dad claps his hands. 'Darling, how lovely! Bravo you!'

'I just have so much time during the day, you know?' I reach for the water and pour myself a slightly shaky glass. 'I thought I could put it to good use and see if anything came from it.' If

Charlotte changes her mind about me, just disappears and I never hear from her again, I'm screwed.

'Well come on then – what's it about?' Dad says eagerly.

'It's a thriller.' I gulp quickly and end up coughing a bit. 'Excuse me.'

'What sort of thriller?' Dad forks up a bit of chicken. 'Police procedural? Crime? Or Domestic Noir, as I believe it's called?'

I stare at him blankly. Damn his newly retired, obsessive daily newspaper habit; from current affairs through to property, arts reviews, business and culture there's not much Dad doesn't have at least a basic working knowledge of. 'It's cross-genre?' I hazard, and Dad nods, impressed. 'I probably shouldn't go into the nuts and bolts of it now.'

I look pointedly at the boys, and Kirsty says quickly: 'Yes, thank you. That would be great, if it's unsuitable.'

'No problem.' I look down and pretend to concentrate on cutting a parsnip while I try to gather my rapidly scrambling thoughts, but now it's Mum's turn.

'Well, you always were filling notebooks with pages and pages of imaginings when you were little,' she smiles at me, 'but you've not mentioned a single thing about this? I mean, it's wonderful, but a bit surprising!'

'I didn't want to say anything in case I didn't finish it and it was just a… I don't know… whim. You know me.' I reach for the pepper. 'But, I did and now I might have a go at seeing if someone wants to publish it.' I clear my throat. 'I've been told that publishers really like debut authors, and my already being an actress and having a bit of a profile is helpful too, apparently. So we'll see…' I exhale. 'I don't want to get your hopes up though, it might not get anywhere at all.'

'Or, you might be the next J.K. Rowling,' Bill says, through a mouthful. 'That'd be a smart move; a wizard James Bond. Jack Reacher does magic. That's what *I* call cross-genre. Sounds good to me!'

'I can see that it might bring you some added publicity,' Mum says sensibly, ignoring Bill, 'if you had a book published. The two careers could feed off each other. I expect that was your thinking, wasn't it?'

She is *so* sharp.

'Exactly.' I pick up my water again, wishing I'd kept my stupid mouth shut. 'But please, guys, let's not get ahead of ourselves. Writing a book is one thing, getting it published is a whole different story.'

'No pun intended,' says Bill, tapping his nose and pointing at me. 'I like it. You're already talking like an author. So what do you do next, take it to your agent?'

'Probably. I should see what he recommends.' I'm starting to feel a bit hot and I absolutely can't look at my mother. 'I'll keep you all posted.' I smile widely and put my glass down firmly. 'Can we talk about something else now?'

'Of course we can,' Dad says. 'But I have every faith in you. When one of our girls turns her mind to something, watch out world!'

Kirsty smiles faintly, but shoots me a worried look. Something tells me I'm not going to have heard the last word on this.

'But if it doesn't get where you hope it will, it is still an enormous achievement and we are very proud of you.' Dad reaches out and squeezes my hand. I have to swallow a lump in my throat. 'Have you met my daughter, the actress and published author?' he pretends to ask the company of the table.

My nephews look between each other, confused, and Mum says gently: 'All right darling, let's leave it now… too much pressure,' she murmurs, not quite discreetly enough, picking up her napkin again.

'*Please* can we talk about something else?' I beg desperately.

'How's your love life, then?' says Bill, sitting back and trying to pick a bit of chicken from between his teeth. 'When are we finally going to get to meet this new bloke?'

Kirsty rounds on him furiously. 'Could you be more socially challenged?'

Thankfully, we are spared an answer to that, because my brother FaceTimes us from New York with my sister-in-law and my other nephew and niece. They are about to brave the cold, wrap up warm and head out for what they call Sunday Second Breakfast, because the kids had cereal at 7 a.m. but could now force down a pancake or two, while the grown-ups want to get stuck into some coffee. I'm incredibly grateful to have the spotlight taken off me, and everyone is in a cheery mood once they've gone and we clear the plates; a little NYC glamour having dusted our day like the first flurry of snow, or sifted icing sugar falling on French toast. Bill starts talking about getting a new sledge for the boys, Dad suggests we all watch a Christmas movie together after lunch, while Mum and Kirsty protest that it's *much* too early to be feeling this festive. The heat is no longer on.

*

Until Kirsty intercepts me coming out of the downstairs loo, once we've washed up.

Mum is putting plates away, Dad is making a selection of decaf and caf tea and coffee for everyone and Bill seems to have sloped off with the papers having let the boys disappear upstairs again.

'So – this book of yours then?' Kirsty smiles as I emerge. 'I have a couple of questions.'

'Do you think they're OK up there?' I try to distract my sister, nodding up towards the bedroom. 'They've gone very quiet. Don't you always say that's when you really have to worry?'

'They're fine.' She doesn't take her eyes from me. 'What's it really about then?'

'Um.' I look away. 'I don't really want to say at this precise moment, if that's OK?'

She continues to stare at me. 'I thought as much. You've based it on Hugo leaving you for Ava, haven't you? That's why you were reading that other book about an affair, to see how other authors have done it, and if it's too similar to yours?'

It's both very plausible and yet also such complete bollocks, I genuinely don't know what to say.

She leaps on my silence, instantly.

'Oh Amy, please don't do this,' she begs.

'Mia!' I correct her sharply. 'I'm not Amy anymore. I'm never going to be that pushover girl again. You know it's important to me. Please try and get it right. Sometimes it actually feels like you do it on purpose.'

'Sorry – Mia. I meant Mia. It's just when I get stressed I forget and…' She exhales heavily. 'Sweetheart, I don't know who encouraged you to start this book – if it was one of your counsellors' ideas to get it all out of your system in some sort of cathartic way – but don't put your own thinly veiled story out there, please. People are so vicious – they'll tear you apart and I'm worried you're not strong enough to take that.' She puts an earnest hand on my arm and I can see genuine fear in her eyes. 'It's different being a character in a play or on TV, you can hide away behind them. But putting yourself and your own experiences up for grabs – that's something else completely. I know you're going to tell me you've not based it on what happened, but you were obsessed by them being together at the time when you must have started writing this book. They were all you could think about when you were… ill and at The Pines.' Her eyes fill with tears and she looks crossly up at the ceiling. 'Shit! Sorry,' she whispers and wipes them away angrily with the sleeve of her jumper. 'I'm sorry. What I mean is, I don't want you to have to think about this anymore. You've moved on. You're doing so well.'

I reach out with my other hand and take hers, firmly, in mine.

'I had a breakdown for lots of reasons that weren't just about Hugo and Ava, although yes, they kicked it all off and were definitely my focus for quite an unhealthy length of time. I know that when I was really bad – that bit when I was in The Pines in particular – you were terrified I was going to hurt myself and we both know I came very close.' I don't hide from this fact. It's too important. To pretend it wasn't that big a deal after the event isn't fair to her or me. It invalidates the support she gave me and how hard *I* worked too. 'I'm so sorry you went through that. Kirsty, look at me.' I wait until she does as I ask. 'I *promise* you, I will never publish a book based on my actual life. It's not about Hugo and Ava – I swear. I wouldn't give the egotistical bastards the satisfaction, for one thing.'

She shakily half-laughs. 'Promise?'

'I promise.'

'OK.' She swallows. 'Then I sincerely hope it gets picked up by someone, they pay you a truck load of money for it and you wipe the floor with Hugo. I hope it's *everywhere* and your success sticks in his throat every day he sees it.'

'I'm not sure that's a healthy motivation. Have you considered therapy?' I deadpan and she shoots me a look.

'Hey, listen,' she squeezes my hand back and then lets me go, 'I hate my husband's lack of tact, but… how *is* your love life and when *are* we going to get to meet this new bloke?'

I shrug. 'I'm not deliberately hiding Seth away, it's just hard because I've been working, he's working when I'm off… and at least every other weekend, like this one, he has his kids.'

Kirsty doesn't say anything, just looks at the floor.

'Now what?' I say lightly. 'Go on, spit it out.'

'Nothing, it's nothing,' she replies quickly. 'I just wish he didn't already have kids and baggage, that's all. I don't want that for you. I want something easy, fun. Not an ex-wife – no matter how nice she may or may not turn out to be – and all the shit that goes with that. And if you hadn't gone for an older man, *again*,' she continues, as I start to protest, 'you wouldn't have to be sharing him at weekends. It's going to be like this, *always*. Disruption, fitting around someone else's demands and requests – and it doesn't have to be this way. You're too little to have to deal with all of this shit.'

'I'm twenty-five, he's only forty-one, he's also not HugeEgo,' I try to lighten the tone by using the nickname she herself coined for Hugo, 'and it is what it is.' I gesture helplessly. 'You can't help who you fall in love with.' The words are out there before I can stop them.

'Love?' Kirsty looks shocked.

I nod, almost guiltily.

'Wow. OK. Well – we better meet him soon then, hadn't we?'

'You'll be nice to him, if I bring him here?'

'Of course I will,' she replies irritably. 'Probably. But what about if you want kids of your own with him at some point? Have you even thought about that? I know you've been seeing this guy for all of *three minutes* and while I know that won't seem imp—'

'Kirsty. Stop. Please.' I hold up my hands. 'You're right. A couple of months is still very early days. I'm being cautious. But I don't think I need to worry and neither do you. You'll like him. He's funny – and kind.' I reach in my pocket and pull out my phone, finding a picture of the two of us. Seth is holding the camera above us and grinning, as I smile, my arms around his neck. 'See? Look at that lovely face!'

'Hmmm.' Kirsty studies him. 'He's very good-looking, yes.' She looks away and instead reaches out, smoothing my hair. 'You *are* tired, aren't you? Mum's right, it'll do you good to have a bit of a break after this run.' She hesitates. 'Listen, when I was putting the book back in your bag before lunch, I noticed a load of mints. I wasn't snooping, I just saw them.'

'I'm not smoking again,' I say honestly, picturing myself knocking back the drinks on Friday night and hoping she can't actually read my mind.

'Just, be sensible, please. That's all I'm saying.'

Mum appears in the kitchen doorway, wiping her hands on her apron. 'Everything all right?'

Neither of us reply and she reaches into her pocket for her mobile. 'I want a picture of my girls. Come on – arms round each other. That's it – Lovely!' She beams, inspecting it and then turns the screen round for us to see.

'Ah – sisters,' I say, looking at the picture.

'It's a beautiful one. Thank you, both.' Mum slips the mobile back in her pocket and starts off upstairs. 'I'm going to see what those boys are up to.'

I turn back to Kirsty who is still studying me.

'I'm OK, I promise.' I lean out and flick her right on the funny bone, like I used to when I was little and wanted my big sister to play with me instead of being sat at the table doing her homework.

I mean it as a joke and grin expectantly, but she just sighs, reaches out and pulls me into a long, tight hug, kissing my forehead furiously before spinning on the spot and marching off into the sitting room without another word.

*

I arrive home to a cold, unwelcoming flat. I forgot to turn the heating on when I got up this morning and the temperature has fallen away. I shiver as I make myself a hot chocolate and take it through to the bedroom, flicking on the TV and climbing under my bedcovers to watch Graham Norton on catch-up. There are fireworks banging and whizzing outside, but I can't be bothered to get up and look at the sparkles.

I love Claire Foy. I want her career and her Crown. I want to be sat on that red sofa being amusing about *my* forthcoming Hollywood movie, not under this duvet – and all that separates us, really, is opportunity. Exposure. And look at David Walliams there, next to her and Kurt Russell! A one-time comedy show and this year his children's books are everywhere. They're all my nephews read. I sigh and feel miserable as I remember the proud look on my Dad's face earlier when I made my 'announcement'. What was I thinking? I'll just have to tell them it got rejected or something, which will make them feel even worse for me, or that I changed my mind about doing it. Except why I'd do that having supposedly written the whole thing I don't know. Especially as my phone isn't exactly ringing off the hook with other opportunities.

Unless... I swear under my breath and snatch my mobile up. I google Charlotte Graves, writer, and her website comes up straight away. Would it hurt to meet her again, just to see what she has to say in more detail about this master plan of hers? I find the 'contact me' page and stare at the blank form for a moment, remembering her instructions that *she* would get back in touch with me. But that was on Thursday. It's now Sunday. There's no point in her treating me mean to keep me keen – I'm as keen as I'm ever going to get. We might as well just do this... my fingers start to type... I enter my name, email address and under 'your message' I put:

Hello! I hope you don't mind me contacting you. I read one of your books over the weekend and really enjoyed it. I'm just starting out in my writing career and don't know any authors. Would I be able to talk to you for a bit of advice? What pitfalls to avoid etc? Perhaps I could take you to coffee if you're ever in London?

I sit back, pretty pleased with that. She can't object to anything I've put there, but she'll also get exactly what I mean. I'm clearly saying yes, let's go for it.

I chew my lip, looking at the words, suddenly unsure, but again – as if they are under the control of some part of my subconscious so deeply powerful I'm almost a spectator to the decision I'm making – my fingers click send...

A frisson of excitement whispers through my body. It's gone. My new-new counsellor asked me only last week, what is it about impulsive actions that I find so addictive?

It's not complicated. They make me feel good.

'But only in the moment,' she'd argued, 'what about the long-term ramifications?'

Whatever. I'm going to 'write' a book. I'm going to sell it for a lot of money. I have a feeling in my bones that, pretty soon, I'm going to be looking back on meeting Charlotte Graves for the first time and genuinely will pinpoint it as the moment my life changed forever.

CHAPTER SEVEN

CHARLOTTE

Clara, in particular, is enchanted by the fireworks, jumping up and down in delight as they explode above her head; golden reflections catching in the river and her eyes, while turning her perfect skin pink, green, red... She claps her gloved hands and gasps: 'Look Mummy! They are so beautiful!'

I pretend to watch, and make all of the right noises, but really I'm sneaking glances at her instead. *She* is so beautiful. It makes my heart hurt. I look at Teddy too – stumpy in his thick coat and wellingtons, his mittened hand reaching up to mine.

'Mummy, I need a tissue.'

I dutifully reach into the pocket of my coat and find one, wiping his nose. He holds his arms up.

'Hug!'

He's too heavy for me to comfortably lift up anymore, but as long as I can do it at all – I'll take every opportunity I've got. I haul him onto my hip, and he tightly wraps his arms round my neck, trapping my hair and getting a bit of snot I missed on my cheek, as he plants kiss after kiss, but I've already closed my eyes to try and lock this memory away where nothing will be able to hurt it. Even when he's finished, still not wanting it to be over, I greedily snuffle his neck, breathing in the biscuity-warmth of him. I love him so much. He's had enough though, and wriggles to get down again, before starting to jump up and down alongside Clara, not because he's that excited about the fireworks, simply because he wants to copy his beloved big sister. She looks down at him, laughs and mimics *him* in return.

Moving to stand slightly behind them, hands buried in my pockets, I watch them both dancing about under the dark sky and blink back tears. They are such amazing children – a proper team. I'm so glad they will always have each other, even when they no longer want to dance like this. I would be lost without Flo. Clara turns to check I haven't gone back inside and smiles excitedly at me. I don't want her to have to grow up.

Tris comes running out of the gloom across my parents' lawn. 'Stand back!' he instructs, and I see the red glow of my father's taper bobbing hurriedly across the garden; the men moving away as the firework bursts into life, showering warning sparks, about to explode into action.

My husband slips an arm round my shoulder and pulls the children back towards us with the other hand. 'Huddle up!'

'I still think we should be watching from inside.' I repeat my earlier concerns, and Tris rolls his eyes.

'We're *fine*, fun police. Right, this should be a biggun! Keep watching, kids!'

'Wow!' They both exclaim as a first, then a second almighty boom sends fountains of sparkles cascading through the air, burning brightly, flickering and finally dying away into silence and smoke. It's very pretty, but not quite a showstopper. We wait, uncertain in case there are any more, but…

'That's it!' Dad calls from somewhere behind the rhododendrons. 'All done.'

'Oh!' Tris sounds a little surprised. 'I thought it might be a little more impressive than that; it looked amazing behind the glass in the shop. Never mind. Thanks, Grandpa!' he calls out, clapping his hands and nodding pointedly at the kids.

'Thank you, Grandpa,' they chorus dutifully as Dad appears, coughing slightly.

'Time everyone went back inside, I think.' I frown at Dad, worriedly. 'It's very chilly and very damp out here tonight. It's got so much colder over the last couple of days. In we go.' I begin to herd the children towards the house. 'Now – five minutes of watching CBeebies and then it's going to be sausages in buns time. After that, it's straight in the car. We've got a long drive and you've both got school in the morning.'

'Thank the Lord we did baths and hairwashes this morning,' Tris says cheerfully, as we all kick off our boots in the hall and unzip coats. 'Good call, Mummy!'

I don't reply, but he doesn't really notice – too busy helping Teddy put his socks back on that came off with his wellies. 'Come on, you two – I'll sort the TV out.' He follows the children into the sitting room, and I turn left into the kitchen, to find my mum and sister.

Flo and her new boyfriend, Harry, are buttering hot dog buns, while Mum messes around on her phone, supposedly keeping an eye on the sausages in the oven. I'm not sure what to make of Harry yet. He's good-looking but in a boyish way: dark eyes, pale skin, floppy hair. I wouldn't be surprised if she said he was an academic of some kind. Not Flo's usual six-footer, reeking of testosterone, that's for sure. I glance at him again... vulnerable. That's the word. He looks vulnerable.

'Mum!' Flo says sharply. 'They smell like they're burning.'

Mum jumps, puts her phone down and yanks the tray out. 'No! All fine!' she says in a sing-song voice.

'I'll get some plates,' I offer, crossing the room to the tissue box on the side and blowing my nose first.

'You OK?'

I look up to see Flo looking at me intently. I nod. 'Just coming into the warm from outside.' I clear my throat and look away.

'Oooh!' Mum tries to unstick a sausage from the foil, only to accidentally flip it on the floor. 'These wretched, skinny little chipolatas.' She bends, picks it up, inspects it quickly, shrugs and moves towards the big plate I've just got out.

'No!' Flo and I chorus simultaneously.

'There's cat hair and God knows what else down there, Mum.' Flo wrinkles her nose.

'No, there most certainly is not!' Mum responds indignantly. 'How rude!' She waves it around and dusts it off. 'There's nothing wrong with it.'

Tris comes into the room and Mum holds it out to him, smiling sweetly. 'Sausage going begging if you want it?'

Before we can say anything, Tris reaches out, eats it whole and starts to chew before stepping across the room to grab a tea towel. He holds it aloft. 'Teddy's just spilt his drink, but it's only water. Thanks for the snag. Very nice.' He disappears back out again.

'See?' Mum says. 'What the eye doesn't see, the heart doesn't grieve after.'

Flo glances quickly again at me. Our eyes meet, and she looks away silently.

'Can I just say, for future reference, I don't ever want to be offered a cat hair sausage?' Harry puts his hand up. 'If that's OK… I'm more of a dog person.'

I half-smile.

'Honestly,' Mum scoffs. 'You're all snowflakes.'

'Mum, you are spending too much time online,' Flo says.

'No, I'm not! What possible evidence do you have for that?' Mum waits for a nanosecond. 'Exactly – you don't have any. You can't just accuse someone of something without any factual basis for it.'

'Seriously. A little less time on Twitter, OK?'

'Look, he was perfectly happy not knowing what had happened to his sausage before he popped it in his mouth.'

Ordinarily, Flo would make a quip about this, and I would laugh out loud. But not today. Harry looks up, as if to catch Flo's eye, but she doesn't look at him and he glances down again, disappointed. I feel bad for him. Meeting the parents has not gone with a bang.

It's almost a relief to make it to the goodbyes in the hall, Tris looking at his watch, repeatedly chivvying us all with: 'Come on! Come on! Time to go! We've got a long journey ahead!' Mum ignores him, leaping around the children crooning: 'Kiss Nona goodbye! Ciao, Bella!' while Dad tickles Teddy, getting him helpfully all riled up.

'OK. Let's do this. Bye, Harry! Nice to meet you.' Tris, standing in the doorway, holds up a hand in a farewell to Harry, who is absently leant against the wall on *his* phone, messaging away. He doesn't look up. Tris turns to me and thumbs at him like, 'Who is this guy?' gesturing widely in disbelief when Harry continues to ignore him. Tris gives up, shooting Harry a quick look of disgust, before turning on the spot and walking off down the path. Flo glances at Harry – oblivious and still staring down at his screen – then quietly disappears into the sitting room.

Mum and Dad follow the kids down the path to the car, so when Harry finally looks up, it's only me still there, fiddling with my shoes. He looks surprised and then embarrassed to see everyone has vanished.

'I'm so sorry, my mum is ill at the moment. I was just saying I'll call her when I get back to mine.'

I smile sympathetically. 'It's totally fine. Don't worry at all. And I hope she feels better soon.'

'Thanks. It's not really that sort of gig. More of a long-standing thing, but thank you.'

'I'm sorry to hear that. Bye, Harry. You take care.'

I very much doubt I'll see him again. Which is a shame. He seemed nice.

*

I don't normally write on Sunday evenings, but once the kids are in bed, Tris gets out his laptop and I decide I might as well. In any case, I'm so woefully behind, I don't have much choice. Since finishing work on 'Mia's' book, I've had to return to the one I owe my own editor under my own name. But despite having been completely in the zone on Friday – the words flying furiously from my fingers – tonight I'm completely stuck. It's like pulling teeth with blunt pliers. I dick around on Facebook for a bit, check my Amazon reviews and wish I hadn't – there's a new two-star annihilation of my latest release which concludes: 'I found myself wondering, what's the point?' – get up, eat a few cheese straws and a biscuit, go back and try another jump start, but by 9 p.m., I've only managed a paltry 286 words. I've been doing this long enough to know it's just a blip and I'd be better off packing up shop for the night and attacking it again in the morning afresh, so I take the Sunday magazines upstairs and sneak off to bed.

I can't even concentrate on *them*, however, and give up – turning instead to my phone. All I can think about is my offer to Mia and how Flo would be furious if she knew what I've done. I don't want to have to think about it. Just for five minutes I want to step away from what I've started and have a few moments of mindless peace. I want to leap-frog from Facebook, to Twitter, to Instagram – blanking my brain, filling it up with pointless sponge information that won't leave room for anything else. But instead, a text from Flo comes in.

> Checking you're OK. You seemed very on edge earlier. Anything you want to discuss?

Very much not, thank you.

Totally fine. You? Harry seems nice?

I wait a moment or two, but as expected, that elicits no response. I leap next to checking my email, but as they load up, one name immediately stands out – and I sit up in bed, swearing under my breath. I told her not to contact me. I was explicit about that – but nonetheless there is her name, right in front of me: Mia Justice… She has begun a paper trail. Something that can now be traced back to me, with little or no effort whatsoever. Idiot!

Out of nowhere, Tris walks in, carrying two glasses of water. As he sets one down on my bedside table, I scramble to hit the home screen and Mia's message disappears.

'I thought I'd come to bed early too for once,' he says quietly and walks around to his side, carefully setting his glass down; but the second he does, Teddy starts to cough in his bedroom across the hall. Tris freezes. 'That wasn't me,' he says, then swears as we both hear Teddy wail: 'Mummy!'

I sigh heavily, and Tris's shoulders sag. 'I'll go. It's my fault.'

I hold up a hand. 'Just give him a moment. He might sort himself out.' We listen as we hear the familiar sound of Teddy reaching for his water bottle and gulping from it, before settling back down. Another second or two passes, and just as I'm starting to relax, he coughs again.

'Great,' says Tris, unbuttoning his shirt. 'Your dad didn't sound a hundred per cent today. They've probably caught this off him.'

'Not in under three hours,' I say, wearily. 'It's more likely to be a side effect of the flu vaccine they had on Friday. It can give them runny noses and coughs.'

'I didn't know you'd been to the doctors on Friday?' Tris unzips his trousers and flings them in the direction of the dirty clothes bin. They miss and land next to it, in front of the door – perfect positioning for me to trip over them when I inevitably have to get up in the dark later to go and see to Teddy. I wait for him to walk over and pick them up. He doesn't and I don't want the row, so I get up and do it myself, before climbing back into bed.

'Maybe they caught something in the waiting room?' He peels off his socks and gets into bed in his boxers, shivering.

'They didn't go to the doctor. They had the nasal spray at school. I filled in the form at the start of term.' I'm emotionless, just presenting the facts.

'Oh. Right. Well, maybe it is that then. Oh come on… not her too?' he groans, as Clara begins to cough, disturbed in her sleep by Teddy. 'You spend all summer waiting for it to get cooler at night, then it does and instead you're up for hours with two barking dogs. I've got such an early start in the morning. I so don't need this.' He stares up at the ceiling, hand on his head.

'You're in Sheffield tomorrow?' I ask, and he nods. 'I did tell you.'

'No, you didn't, but no worries.' I turn away from him, pick up one of the magazines again and lie down myself. He listens to the kids coughing for a moment more. 'Was your sister OK today?' he says suddenly.

I carry on reading. 'I think so? Why do you ask?'

He continues to stare up at the ceiling. 'She seemed very quiet.'

'She's fine.'

'I didn't think much of that new bloke of hers.'

'Yes, you made that quite clear. I liked him.'

Tris turns and gives me a look. 'Based on what? He was barely three-D. It's like saying "I like clingfilm".'

Clara explosively coughs again. Tris groans. 'Isn't there anything they can have?'

'I've already done Calpol. They don't need Nurofen as well.'

'Mummmmmmy! Where are you?' Teddy is now wide awake.

I get up just as Tris does, gathering his pillows, water and his book. 'I'm sorry, but I really need to get some sleep tonight. I've got such a long drive in the morning. Plus if I go in the spare room you can at least bring them in here with you if you need to.'

I look at him steadily. 'OK. Sure. You do that. I don't want you crashing on the motorway.'

I leave the room before he can answer and when I come back to the now-cold bed, some twenty minutes later, after both kids seem to have mercifully settled down, he's not there, but I can hear him snoring across the hall.

I climb back in, on my side, and return to inspecting Mia's message… her confirmation that yes, she'll do it. She'll pretend to be me and make us both a lot of money.

I close my eyes. I promised Flo.

I swear and delete it quickly, both from my inbox and then Gmail itself before turning off the light. I lie there in the dark, listening to Tris snoring and coughing across the hall. It starts to rain outside. Blustery gusts thwack against the window, but my babies are safe in their beds – all is well in their world.

The rain doesn't stop. I can hear it pouring through the hole in the gutter I told Tris about ages ago. In fairness I could have just had it fixed myself.

It's a very long time before I finally get to sleep.

*

'So I can't call my shop John Lewis?' Clara holds a felt tip over her notebook, snuggled in our bed, watching her daddy get ready for work.

'No.' Tris is staring down at his phone. 'Because there's already a shop called that and people would get confused. You need a new name that's all your own to make as famous as John Lewis. That's what we call a *brand*.'

Oh come on! Really? She's seven.

'I'm going to call MY shop "Edward loves fruit cake",' Teddy says confidently, tucked in on the other side of me. I can't help smiling at that and Tris looks up too, catching my eye, equally amused.

'Can you really not just tell work you have to be London-based today?' I say suddenly.

Tris doesn't answer, just slides his mobile into his pocket and pats the others, to make sure he's got everything. I know he heard me.

'Clara, Teddy – as you're not going to school, you can go and get the iPad if you want,' I say instead. 'It's in the kitchen. Take it into Clara's room and watch it in her bed. I want you to stay warm. Just CBeebies.' I call after them as they scramble out, and Tris says: 'Mind my stuff please!', grabbing onto the open case on the bed as Teddy almost knocks it flying in his haste.

'I thought we weren't letting them watch it during the week?' Tris turns and glances at himself in the mirror, fiddling with the front of his hair then flaring his nostrils, peering up them briefly.

'They're ill. It's fine just for this morning. Tris, surely you're senior enough to pull rank now and say you can't go to Sheffield today after all and someone else has to do it?' I try again. 'Just be honest. Say "my kids are ill again, they can't go to school today, my wife is going crazy not being able to work and I need to be at home this evening to help her".'

'It's *because* I'm senior that I have to go,' he explains. 'I know it's not glamorous and you're thinking "it's only Sheffield, not Frankfurt", but I've told you before, this client is huge. People make the mistake of writing firms off just because they're regional. It's elitist and unfair. Yes it sucks that the kids are ill again and yes I'm really, really sorry that I can't stay and help today, but there is nothing I can do about it. I'm genuinely sorry – but there it is.' He looks at his watch. 'Shit. It's already half past six. I've got to go. The M25 is going to be horrendous. I should have left at 5 a.m., really.'

'I'm not asking you to take the day off, just to work in town instead. That way you can take over this evening when you get back, so I can write then. Please?' I beg. 'They're going to be up and down all evening with blocked noses. I'll get nothing done otherwise and I'm so in the zone at the moment.'

He looks up at me from double-checking the contents of his wheelie case and raises an eyebrow.

I cross my arms. 'I know you think that sounds wanky, but it's honestly like asking someone to hit pause when they're just out of the blocks. This bit when the words are just pouring out happens for ten seconds of the race and that's it. It's like magic and I can't even explain the frustration to you of having to just stop when all I want to do is write. Again. Like last time they were ill.'

'I get it – honestly I do – but like you said last week, one of the few great things about your job is flexibility. You don't have a boss to call who will go nuts at you for not coming in like I do. You'll make the time up – like you always say, you write fast. I don't feel good about the fact that I have to go again and leave you with this shit to deal with, of course I don't.' He zips up the case. 'Funnily enough, I do also miss you and the kids when I'm away. Isn't there anyone else who can come and help you tonight? What about your mum? Or your sister?'

I pull the duvet around me more tightly, defeated. 'Forget it. I'll sort something out.'

'I can ask my mum and dad to come down if you like? They'd love to help out.'

'Christ!' I picture Moira framed in the front doorway, grimly rolling her sleeves up and snapping on the marigolds. 'No, thanks.'

'Fine. Well, I've offered solutions. I know it's grossly unfair that just because I have a comparatively traditional job, I can't ever be the one to take up the slack, and it always falls to you. I'm sorry, but I don't know what else to say. It's also my job that largely pays the bills, so...' He shrugs, picks up the case and leaves the room, calling: 'Guys? Daddy has to go to work now! Where are you? I need a kiss.' I even hear him say to Teddy: 'be good for Mummy while I'm away, OK?'

'Tris!' I call desperately and he reappears in the doorway. 'I want you to call in sick if you genuinely can't not go into the London office today rather than Sheffield. I never, ever ask you to do this, but I need you to today.'

'No,' he says simply. No negotiation. That's just it. 'I can't.'

I feel prickles of anger start to puncture the tears at the back of my eyes. 'I have a job too, that is just as important as yours. The children are your responsibility as much as they are mine.'

He sighs and looks up at the ceiling. 'Oh my god… No one is saying it isn't important. I'm simply saying I have to go to Sheffield today. Can we please not make this into a nine-act drama where you start telling me we don't live in the 1950s anymore? I know that. I just don't have the job freedom and flexibility you do. That's all.'

'You're a fucking selfish prick.'

His eyebrows flicker with surprise as I spit out the words, but he stays calm, looking at me meditatively. 'And you're toxic.' My mouth falls open in shock as he turns and walks out of the room, shouting: 'bye, kids! Love you!'

'Bye, Daddy!' I hear them call back.

I stay sitting on the bed as the tears start to leak down my face. I try really, really hard to make life as good as it can be for my family. I am *not* toxic. I hear Clara calling me and get up quickly to wash my face in the en suite – I don't want her to see I've been crying – before going downstairs to make the breakfast. Keep calm and carry on. What's the alternative?

Unfortunately, while both of the children have temperatures, they are not quite ill enough to sit quietly on the sofa and watch movies while I work alongside them. We limp through the morning somehow; a blur of colouring, stickers, junk modelling and Play-Doh, while I hear Tris call me toxic on repeat, in my head. I see myself walking confidently into his office – over ten years ago now – in heels and a pencil skirt, to interview him for the recruitment magazine I was working on at the time. I picture him jumping up politely and, rather flustered, shaking my hand. I was aware of the effect I was having on him and I liked it. Somewhere, I still have the tiny cassette of our very first conversation. He was funny – I laughed a lot. I looked online recently to see if I could buy one of the old-fashioned Dictaphones to play it back on, but they're about a hundred quid. It seemed a waste of money.

I glance down at my yoga pants, black jumper and odd socks as I load the plates into the dishwasher after lunch. I look a state. How the hell did I get here? I pick up my phone as I put the kettle on, checking my emails. A new one from Johnnie Boden – 30% off ends at midnight tonight! and then Sky – Charlotte, your latest Sky VIP rewards! Enter to win tickets for Disney on Ice Skate with the Stars. Nothing from my agent, or my editor.

'Mummy!' comes a shout from the sitting room. 'Teddy just pinched me! OW! And now he's hitting me!'

I stare up at the ceiling and take a deep breath. 'Coming!'

After I've been called a poo, had a few tears (him, not me) but he's said sorry and calmed down, we all make the train track, play Hungry Hippos, build Lego, sort out the dressing-up box and somehow, mercifully, it creeps round to 4 p.m.. The children *finally* settle down and select a DVD, and with huge relief, I immediately seize the opportunity to snatch a crumb of work time. Unfortunately they choose a compilation of Disney shorts, which means I have to stop every five minutes, yank my headphones out and select a different mini movie for them. I'm trying to kill someone, which is a hard enough scene to write at the best of times, requiring detailed concentration, unless I want my murderer to get caught immediately by a particular breed of Amazon reviewer who lives for errors in books:

★ **Not thrilling OR suspenseful.**

I also noticed immediately that in chapter seven the killer was NOT EVEN WEARING GLOVES and would have left prints all over their glass. How does this rubbish get published?

'Can I have a hug?' Teddy appears at my elbow.

'Of course you can.' I put the laptop down – hug him, then settle him on the sofa next to me and pick up the laptop again.

'Can I press some buttons?' He leans over and gets in a 'fwtdklae;87w4i6hla' surprisingly quickly before I lift his hand away.

'Not right now, darling.' I manage to smile – but the hurt I've squashed down all day is shape-shifting back into rage again and starting to bubble ominously. I think about Tris wheeling his case out of the door, shutting it behind him and just walking away – simultaneously realising the chicken I put in the oven and forgot about will now be overdone and I haven't started the rest of tea yet. I'll bet Lee Child doesn't have to stop mid-chapter to make a fucking cauliflower cheese.

I've just got it in the oven when it all kicks off again in the sitting room. Teddy deliberately wallops Clara with a cushion for overruling his choice of film and the zip catches her cheek, making her cry. Teddy cries too, first with genuine regret when he sees the small line of blood on her face… then with fury when I have no choice but to sit him on the stairs again.

'I hate you, Mummy!' he bellows, then bursts back into the kitchen – where I have just sat down – grabs something and runs back out. I follow him out to discover it's his harmonica. 'I'm going to sit on the stairs and PLAY SAD SONGS!' he announces dramatically.

I manage not to both laugh and cry. Instead, I make him apologise to Clara, again, re-settle them and return to wash up the cheese-sauce pan and lay the table. As I walk back to the kitchen I consider texting Tris to tell him what Teddy has just said. Normally, that's the kind of thing I would do, message him with the funny anecdotes, so he doesn't miss out – but my phone is already lit up on the table when I pick it up.

All OK? Just got back to hotel. Cold here. Miss you all. Back Wednesday xxx

I place it back down carefully, sit down and put my elbows on the table, clasping my hands as if in prayer and rest my chin on my outstretched thumbs, thoughtfully. The lid on the broccoli is lifting and jiggling as the steam gathers in the pan beneath it. It's ready to come off the hob. The water will boil dry otherwise, out of sight and start to burn, getting hotter and hotter.

I sit and think for a moment, then find Mia on Facebook. Via Messenger, I tell her that, coincidentally, I am in London tomorrow and am available to meet her at 11.30 a.m. on the steps to St Martin-in-the-Fields, should that be helpful, and I'm very flattered she would like my advice.

I do not regret it the second I've sent it.

Quite the opposite, in fact.

CHAPTER EIGHT

MIA

Charlotte stirs her tea slowly, tucked away at our table in the corner of the Crypt restaurant, her back against the wall.

'I told you not to contact me.' She places the spoon carefully on the saucer, reaches for a napkin and delicately wipes her fingers. 'I shouldn't even be here now given you pretty much failed at the first hurdle.' She sits back, crosses her legs and rests her now-spotless hands lightly on her knee. 'When my first serious boyfriend was at university,' she lowers her voice, like she's telling me a secret, and I find myself leaning in, 'he applied for a graduate recruitment scheme in Customs and Excise, but a *different* department within the civil service contacted him instead, asking them to come to an interview with them. Could he report to London on such and such day, but with strict instructions not to discuss this request with *anyone* at this stage, please? He was very excited. Practically started referring to himself as 007.' She picks up her tea and takes a small sip. 'He dutifully turned up at the specified address and announced to the receptionist "I'm here for the MI5 interview".' Charlotte smiles brightly at me. 'He did not get the job.'

I let my gaze fall, chastened. 'OK. I'm sorry,' I stammer. 'I just thought you might have forgotten what we discussed.'

She gives a short, sharp sigh. 'You can't possibly think I've asked several girls if they want to pretend to be me? How long do you think that would take to get around?'

I hesitate. She's got a point.

'If people start to gossip, this won't work. You were my first choice. You are my *only* choice.'

Brightening, I look up again.

'Yes, you're right.' She isn't smiling anymore. 'I need *you* to make this work. So please don't force me to have to walk away.' She reaches for her cup again. In contrast to last week's vintage glam, today she is more conservatively dressed. Her dark hair is in a sleek ponytail and her pale skin is accentuated by a black polo neck tucked into tailored trousers, over heels. She looks like she's stepped out of a full day of board meetings to take an early lunch.

'From now on, if you need to contact me, please do it via direct email only and make no mention of our arrangement whatsoever. We'll have to carry on pretending any contact between us is simply about me offering you advice now, after what you put on Sunday night.'

'Well at least that's plausible, I guess?' I try a smile.

'Not really, no,' she says crushingly. 'Normally at most I'd send a wannabe writer a brief email with some useful weblinks. I'd never offer to meet someone in person like this.'

I can't help but think all of this secrecy and trail covering is a bit over the top, but remind myself she's a thriller writer. It's probably an occupational hazard. I bet she sticks a plaster over her computer lens in case people are watching her remotely, too. 'Would you like to get me a pay-as-you-go phone instead?' I'm joking but she doesn't react. 'My point is, 'I try again, 'what we're doing isn't illegal, is it? If it all came out at some point, it wouldn't be the end of the world. It would probably result in *more* publicity.'

'Not the kind that would help *us*,' she replies. 'It would wipe several zeros off the value of the deal for a kick off and, reputation-wise, you'd be OK, but I'd be ruined. At best I'd look desperate, pathetic – slightly mad, in fact – at worst I'd be shunned for barefaced lying and trying to cheat the system everyone else has to suffer. I'm risking a huge amount here, Mia.' She clears her throat and holds her head high. 'So, last chance. Take this seriously. There's got to be nothing linking me to your book. We do this properly, or not at all.' She reaches down into her handbag and pulls out a memory stick, pushing it across the table. 'This is the manuscript. Are you in, or not?'

I still want to giggle at the 'Mission Impossible' nature of it all, but I actually think it might be partly due to nerves. She's not messing around.

Have you met my daughter, the actress and published author?

Dad's words echo in my mind. He was so proud. I take a deep breath. 'Yes, I'm in.'

'Well pick it up then.' She gestures at the memory stick. 'Have you got a computer?'

'Yes, of course. At home. I'll download it when I get back tonight.' I slip it into my coat pocket.

'That's no good. We need to send this book out today.' She chews her lip and thinks. 'OK, in a minute, I want you to call Ruth.'

I'm puzzled. 'My agent's assistant, Ruth?'

'As opposed to my great-aunt Ruth who lives in the Cotswolds?' She retorts. 'Yes, of course your agent's assistant.'

'I don't think there's any need to be mean.' My voice wavers slightly. 'How do you know her name anyway?'

She closes her eyes briefly, as if frustrated and trying to calm down, then continues evenly. 'Because I've done my homework. I'm sorry if I upset you, Mia. I wasn't trying to be "mean". As I was saying, you're going to need to call Ruth, because you don't have a direct line through to your actual agent, Cary, do you? That treatment would be reserved for one of his major clients like Cate, Emily or Gillian. Not someone much lower down the pecking order, like you.'

I flush, silenced by her humiliating accuracy.

'Don't feel badly about that.' She sounds more kindly. 'The point is, he *is* your agent and his name alone opens doors. For our purposes that's all that matters. You need to tell Ruth you've written a book that an editor you know socially has offered to buy from you direct… but you thought you ought to run it past Cary first.'

'I'm going to need to write this down if you want me to learn lines.' I start to dig around in my bag, finding a biro, but no paper.

Charlotte picks up her leather-bound notebook, rips out a page and pushes it across the table. 'Here.' She waits for me to start scribbling. 'Tell Ruth you're getting quite a lot of pressure from this editor friend of yours to sign. You need to make it sound like she *really* wants it. If Ruth asks for more detail, tell her you'd rather not say at this stage, but you'll drop the book in on your way to work. Normally you'd just email it, but let's give them something to physically hold in their hands, make it all feel a bit more real.' She pauses to think. 'There's a photocopy and print shop on Shaftesbury Avenue. Take the memory stick there and ask them to run off a copy for you. That'll probably cost about forty quid. Here.' She reaches into her bag again, pulls out a smart purse and holds out two crisp £20 notes.

I stare at her, my mouth having fallen open. 'I'm not a bloody intern! I actually do have to go to work today, thanks very much!'

Her expression doesn't change. 'They'll print it then and there, and your agent's office is in Soho. That's about ten minutes' walk from the theatre at most. You've got all afternoon. If I can write the "bloody" thing,' she mimics me, 'the least you can do is deliver it.'

I fall silent, reach out and rather sulkily take the money.

'That's better. Now listen, because this bit is important. You need to start reading this book tonight when you get home. Yes, tonight!' she repeats, exasperated, when I start to protest again. 'You're telling me you wouldn't read a script overnight if it was attached to a role worth half a million? Because that's what this is. Your script – and if I'm right, whoever reads it in the books department will be coming back to you within a day or two. Cary is royalty. So read it.' She picks up her phone and checks it. 'Any questions?'

I scan everything I've noted down. 'This is why you wanted me then?' I say eventually. 'Just because Cary is my agent?'

She looks at me sympathetically. 'Not just that. I told you, I remembered you from Edinburgh. I knew you were the right sort of age and I also knew I needed someone who, for whatever reason, hasn't quite had the professional luck she probably deserves.'

I suppose I should be pleased. Being a bit shit has never got me a job before. I try to smile.

'Come on, chin up!' she says briskly. 'You have a *really* good agent, Mia. Let's use him. Make him kick down some doors for you, hey?' She leans forward and smiles properly for the first time, like we're in this together. I feel better immediately. She's very good at making people feel special when she wants to.

'I read your first book,' I blurt. 'Your first published one, I mean. The one you told me about last Thursday in the bar. I enjoyed it.'

She glances at me as she stands up. 'Thank you.'

'Did someone cheat on you in real life? It read like it did… my fiancé ran off with my best friend.' I add on the last bit by way of explanation but, instead, it just sounds like a very lame teenage attempt at bonding.

Charlotte stops, frowns, sits back down slowly and puts her coat across her lap.

I clear my throat awkwardly. 'I recognised a lot of the feelings of grief when a relationship ends and there's nothing you can do to stop it happening, however hard you try. That's what I mean.'

'Aren't you a bit young to have been engaged?'

I shrug. 'By today's standards, maybe, I guess? My mum was married and had my sister by the time she was my age though. She's still happily married to my dad.'

'I'm sorry to hear you had a rough time. That must have been very difficult for you.'

Out of nowhere, like a prat, I feel a lump rise up in my throat. One day it'll all stop having an actual physical effect on me. 'It was a bit,' I admit. 'I didn't handle it very well. I didn't pull any of the tricks in your book,' I add quickly. 'I just mean I was unhappy and it sort of triggered some stuff that made me a bit ill for a while. I'm adopted,' I confess. 'In fact in Edinburgh, I was…' I hesitate, look at her and change my mind about continuing. 'Actually never mind that.' I cough and start again. 'When my fiancé dumped me for my best friend, I was devastated. I thought we were going to do the whole thing: wedding, children… be a family – I was really shocked. He was basically saying I wasn't enough. I was sort of coping with that in the normal way but I'd also started trying to get in contact with my birth parents when I thought I was getting married. It had stirred up a lot of stuff about not knowing who I really was, them not being at the wedding when this *huge* thing was happening to me…. Anyway about a week after we split, I discovered my birth father wasn't alive anymore and *all* of it just *exploded* in my head.' I take a sip of my now-lukewarm tea and wish I hadn't. 'I couldn't cope with that much loss. My birth parents weren't ever together, it's not like they were ever out there being a family without me, but it still felt… hard. Then I started going through this period where I found it really difficult to be around my adoptive family. Basically I felt guilty for being so upset about my birth father when he wasn't the one who'd done so much for me. It got messy.' I stop to take a breath.

Charlotte doesn't say a word. Just waits for me to continue. I can't work out what she's thinking, which makes me more nervous and like I need to carry on talking. She'd be a good counsellor. 'I kind of *did* go a bit mad after that, if I'm honest. I ended up sort of transferring my grief onto what had happened with Hugo and my best friend, which gave it a disproportional power over me, you know? Plus, my real name is Amy, but I dropped it completely. I didn't know how to be her anymore, or who she even was, so I kind of made myself into Mia full time, instead. This probably does sound mental, doesn't it? I should shut up. I'm sorry.'

'It doesn't at all. I knew a little girl called Tara when she was born and for various reasons her name was changed when she was six months old. She wouldn't have remembered, but I've often wondered if it made any difference to her, subconsciously. If she ever felt like someone she wasn't.' Charlotte shrugs. 'From what you say, perhaps it did.'

'For me it was about taking back some control, I suppose.'

'Yes,' she agrees. 'That's really important after something that shakes you to your core. I had an absent parent for a large chunk of my life and that was bad enough. I told all of my friends he was a spy and wasn't allowed to tell us where he was.' She briefly smiles. 'I'm sorry for your troubles.'

'Thanks. You too.'

'Do you have any contact with your birth mother now?'

'No, she doesn't want to.' I shrug. 'It's cool. I'm grateful to her for putting me up for adoption and wanting a better life for me, but my mum, dad, brother and sister are the ones that have been there my whole life. They're my family.'

Charlotte nods silently, which is fair enough. What can you say really? As usual, I've said too much. 'Sorry. I didn't mean to end up talking about *my* ex.'

She half-smiles. 'It's OK. How did you meet your current boyfriend?'

Oh, she's really good; the classic counsellor trick of closing a negative experience by asking about a positive one instead. But I'm happy to share. I could talk about Seth all day long. 'On a train station,' I say shyly. 'I was going through London Bridge at the same time every morning while we were in rehearsals for the play I'm in now. On the last day in that location – I wouldn't have been there the morning after that, he'd have missed me – he came up and said he'd noticed me. He didn't want me to think he was a weirdo perv, or something.' I laugh. 'We had a coffee and just clicked, although Seth would probably tell you I talked too much and he just listened. He's very kind. Last night he just turned up after work with flowers for me, even though it was really late and he'd had to hang around after work for ages waiting for me to finish.'

She smiles. 'That's sweet. He sounds nice. Well, as we're exchanging confidences... sealing the deal, as it were... I'll tell you something no one else knows. In answer to your original question, yes, my first serious boyfriend – the wannabe 007 – who became my fiancé, did the dirty on me.' She sits back, reaches into her bag and pulls out a packet of cigarettes.

For a mad moment I think she's actually going to light it in here, but she doesn't, just pulls one out and holds it between her fingers. 'I found out about it but I didn't tell him. I waited to see if it would finish and lo and behold – it did.' She gestures with her hands, holding them wide as if something has vanished into thin air. 'I don't think it was actually anything more than a two or three night stand in reality, but everything in that book you read is the hurt I felt, turned into words.' She peers in her bag and pulls out a lighter.

'At the time I thought I was getting it out of my system, but now I think my real motivation was wanting to show Daniel that I knew. I'd known all along and I wanted him to see how it made me feel.' She shrugs. 'It didn't hurt anyone else. I exorcised a few demons and I got a book published into the bargain. All of the characters were made-up, of course, and no one else knew about his affair apart from my sister. However,' she points the unlit cigarette at me, 'he had the final word, after all, because he never actually bothered to read it and was totally oblivious to my silent protest. So there we are.' She laughs.

'Why didn't you just leave him?'

'I was also pregnant, very young and very frightened. He was my childhood sweetheart. We'd been together since we were fifteen. I loved him very much. I was very stupid. Take your pick.'

'What happened then? You just stayed with him?'

She clears her throat. 'Well, I lost the baby.' She rubs her forehead, briefly touches the cigarette to her lips and pulls it away again. She's obviously completely desperate to light it. 'And two years after that, Daniel sadly died.' She turns her unflinching gaze back to me.

'How?' I whisper, spellbound, before I even realise how inappropriate a question that is.

'He fell from a balcony while we were on holiday in Tenerife of all places. He was very drunk.'

I gasp. 'I'm so sorry!'

'Thank you,' she says quietly.

I don't know what to say after that and, it seems, neither does she. She stares into space for a moment then starts, making me jump too and looks around her, gathering her things again.

'I'm sorry, Mia. I have no idea why I just told you all of that. I apologise.' She stops again, still holding her cigarette. 'I suppose the point is…' She peters out and sighs. 'Actually, I don't know what the point is, or was. He was far too young to lose his life.'

'That's so tragic.'

She sighs again, much more deeply this time. 'Yes it was, and repatriating a body is not something I'd wish on my worst enemy. Later, there were also ominous mumblings that I might have had something to do with it, purely on the basis of the kind of books I write. Which was nice given I'd lost my fiancé.'

'From the police?' I'm astounded.

'No, an ex-friend started the rumour. Once I'd first killed someone in a book, in fact. Much as I try to explain to people that it's all fiction and I haven't slept with a seventeen-year-old boy, murdered a diabetic in a forest, had a one-night stand with an ex, run someone over or burnt a house down either, I'm not sure anyone ever really believes you lead an innocent life. Not once they realise you know how to plan the perfect crime.' She laughs. 'Every single ex-boyfriend I've had has contacted me to say they know I've based books on them, and of course, I haven't. You must get the same thing when people confuse you with characters you've played.' She shoves the cigarette and lighter back in her bag after all. 'I loved Daniel very much. I would never have hurt him. What I'm trying to say – and no writer uses five words when they can use five hundred – is I understand how you felt when *your* fiancé blew your life apart. Thankfully we both recovered and met the man who *is* right for us. We're survivors, Mia.' She reaches out and pats my hand briefly, before standing up again. 'Come on, we've got a book to sell.'

*

And yet that statement doesn't feel real even at the printers, despite my staring down at the cover sheet of the manuscript in my hands and seeing my name under the title.

Complicit
by
Mia Justice

Perhaps because I'm so used to pretending all of the time, I don't actually feel freaked out in the slightest as I lug it up Old Compton Street. I'm too busy thinking about Charlotte and everything she told me. Why would she tell me something so intimate? Maybe she made it all up to make me feel better, because I'd already stitched my heart onto my sleeve with a blunt needle, telling her all that stuff about Ava and my parents. But her admission had the ring of truth about it. I've worked in showbiz long enough to know when someone's bullshitting me and when they're telling the truth. How horrendous to have someone think you might have hurt your fiancé simply because of what you do for a living. I turn left, then right, past the NCP car park and finally left again.

When I buzz the door at the agency and announce at reception that I'm dropping something off, I remember just in time what Charlotte told me to do as we parted on the steps of the church.

'Actually, can you ring Ruth and ask her to come down and pick it up now? Or I'll take it up?' I smile winningly as I loll against the front desk.

The receptionist places the call. 'She's coming right down.'

I cross the lobby and sit down on the rock-hard sofa to wait. It's impossible to recline on – only perching allowed. As I scan through the book, making sure the pages are all in order and reading snatches of it here and there – it actually looks really good – that's when it suddenly hits me. I am sat in my agent's building, actually about to pass off someone else's book as my own. This is insane… actual fraud – but I can still change my mind. I can walk out right now. I *should* do exactly that. I will…

I wobble to my feet, and bend to quickly to gather my stuff, right as the main doors open and a small huddle of people sweep in off the street and into the lobby. The energy changes instantly, the receptionists sit up straighter and I realise right at the centre of the group is Emily Blunt herself, head down, as several people talk around her, one of whom is Cary. I quickly plaster a big smile on my face, but he attentively ushers Emily straight into the lift without even noticing me, unless – even worse – he does and I have just been blanked by my own agent.

The lift doors close, leaving me frozen to the spot like a fool. I'm not sure the shitshow that is currently my career could be summed up any better than this pathetic interlude. I feel sick and wonder if anyone else just saw what happened, but when I sneak a glance at the receptionists, they've already got their heads down again. Nobody even cares.

When Ruth bounds down the stairs, seconds later, I am ready with a second big bright, *determined* smile.

'Mia!' she exclaims, holding her arms out. We exchange kisses on both cheeks and she points at the book on the sofa. 'Is that it? This is so exciting!' She claps her hands. 'Everyone is on tenterhooks to read it.' She picks it up and reads the cover sheet. 'Ooooh! I love it! You little diamond! I had no idea!'

'I haven't told anyone… except for my editor friend.' I remember quickly.

'Yeah, well say nothing, do nothing, but most importantly *sign* nothing until we come back to you, OK? Standby!'

I nod obediently and put my bag over my shoulder. 'Will do.'

She makes big wide eyes at me, inhales dramatically, crosses her fingers and trots off to the stairs, turning on the spot again as she reaches them. 'Try and relax, darling,' she calls. 'I've got one of my good feelings about this!'

And just like that, I've written a book. I am, indeed, complicit… but what have I got to lose? Absolutely nothing.

*

The call comes the following morning. I've come in early because I have the dreaded Wednesday matinee and am shivering on a bitterly cold platform at London Bridge waiting for my connection. My bad mood falls away immediately, however, when my screen lights up with the magical announcement:

AGENT!!!

I *always* get a thrill when I see it display like this because it means business potential: a job! Out of habit, because I'm expecting Ruth, I answer with a familiar 'hello!'

'Hello! Now, would that be Mia Justice?' The unfamiliar man's voice is warm, confident – almost amused.

'Yes. Speaking?'

'This is Jack Cartwright from… your agents!' He laughs. 'I read your book last night, Mia. In fact, I stayed up *most* of the night reading your extraordinary book. I wonder if you might be able to have lunch with me today?'

Ooooh! This sounds promising – except I haven't read it yet, so blatantly the answer has to be no. 'I'd love to but I have a matinee this afternoon. Could we maybe do tomorrow, instead?'

He laughs again. 'You can't make me wait another twenty-four hours! I don't think I can bear it. Go on then, let's have coffee this afternoon instead – in between shows – how about Paul's on Bedford Street? Shall we say half past five?'

I blink. Um, slow down there Mr Pushy. 'That would be great but—'

'Excellent! I'll see you then.' And he hangs up!

I stare at my phone in astonishment. I just got manoeuvred. BIG time manoeuvred.

Frowning, I phone Ruth, who picks up immediately with an excited: 'MIA! I told you! Didn't I tell you I had one of my feelings? Has he called you yet?'

I hesitate. 'Has *who* called me yet?'

'OK,' she lowers her voice. 'You know how Cary is King agent for the actors here? Well the King agent for the authors is a man called Jack Cartwright. He handles all of the really BIG writers – I mean like the ones you've actually heard of – negotiates all of their contracts for them, gets them huge deals. Heads up, baby girl – *he's going to be calling you for a meeting!* Arghhhh! It's so exciting!'

I feel a bit faint. 'So I should definitely go then?'

She laughs like I've just said something hilarious. 'I know, right? I'm beyond thrilled for you!' She lowers her voice to a whisper. 'You should know he's already been in with Cary this morning.

They were fired up and totally smelling the money, which must mean they think this is going to go *big*. You see? I told you! Go get 'em girl!'

I immediately google Jack Cartwright when I get off the phone – and turn cold when I see who he represents; Ruth wasn't joking, they are proper authors who win prizes and everything. And I'm going to have a meeting with him in eight hours about a book I'm meant to have written that I haven't even read. This is going to be an even worse version of the casting when I'd put fluent French on my CV, the producer chattily started speaking to me in French and all I could say was 'Pardon?'

I whimper aloud. Charlotte told me to read it and I really meant to, but I went to see Seth at his flat after work instead. All that talk about Ava and Hugo yesterday unsettled me. I wanted to be held. I wanted to have Seth kiss the bad memories away and replace them with happy ones. At least I didn't stay over at his, like he wanted me to, otherwise I wouldn't even have uploaded the book – which I did when I got back from Putney at 1 a.m. But still. I should have listened to Charlotte and done as I was told.

So now what? Cancelling the coffee is clearly not an option, having had his status update from Ruth. He won't even be able to remember the last time someone said no to him, I bet. I'm going to have to go – this is too important, but I can't possibly read the whole thing *and* do a matinee in the next eight hours, even though, thank you God, I do at least have my laptop in my bag.

I could tell Charlotte, come clean and admit I haven't read it so she can at least give me a summary of the story? But she'll be understandably furious. I picture her face and immediately decide against that as an idea, plus I don't want to disappoint her. I said I'd take this seriously and I must. I'm just going to have to wing it.

I take myself to the top of Foyles to channel 'writer' and get into character. How would I feel if I really had written a book and someone like Jack said it was 'extraordinary'. I'd be… embarrassed? Thrilled, certainly. Grateful that he'd read it. Grateful for anything probably. Plus he knows I'm an actress, so he's also going to be expecting a lot of self-doubt, but plenty of charm. In fact, while I might be confident in my abilities as an actress *this* would all be new to me, so I'd be nervous and eager to please. I picture myself walking into the book department at the agency. I bet it's calm, quiet – intelligent. I think it would make me feel pretty deferential and very out of my depth. Well – that won't be a stretch to play, at least.

Now… why have I decided to write a book? I sit back in my chair and chew my lip. Because I had the time in between castings and jobs, plus… I like the escapism, I like the space it gives me. When you're turning up to auditions and rehearsals… constantly *performing* and giving, it's draining. People take from you all the time. There's so much rejection. This book was what I held back, for me. I like the peace that writing gives me. I've enjoyed stepping from one life into another. Yeah – he'll like that. *That's* what I need to make feel real to him. He's already on board with the book itself.

And talking of the book… I get my laptop out and switch it on. He's almost certainly going to ask me how I came up with the idea for it. I read the first chapter hurriedly… and God bless Charlotte, I realise there's more than enough to get a handle on. I can do this. I know I can.

*

What I don't bargain on is the twenty-four carat gold charisma of the man. He's nothing to look at – at best a cut-price Patrick Dempsey; not as tanned, a little fatter. Brown eyes not blue – but sweet Jesus, he's one of the best snake charmers I have *ever* met. I can feel myself falling for every word he says.

'I can't tell you how excited I am!' He exhales in wonder as he looks at me. 'You are the whole package. Bright, glorious company, heartbreakingly photogenic, you have a press-worthy backstory, more than enough social media presence and you write like an angel. It's *dazzling* to watch the stars align like this! You have no idea how life-changing this is going to be!'

'It is?' I find myself genuinely intrigued. 'Tell me.'

He laughs. He laughs a lot, in a 'isn't this a wonderful time to be alive?' sort of way; I like it. 'This is your big break, Mia. The one you've been waiting for.' He leans forward and whispers: 'the one you've always known you deserved.'

I blush and clear my throat. 'I'm so glad you think *Complicit* has got potential. When I was little I used to write endless song lyrics in notebooks. Somehow in dressing rooms, on trains, waiting for castings, at the back of coffee shops in between shows, that passion has turned into a book. I've loved every minute of it.' I imagine myself actually doing this and it begins to feel real.

He shakes his head. 'Potential? You have no idea how good you are, do you?'

I feel excited for Charlotte to hear him say that. I must tell her.

'That opening to the book… you had me in the palm of your hand. Our heroine is at home, doing her grown-up children some Saturday night tea… she's bored, messing around on social media – I mean, don't we all?' He takes a thoughtful sip of coffee. 'She's got that nagging, empty feeling that something is missing from her life; she thought it would all be a bit more exciting than this; pretty much something *every* reader will identify with.' He puts the cup down, excitedly. 'And then – boom! – the WhatsApp video comes in from a number she doesn't know telling her she has to get out of the house, now! If she's watching this, it's because something catastrophic has happened. Her whole life is a lie… she must go and look in the mirror for the tiny scar on her head; the evidence of the surgery that was performed to make her forget everything she used to know… and it's impossible to believe this can be a hoax, because the woman telling her what she must do – is HER!' He laughs. 'It's a gloriously mad mash-up of Harry Potter meets Lisbeth Salander!'

He grins. 'I could see the jacket of the book straight away. The title itself isn't great – too literary – but whoever publishes it will change it anyway. What I totally bought into with Layla, your heroine, is that she's *interesting*. She's not necessarily likeable and that's quite a departure for this kind of fiction. It's rather the golden rule that you must at least have one character readers can identify with and this doesn't – but I was intrigued by the question you pose: what indeed *does* make a woman with a very ordinary home life – she's a wife and a mother – walk into a room to negotiate with men that want to kill her? You also write about parenthood very convincingly.'

'Thank you,' I murmur, not thrown for a second. 'There's a big age gap between me and my older brother and sister, but I've been lucky enough to be very involved in helping bring up their children – my sister's especially – but because we *are* sisters, she's also very candid with me about the realities of motherhood. She doesn't sugar coat it.'

'No, I can see that!' he agrees. 'I think it's a brilliant take on someone leading a double life.' He sits forward, urgently. 'Mia, I want to do this for you, for *us*. I want to bring your book to the world. And I do mean, the *world*. I want everyone to meet Layla. This is what we're going to do.' He pulls a pen from his pocket, reaches across the empty table and snatches up three clean napkins. 'I am going to get you at least this much money when I sell your book in this country.' He scribbles, passes it over and I have to fight not to let my eyebrows shoot up in shock. 'At the same time, I'm going to sell it in the States for at least *this* much money.' The next napkin flies over the table, and I gasp when I see the figure he's written. 'And then I'm going to sell it in France, Germany, Italy, The Netherlands, Poland, Spain, Denmark, Norway, China – possibly *not* Russia,' he laughs, 'but Hungary, Estonia – you name it – for at least, collectively, *this* much.' He waits as I pick up the third one and swear under my breath. 'And that's before we even think about the film of the book.'

'I can't believe this,' I say truthfully.

He frowns soberly 'You really are *completely* unaware of how good you are… I don't think I could bear it if someone came along and took advantage of that.' He sighs heavily. 'Forgive me, Mia. It's just I become enormously invested in my writers. I'm so proud and protective of them all and it's such a joy to see their books go on to delight the whole world when they started out as those scribblings in between shows, on the train home, in that coffee shop.' His eyes twinkle… 'It's *magical*.'

I am spellbound.

'We are going to have *such* an adventure!' he whispers. 'May I start the wheels turning?'

'Yes!' I exclaim, so completely caught up in the moment I feel genuinely excited.

'Ha!' he claps his hands, delighted. 'Well then, we have begun! I'll get the contract drawn up – but the *important* bit is, I will now send your wonderful book out to the best publishers in the business so they can begin vying for your hand. Hold onto your hat, Mia. The next couple of days are going to be a *lot* of fun!'

*

By half past six I'm running down The Strand to Embankment Place, to see if I can catch Seth – just for five minutes before I have to double back to work – because I can barely contain myself. I did it! Jack totally bought into me. I know I can't tell Seth because I promised Charlotte I wouldn't breathe a word, and I won't – yet… but I need to share this excitement and this moment with someone. I phone him breathlessly from outside the building.

'Hey! It's me, are you still up there?' I ask, when he answers. 'I'm outside, can you come down? Just really quickly?'

He appears moments later, looking around him, his face lighting up when he finally sees me.

'I'm so sorry to disturb you at work.' I don't kiss him because I'm very conscious of lots of people spilling out of the doors of the building. No one wants to see the boss snogging on the doorstep. How unprofessional would that look? 'I've just had the most incredible day and I can't wait to tell you all about it just as soon as I can.' I smile. 'That's all really – that's what I came to say. That and… I love you!' I blurt it out, just like that and immediately cover my mouth with my hands, horrified.

His eyes widen with surprise, and I quickly look up at the already dark sky feeling my face burning with embarrassment, but excitement too.

'I didn't plan on telling you that yet,' I admit, and I hear him laugh. 'I'm just so happy, that's all. But it's too soon. It's much too soon.' I risk a glance at him. 'And I absolutely DON'T want you to say it back, just because I've said it to you. In fact, I'm going now.' I turn and start to literally run up the street. 'I'll call you tomorrow!' I yell over my shoulder.

I get to the top where the road bleeds into The Strand and, breathless, have to stop, bend and drop my hands to my knees. I can feel him still watching me and, sure enough, I hear him yell 'Mia!'

I half turn back, he's made a heart shape with his fingers and thumbs which he's holding up above his head – high enough for me to see.

My face splits into a huge smile of relief and happiness. He loves me too, but I already know he does. For the first time in my life, I actually don't even need him to say it. I laugh, and keep on walking.

What a day!

I'm so glad Charlotte chose me.

CHAPTER NINE

CHARLOTTE

Hi Charlotte!

    I just wanted to let you know, that following your excellent advice, I had a meeting with an agent called Jack Cartwright today and signed with him! He's really excited about my book and thinks I have a very big couple of days ahead. He's already sent it out to people. I can't thank you enough for all of your help. Could I buy you a drink to say thank you next time you're in town? Mxxx

Hi Mia,

What great news and how excited you must be. He's an excellent agent and whatever he secures for you will be a really great opportunity. Keep me posted and of course, re the drink. I'll no doubt be in early next week, so delighted to catch up then and celebrate with you!

    All best,

    Charlotte.

I hit send. He actually signed her. Today. Less than twenty-four hours after she dropped the damn thing off.

And it could be a big *couple of days…*

It took me five months to get a deal for four grand last time. Almost half a year. I can't believe this has happened. *It's actually happened.*

I hear Tris slide his key into the front door lock, and slam the lid shut on the laptop. I exhale, shakily, and take a couple of deep breaths to steady myself as he appears in the kitchen doorway, bag over his shoulder, overcoat still on, car keys and a bottle of wine in one hand, mobile in the other. He's staring at the small screen and looks tired.

'Hello.' I get up. 'Must have been a long drive, you poor thing. You're really late. Have you eaten?'

'No, I haven't, but don't worry – I can sort something.' He shoves his phone in his pocket.

'It's OK. I've got lasagne. Do you want me to open that?' I nod at the wine.

'Only if you want some.' He passes it over to me. 'I'm all right. You look nice.'

'Thanks. I washed my hair.' I briefly think back to yesterday and how gross I felt in London with my scraped-back, grubby ponytail – wearing old office clothes. They were the only things in my wardrobe that didn't need ironing… thus saving the extra minutes I needed to complete the school run and dash to the train station. I was Melanie Griffith in *Working Girl*; a look so dated I was almost ironic, in comparison to Mia's Instagram-influencer chic, waiting for me on the steps of St Martin's in a very tight Fair Isle jumper, furry coat, cropped jeans and knee-high boots. Ridiculously beautiful. When I packed her off to the printers like a grumpy teenager, clutching her memory stick, I watched her stride off up Charing Cross Road and a besuited man twice her age literally stopped in the street and stared at her as she walked past him.

It just overtook me. Red mist, white rage – all the colours of a psychopathic rainbow. Opening my water bottle, I ran down the steps, and as he turned back to continue on his dirty old bastard way, I slammed into him, deliberately pouring my water all down his front. 'Oh my god, I'm so sorry!' I gasped, putting my hand over my mouth, genuinely appalled at what I'd just done.

He looked down at his shirt front and crotch dripping with water, and said incredulously: 'you stupid bitch.' I didn't feel so bad then, after all.

'How are the kids?' Tris walks over to the side and sifts through the post, before taking his laptop bag off his shoulder as I open the drawer for a corkscrew.

'They're fine. Better.'

'That's a relief. Did you manage to get some work done today? Any news?'

'A bit thanks,' I turn away from him, 'and no, not really.' I reach for two glasses. 'You?'

'Really – no wine for me, thanks.' He holds out a hand. 'And no, nothing exciting. Sheffield was…' he sighs… 'predictably shitty. Listen, you're not going to be happy, but I've got to go up again for the day on Friday and then this weekend it's Richard's stag do.'

'I told you ages ago.' He continues, when I look blank. 'Richard from work. That ridiculous SAS course and then clay pigeon shooting, in Wales – ten of us in a cottage.' He rubs his eyes tiredly. 'I appreciate this is about the worst timing ever and you have every right to go ballistic about me going, so I'm more than happy to cancel it if you like. I'll still have to pay a couple of hundred quid for my place, but that's fine.'

'Ah, so that's why you've brought wine,' I say lightly. 'A peace offering. We could have just opened one from the new case though?'

'I'd rather save them. They're too nice for a school night. I really don't want to go, obviously. I should have just said no in the beginning.'

I shove the spike into the cork and twist. 'Whatever you think. It's a lot of driving to do Sheffield and back on Friday, then go to Wales from here on Saturday morning though?'

He hesitates and I realise he was about to admit the plan is actually to go straight from Sheffield to Wales on Friday night. He bottles it though, biding his time. 'I'm just going to get changed.'

He undoes the top button of his shirt. 'Would you mind putting that lasagne in, if it's not too much trouble?'

'Sure.'

'Thanks, that's kind.'

He disappears, and I pour my wine, listening to it glug from the bottle, then head back over to my laptop, delete Mia's message and my response, before taking a sip and sitting down on one of the tall stools next to the island. I wanted to believe it would happen this fast. I knew that it could, in exceptional cases – but now that it actually is… I breathe out slowly and close my eyes. Shit. Not that there's any point in wondering have I done the right thing, because it's too late now. The book is out there.

I force a few deep breaths and when Tris appears in the doorway again, I know I look totally normal, even though inside my mind I'm running for my life. I can still catch up before it all slips away and out of reach, forever.

Tris looks around hopefully and I remember what I'm supposed to be doing. 'Sorry. The lasagne.' I get to my feet.

'It's OK. This is it, right?' He moves over to the covered plate on the side and opens the microwave. 'I can do it. The last thing you want to do is cook again.'

'It's not cooking. Just reheating.' I watch for a moment as he peers at the controls, then step forward and take over. 'Let me. Go sit down.'

He does as I tell him. For once, no phone, no iPad, no paper – just frowns at his clasped hands resting on the table. The only noise is my moving around the kitchen opening drawers and getting cutlery, finding a plate, filling up a glass of water, then the bleep of the microwave finishing.

'This is one of those Charlie Bingham ones, isn't it?' he says as I place the food under his nose. 'There are about a million calories in half a portion.'

Even if it were – which it isn't – just a simple thank you would do. 'No. I made it myself.'

Mollified, he starts to eat silently, and I begin to sort my stuff out to go and put it away in the other room.

'Martin came into the office today,' he says suddenly. 'We had a team debrief. He looked like absolute shit. He said the twins had been up every ninety minutes last night.'

'Well, babies do that, don't they?' I zip up the case on my laptop. 'They have such tiny tummies at that age and they're probably having a growth spurt. Remember how Teddy was up every forty minutes at one stage? It'll pass. Martin will survive.'

He grunts. 'I dunno. He doesn't look like he's long for this world.'

'Well it's probably also the stress of knowing he's got two families to financially support now.' I shrug. 'Caroline and the boys *and* Astrid and the twins.'

Tris sits back. 'I looked at him and thought, Christ – he's the same age as me and he's *just* starting out again.'

I don't say anything, just gather up an armful and make towards the door.

'Charlotte, do you love me?' he says suddenly.

I stop immediately. *Do I love you?* I blink back tears, quickly. I used to drive hours just to kiss you when you lived in some anonymous flat about half an hour outside the M25 on completely the wrong side for me. All I thought about was when I wasn't with you, was you. I jumped in heart first and promised in front of everyone I love most in the world that I'd love you the best of all, and forever. *Do I love you?*

I turn back to look at him over my shoulder. 'Yes, I do.'

He puts his fork down. 'Then why do you flinch when I touch you? Why do I feel like I irritate you all of the time? Why don't you want to have sex with me anymore?'

Oh please. Not now. We're so close to the finish line. My jaw clenches tightly. 'Tris, you have *just* walked in through the door.'

'I feel like one of the children; like then with the microwave,' he gestures at it. 'I can do it but I can sense your impatience with everything, that you expect me to mess up. I know I shouldn't have called you toxic before I left and I'm sorry, but you ARE angry. All of the time. I don't feel like you like me. Let alone love me.'

I turn my body back to the room so I'm facing him, but staying in the doorway. I don't say anything because I'm afraid, if I do, I'll simply explode and I can't misfire. It'll ruin everything.

'We're *both* working flat out,' he says. 'You have a job you love but the pay is shit. I have a shit job I hate that pays well. When I'm at home, you're working every evening, so I either work too or go to the gym for something to do. Then at the weekends it's just the kids. I've stopped seeing my friends. I barely speak to my family. There's nothing left over for me.' He hunches over the plate, miserably.

'I don't think that's true, is it, Tris?'

'Please try not to become defensive and just listen. I can *hear* you thinking "I'm tired too, I work hard too". Of course you are, that's not what I'm saying. We've become… stagnant. Superficially, we've got everything: a nice house, two kids, decent salary – we're privileged and I should be happy, but all I feel is this immense pressure. I know it sounds selfish saying "I need attention too"… pathetic even – I should just keep going. In fact, what I feel is irrelevant really, because I can't do anything about the—'

'There's nothing superficial about it,' I interrupt. I can't help myself. 'You *have* got everything.'

'Please,' he holds a hand up, 'let me speak. I have major financial commitments. I'm not going to shirk them, or just walk out on my job, but what I can't cope with anymore is the pressure to keep achieving alongside the lack of intimacy between us. There's this distance that's getting worse and worse. When I do try and touch you, I feel like I'm bothering you, which is… horrible. Men need sex, Charlotte.' He shrugs. 'I know it sounds shit – but we just do. We're different. It's a genuine biological need. I can't stay in a relationship for the rest of my life that doesn't feature sex.'

Still I don't respond. I can't let myself. Now all I can see is younger versions of us lying in various beds on luxury holidays and weekends away we never properly appreciated… but also in his flat on lazy long Saturdays, blissed out, laughing and whispering. Kissing each other… when we were happy, because we were, I know it.

He waits, then gestures helplessly. 'Do you hear what I'm saying? Do you even care?'

'I'm very tired,' I whisper. 'I just want to go to bed.'

'This is important.' He sits back in his seat and folds his arms. 'OK, so do you think it's a loss of sex drive full stop, or do you just not want sex with me? I've looked it up online and I think you might be perimenopausal, but perhaps I'm wrong? I get that it's *shit* that a bloke can take a pill and get a hard-on and there's no equivalent for women; no quick fix – but let's start with the basics you say are there. Do you even find me attractive?'

'I'm going to say it again: you've just walked in through the door after two nights away, I'm shattered – on my knees exhausted – and you want to know why we're not having sex anymore? If I get naked now, right here on the table – will that fix everything? Will you be less bored then?'

'I'm trying to be honest.'

My heart beats double time. 'Really? How admirable of you.'

'Admirable?' He shakes his head, exasperated. 'What is it you're not telling me, Charlotte? There's something, I'm sure of it. You can play it down as much as you like – but you forget I know you. Please, just *talk* to me! I have tried so many times to discuss this situation with you, to make you understand I can't—'

'Telling me repeatedly that our relationship is shit and I need to do something about it, is not "discussing a situation", it's little more than a profit warning,' I interrupt. 'Yes, I love you, but I want to go to bed now. I don't feel so good. I'm going to say good night.'

He stares at his untouched food. 'Charlotte, I don't want it to be like this anymore. I feel like I'm imploding. I've tried to reconnect with you. I love my family more than anything in the world, but when I get back from Wales, I think we need to properly talk, OK?'

There's a long pause. I stay very still because now the hairline cracks are snaking through the ice beneath my feet. 'You want to leave?' I say lightly. I hear Flo's voice in my head: *You told me that you had no intention of letting this change your life, or your family set-up. That you want everything to stay as it is.*

'Maybe you're right; expecting the solution to my problems to come from others just isn't realistic. I think it's time to consider all options, yes.'

Do not shout. Do not become emotional. Hold on, just a little longer.

'It's certainly important that we both approach whatever comes next with Teddy and Clara's best interests at heart,' I manage. 'But yes, if you want to – we can talk properly. Just to clarify, you're here tomorrow and tomorrow night, but then Sheffield on Friday and probably Wales on Saturday… so we'll say Sunday then?' I hold his gaze, calmly. 'And you'll sleep in the spare room tonight?' It's not really a question and he knows it.

He stares at me, incredulously, and nods. I think I see his eyes shine but he blinks quickly and looks away.

I manage to hold it together until I get up to our room. As soon as I close the door quietly behind me, my hand flies to my mouth in readiness, but no sound escapes. I'm shocked to discover I'm feeling no pain. There are no more tears; they're done. I stand very still, breathing deeply and looking at myself in the slightly open wardrobe door. Too thin, bending but not broken. Not when I have people that need me to stay strong and focused: children that depend on me.

I think of Mia, out there right now, excited, happy, oblivious – and Teddy and Clara, safely tucked up in their beds on the other side of the wall. Since Flo told me two weeks ago there was something I need to know, I have been very clear that I must fiercely protect the three of them from any more hurt, and that's exactly what I intend to do. I can't afford time for white noise, for Tris and his ultimatums. This is too important and I'm going to see it through by whatever means necessary and no matter the cost to myself.

My phone lights up with a text. It's Flo.

Just wanted you to know am thinking about you all the time atm. You are so brave. Love you so much, my strong, incredible sister. Whatever you decide to do, I will support you 100% xxx

Hmmm. I might need to hold you to that Flo…

CHAPTER TEN

MIA

'I can't talk right now!' I tell Kirsty happily as I cross the road, blinking as the bright winter afternoon sun, already low in the sky, shines directly in my eyes. 'I'm outfit shopping for the after-show party on Saturday night.'

'Oooh. Nice. I'll get it as an early Christmas present for you, if you like?'

'That's very kind. Thank you. I'm just walking into Liberty.'

She gives an amused exclamation. 'I'm sure you are. Turn around, walk straight back out and up to Oxford Street instead.'

'But I want it to be really special!'

'You'll look amazing in whatever you wear and you don't need to spend money you haven't got. I hate to be the voice of reason, but you don't actually have a job as of Saturday and you already owe Mum and Dad enough, don't you think?'

That stings a bit. She's right, but… I hesitate and chew my lip before blurting. 'Yeah, well I'm not so sure about that. I'm about to land a new gig, actually.'

'What do you mean?' she demands immediately. 'You've had a casting? You never said. With who?'

'I can't tell you. It's top secret at the moment.'

'No! I HATE it when you do this!' she exclaims. 'Oh, please tell me. You know I love this stuff. Who else is attached to it? Is it a director you like this time? Film or stage? Or TV? Come on, sing. I won't breathe a word.'

'Yes, you will. You know you will – so I really can't. But my agent has said it's going to be BIG money this time.'

Kirsty gasps. 'How big is big?'

'About a million,' I whisper.

'Mia! That's amazing!'

'I know!' I squeal, then look at my phone as it bleeps in my ear. 'Oh! They're calling me right now!'

'Who?' Kirsty shrieks. 'Who is? Spielberg? David Fincher? Richard Linklater?'

'Kirsty! Susanne Bier? Marielle Heller? Sam Taylor-Johnson?' I remind her pointedly. 'I'll ring you back.' I roll my eyes and hit call waiting. 'Hello?'

'Mia? It's Jack. Tell me – where are you?'

'Right now?' I look around me. 'By the flowers in the doorway of Liberty. Why?'

'Perfect, my fair lady! I want to be able to picture the scene properly when I give you the news.' He pauses dramatically. 'We have already had one very nice offer for your book to take it off the table so no one else can buy it, but…' he stops again and waits to build the expectation, 'I will be turning it down, because tomorrow, everything is going to go crazy with bids. Mia – we are already in the high six figures for your UK deal. I can't promise, but I think we stand a very good chance of hitting seven.'

My mouth falls open as I walk into the store slowly, stopping dead in the perfume section when it dawns on me. Seven figures… that's a million. Just for selling it in this country? Shit!

'Can you be around tomorrow if I need to talk to you?' he continues, 'because I want to have this concluded on our side of the pond before the weekend. Word is getting out that a big, big deal is underway and I want to tie it all up here while everyone is in a feverish state of excitement that will then also get the American publishers nicely hot and bothered. I do just need to ask you – this will be a two-book deal. What have you got lined up for the next one? Have you started working on it already?'

My eyes widen. Charlotte hasn't said anything about that. Like a rabbit in the headlights I stare desperately at the immaculately dressed assistant stood behind a counter in front of me, like she's going to hold a cue card up or something, but she just smiles blandly, turns her back on me and then sticks her tongue out while pulling a face like she thinks I'm mad. I see this because she doesn't realise the mirror to her left has caught her reflection. Classy.

'It's kind of hard to resist the temptation to do something about women putting other women down, to be honest, because that's *everywhere*,' I say loudly and unnecessarily, to make the point that I *did* see, thanks very much. 'I've got a few ideas,' I continue, thinking as fast as I can on my feet, 'but because I literally make it up as I go along, I'm playing around a bit with a couple to see which one grabs me the most. Is that OK?' That was vague enough, wasn't it? Charlotte will have it covered, surely?

'That's fine,' he says breezily. 'I don't need more than that at the moment. And you'd be happy to deliver a second within a year?'

A year? That's ages! 'Oh, absolutely!' I say breezily.

'Wonderful. Right – well, sleep soundly tonight and I'll be back with you soonest in the morning. Standby!'

I hang up. Wow. Should I email Charlotte? Maybe I better hang on until tomorrow, when there's something concrete to tell her. It wouldn't fit with our 'story' otherwise and I don't think she'd be happy with any deviation. I decide to wait and put my phone back in my bag before shooting a haughtily dismissive glance at the assistant. *I* am busy doing seven-figure deals – stick that in your pipe and smoke it.

But as I continue on my way to the women's department, I feel bad for being a bitch. I've seen so many actresses start to believe their own hype and turn into actual monsters. I didn't even write this book. I'm just the public face; I need to remember that. Sighing deeply, disappointed with myself, I reach the women's department… but immediately cheer up. It is full of very beautiful, expensive things, and I know exactly what I'm looking for!

'Excuse me?' I find a far friendlier-looking assistant. 'Could you show me where to find The Vampire's Wife? I had a look online and I think you stock it?'

'We certainly do!' She beams. 'It's just this way.'

I follow her and feel my heart flutter with excitement as she leads me to a rail on which I immediately spy a long, black velvet dress. It has exactly the same languid silhouette as Charlotte's. I reach out and let the soft, slippery material run between my fingers. It's finished with a light frosting of silver glitter that sparkles under the shop lights.

'It's designed to be reminiscent of a starry night,' the assistant confides. 'Would you like me to put it in the fitting room for you?' She's just like Bridget in *Pretty Woman*. In fact this dress reminds me a bit of the black cocktail one Julia Roberts wears when she meets him in the hotel bar for the first time!

'Yes, please,' I say shyly.

As soon as I put it on, I know I've made a fatal mistake. I now have to buy this dress. It's the loveliest thing I've ever worn in my life. I imagine *everyone* staring at me in admiration, Seth proudly looking on – it's the happiest of dreams until I find the price tag and almost faint on the spot: £1,650! I can't – I just can't. It's all right for a proper grown-up like Charlotte to have expensive tastes like this, but Kirsty's right – I'm going to be out of a job as of next week. But then Jack *did* say a high six-figure offer was already on the table. Surely I'm *going* to be able to afford it?… I stare at myself in the mirror, entranced. I'll never be treated like an actress going places unless I start behaving like one, and I won't always have to *buy* dresses like this. It won't be long until people will want to lend them to me. I make a snap decision and that's it, a done deal. I shall go to the ball.

I don't even falter when I hand my credit card over and watch as another assistant carefully wraps the dress in tissue paper. From then on it's easy, the purple bag swinging on my arm as I walk confidently towards the theatre like I always carry dresses worth thousands of pounds around with me. I'm at the far end of Carnaby Street when my phone rings again and I scramble for it – that can't be Jack again already? – but it's only Kirsty.

'You didn't call me back,' she says accusatively. 'I knew you wouldn't. So was it good news?'

'Yes,' I tease. 'It was. I'll be able to tell you more tomorrow, I promise. You'll be the first to know.'

'You swear?'

'Cross my heart and hope to die. Hey, talking of my heart – want to hear my other big news?'

'Always,' she says, but I think I hear a note of apprehension creeping into her voice. I decide to ignore it and plough on anyway.

'I told Seth I love him for the first time yesterday. Just blurted it out in the street then literally ran off like I was Forrest Gump or something.' I laugh, and she sort of does too, before there's a pause and, unable to help herself, she says: 'And did he say it back?'

'No, but I was at the other end of the road by then. He'd have had to shout it right outside his office. It's OK, Kirst,' I say quickly. 'I know what you're thinking, but I'm not worried. I know he loves me. It's fine. It's all going to be fine. Trust me.'

'Sweetheart, I trust *you* one hundred and fifty per cent, but…'

Frowning, I slow down and step out of the way to let other people pass, shivering slightly as I move out of the sunlight and into the shadow of some offices on the right-hand side of the street. 'Go on. What's the end of that sentence?'

She sighs. 'Remind me again why he split up with his wife?'

'Well I can't remind you, because I've never actually told you in the first place,' I say tightly.

'Don't get upset. I'm not having a go. It's just this is all happening very quickly. This is a man you picked up at a train station two months ago, and—'

'Hey! I did NOT "pick him up" at a train station,' I say hotly. 'You could describe *Brief Encounter* exactly the same way and that's one of the greatest romance stories of all time!'

'Yes, with quite the happy ending.'

'Why are you determined to do this?' I demand. 'Are people who have been divorced not allowed to fall in love again? Is that some rule that I wasn't aware of until now?'

'I don't understand why you won't just tell me why he split up with his wife?' she insists. 'What's the big secret?'

'There ISN'T one!' I start to raise my voice, and a woman stares at me as she walks past. 'This is all in your head.'

'No, it bloody isn't!' she retorts. 'He's either divorced or he isn't!'

'I never said he *wasn't*!' I raise my arms in exasperation. 'I meant there's no big drama here. If you must know, he had a really hard time of it with his ex-wife. She's a very difficult person. She—'

'Doesn't understand him?' Kirsty leaps in and, just like that, I lose my temper. It's ONLY my sister that can do this – get right in, under my skin in two seconds flat.

'And THIS is exactly why I didn't tell you,' I say angrily, 'because I knew you'd react exactly as you are! I'm having a really good day, can you please just let me enjoy it, instead of dragging your shitty bell of impending doom around with you and clanging it in my face where it's not wanted?'

'I am NOT clanging a shitty bell in your face,' she says indignantly. 'I'm trying to get you to listen to yourself! "My wife doesn't understand me" is the warning label God attaches to shit-stick fuck-knobs so all sensible women know to stay the hell away from them!'

'"Shit-stick fuck-knobs"?' I repeat. 'What are you – fifteen? And don't sit on the fence, will you? Tell me what you really think!'

'Fine!' she says quickly. 'I will! I don't want you going out with him! I don't want you involved with him. I haven't met the bloke and I can already tell you he's trouble. He won't even tell you he loves you!'

'Because I was at the other end of the bloody road! I already told *you* that! You're honestly saying you don't think it's at all possible, perhaps, his ex-wife could genuinely be a bitch? It has to be all *his* fault, right?'

'Amy – you don't know this, because you've never been married – but trust me – it is very rarely just one person's fault that a marriage breaks down.'

'Mia. My name is MIA – and that's just bollocks,' I say, rudely.

'If he's telling you that,' she loudly talks over me. 'He's lying. You need to—'

'I need to go now actually,' I say. 'Goodbye.'

'Don't you dare hang up on me! I'm telling you that this will—'

'Bye. Catch you later and thanks for completely ruining my nice day. Really kind of you. So glad you called back. Bye.' I hang up shaking with anger and, shoving my phone in my bag, march off down the street so fast the tears in my eyes practically blow from my face.

In less than three minutes my phone starts to ring again. I want to ignore it, but can't, in case it's Jack. Sure enough when I look – it's Kirsty. I reject the call. She tries again. I ignore that too – and a third time. Three minutes later, Mum rings.

'I don't WANT to speak to her, Mum!' I don't even bother with hello. 'You can tell her from me that it's really SAD to be forty-two and phoning your mum to tell tales on your little sister so you can get your side of the story in first.'

My mum sighs gently. 'Darling. She's trying to look out for you. She loves you so much. We all do. She's just worried, that's all.'

'She swore at me. Lots. She was really unkind, Mum. I had to hang up on her.'

'I don't think you *had* to. You *do* know she hates it when you do that, darling, and then won't answer the phone. I'm not sure it's helpful?'

'Why should I have to listen to that stuff about Seth? She's not prepared to give him a chance! She goes off on one like that and then wonders why I don't want to bring him to meet everyone!' I start walking faster. 'He's done nothing to warrant her being like this. Genuinely, his ex-wife is really hard work.'

'I'm not saying she isn't. Kirsty cares about *you*. That's all. Will you talk to her? Please?'

'I don't want to! I—'

'I so hate it when any of you are fighting! Please. For me. Just talk to her.'

I scowl. 'Fine.' I manage eventually. 'I'll message her in a minute.' If there were a can on the street right now, I'd kick it. Boot it as hard as I could.

'Thank you, sweetest. That's all I'm asking. Why don't you bring Seth to lunch on Sunday, if he's around? I'd really like to meet him?'

I hesitate, then sigh, mollified. 'I'll think about it – but thank you, Mum. I appreciate that… I just want to go now, if that's OK. I'm still feeling really angry – but yes, I'll speak to Kirsty. I promise.'

True to my word, once I hang up, I stop again, in the street and message my sister.

You called him a shit-stick. How would you feel if I called Bill names?

I couldn't care less!

She messages back immediately.

Bill IS a shit-stick. All men are!

No they're not, Kirsty! Not all men are out to hurt women! Dad isn't. Neither is Seth. They are GOOD men. I think Bill is too, unless there is something you're not telling me? I can't help it if YOU are unhappy – but please don't take out your stuff on me; "don't write a book about yourself, don't spend money. Seth is a shit." Are you jealous of me and my life? Is that what this is about?

I regret it as soon as I've sent it. I might be annoyed, but I've crossed a line. I've hurt one of the people I love more than anything in the world. I would kill for my big sister.

OK. NOW I'm angry. And heartbroken that you could think that.

I try to call her immediately, but she won't pick up, turning my own trick on me. She's never done that before. I feel frightened for a moment. She has always been there for me. When I was ill Kirsty and Mum kept me tethered to the earth; cuddling me on the sofa on Saturday nights while I stared at a blank screen that was just bright colours and sounds with no picture I could make sense of. It was Kirsty who came to see me every single time I asked for her when I was in The Pines.

I'm sorry. I love you x

She doesn't message back.

*

I can't reach Seth either, which freaks me out a bit. I try him a couple of times after the show has finished but he doesn't pick up. I have to remind myself as the train clatters back to Blackheath, clutching the dress bag on my lap, that Kirsty loves me, that's why she's so protective. It scares her to see me making myself vulnerable again – but she doesn't know him like I do. The fact that he didn't say it means nothing. It's all been taken out of context. He loves me. He made a heart shape. I know that's what he meant.

At home, I slide between the cold sheets, shivering in the bed that feels too big. I briefly consider calling an Uber, getting it to take me to Putney right now, but there will be a good reason why he hasn't called me back. It's coincidence. That's all.

*

It's 1 a.m. when I wake up with a start, unsure why I've disturbed. I check my phone and there it is. A message.

I love you too x

I blink, trying to focus on the screen – squinting in the dark. Seth. The relief is immense… which is so stupid. I have never doubted how we feel for each other. I'm now wide awake. I put my phone down and stare up at the ceiling. I told her. I wish Kirsty could just trust me on this.

I wish *she'd* text me back and tell me she loves me.

*

She still hasn't called me by Friday lunchtime – although I *am* starting to get loads of weird congratulations messages… from people I barely know anymore but have worked with. One actually says: 'Congrats on your book deal!' That obviously freaks me out, and I call Jack, only to be told by his assistant he's in a meeting but will 'shout me back' the minute he can. The randomness of the morning unnerves me completely and by mid-afternoon, Jack still hasn't rung, I've left countless messages of apology for Kirst, am quite tearful and begging Mum to get her to contact me.

'She *will* calm down, Mia. Give her a moment. She's angry and hurt.'

'I shouldn't have said it. I know that. Plus she's just going to blame Seth for this even more than she was already, but she's never been cross with me like this before, Mum. I can't handle it. It's not kind of her to be deliberately punishing me like this.'

'Give her some space. She'll come round. Try not to think about it anymore today. Focus on the show. You only have three left, after all. Put your energies there instead. What do you think you'll—'

'Mum! I have to go!' I say quickly, because a call waiting beeps in my ear. 'It might be her or some really important work stuff I've got going on. I'll catch you again in a bit… hello?'

'Mia Justice! Author and superstar, hello! Do you want the very good news, or the extraordinarily good news?'

'Hello, Jack. The very good news, please.' I wipe my eyes and try to concentrate.

'American publishers have got wind of everything happening here. Several of them are already preparing their bid. Lots of people's weekend is going to go wonky, stateside because whole teams are going to be frantically reading your book. The other very good news is that after a ten-way auction, I have just secured you seven-figures for your UK deal. £1.1 million to be precise, for two books.'

I gasp.

'I know! You may find something gets naughtily leaked to the press about it, just a heads-up.'

'I think it already has been – I've been getting strange messages congratulating me this morning.'

'Really? I'll find out. Anyway, it will come out soon enough in any case, so prepare yourself for that, not least because the *extraordinarily* good news is that ten minutes ago I took a call from a very prominent film studio about optioning the book and making it into a major movie!'

'What?' I exclaim. 'You're kidding me!'

'I never joke about deals,' he says soberly. 'I want to be the first to congratulate you, Mia, for writing such a life-changing book.

We will dot the i's and cross the t's next week when you come in to sign the UK contract and meet your new publisher, but in the meantime you might get an email to tell you how thrilled she is to have secured you, now the deal has formally been done. Her name is Kate and she's very, very nice. Can I offer you a little advice however?'

'Yes, please.' I'm already feeling hugely out of my depth as I arrive at the stage door.

'Take a second to go and sit quietly somewhere. This moment will never come again. You will never again be a debut author on the cusp of such an exciting journey. This moment is to be savoured, privately. Call me if you need me at any point over the weekend, but otherwise, can we say you'll come into the office on Monday at midday?'

'Yes – of course. And Jack? Thank you. Thank you very, very much.'

'You're very welcome, Mia. We're going to have a lot of fun with this, but for now – that quiet moment to reflect on your achievement in finding such an exciting home for your extraordinary book. Congratulations.'

I hang up, stunned. I should email Charlotte immediately… and Seth. And Mum and Dad. Or maybe I should do as Jack said and just—

'Mia Justice! You dark little horse!'

I jump at the shout behind me and turn to see Theo striding up the street. Before I can say anything, he arrives in front of me, breathless and sweaty, leans in and hugs me effusively. I can feel his fat wrapping around me.

'I'm sure there was something in your contract about telling me in my director's capacity if you were secretly writing a mega book that I might want to option, you cheeky little minx.' He leers at me as he steps back and waves the *Evening Standard* in my face. 'Congratulations, darling. I'm thrilled for you. Which studio is it that you're going to go with, by the way?'

I must stare at him blankly because he looks a little uncomfortable. 'Ah – I see you're still understandably upset about our exchange last week. What can I say? It was the wrong technique to use on you. Sometimes, you really can squeeze a little more out of an exceptionally talented actress like yourself by pushing them further into part – but I can see now it didn't do that for you. I misjudged the situation. I'm sorry.'

'You're saying you shouted at me, made me cry and belittled me, to help me "raise my game"?' I say slowly.

He looks alarmed. 'Of course! Nina is a character who simply must come out fighting! Don't say you never experienced that "knock them down, build them up" technique during your formal training and thought I actually *meant* it? Oh you sweet thing! I'm *mortified*. Mia, you are a wonderfully gifted actress. You've been a delight to have in this show and I'm so proud of everything you have achieved. I'm not surprised in the least to discover that you are poised to also achieve wonderful things in the literary world.' He taps the *Standard* again.

'May I see that?' I hold out a hand.

'You haven't yet?' His mouth falls open. 'Of *course*!' He flicks through the pages eagerly. 'Here!' He passes the paper to me.

ACTRESS TURNED AUTHOR SET TO NET £1M-PLUS DEAL AS PUBLISHERS SCRAMBLE FOR 'HOTTEST BOOK OF THE YEAR'

A million pound major auction is underway for the debut book by actress Mia Justice. The twenty-five-year-old, currently starring in The Seagull *at the Wyndham's Theatre, London is the latest hot-property hopeful as publishers looking for the next big thing battle to snap up her book,* Complicit. *Described as a thriller, ordinary working wife and mother to grown-up children, Layla, receives a video message from herself urging her to safety immediately. Nothing she knows is real. The identity she knows as her own has been forced upon her without her knowledge, and has now been compromised. 'Layla is an irresistible heroine,' agrees agent Jack Cartwright, who signed Justice after staying up all night to read the book, the same evening it was submitted to him. 'I read a lot of unpublished material that is a pale imitation of whatever last year's brilliant breakout success might be. Currently I'm being sent a lot of stories about quirkily named ladies who are very well, thanks for asking. Layla stood out as a breath of fresh air when she exploded into my life this week: forced not to succumb to the weakness of emotional relationships in her life, that may or may not be real, in order to survive.'*

While mega deals like this are 'unusual' Cartwright points out that the figures concerned reflect the energy and passion publishers are keen to commit 'to this truly gripping page-turner. I couldn't be more delighted for Mia, a significant new voice who has a very exciting career ahead of her'.

Deals are currently underway in all other major territories, including America, with the film rights rumoured to be heading to Universal Studios.

'May I keep this?' I manage.

'I think the whole world is yours right now!' he grins.

I simply walk off. Not because I'm intentionally being rude, but because I have to phone Seth. It goes to voicemail.

'Hey, it's me,' I say. 'Firstly, thank you for your text last night. It meant the world to me. And, um, secondly – you might see some stuff about me in today's *Standard* that I obviously haven't mentioned to you yet. It's all a bit, mad, to be honest, but… exciting! Anyway. I'll talk to you properly about it all later and…' I hesitate, still feeling a bit shy, 'I love you. Bye!'

More messages start to come in. Still mostly people I've worked with, although someone helpfully posts a link to the *Standard* article on my Facebook page, as it seems to have gone online now, too. Cary *himself* rings to congratulate me; 'I'm already getting casting calls – enjoy your weekend off, you're going to be a busy, busy little bee next week.' My parents and brother are stunned but delighted when I call them. Even Hugo weasels out of the woodwork to ring from a new number and let me know he's been telling everyone how clever his ex is, how pleased he is for me, how much I deserve it. I'm shaking with anxiety when I hang up. And yet still I hear nothing from either Seth or Kirsty. It's too late to go down to Seth's office and I don't want to make a habit of that anyway. Instead, in my dressing room, I email Charlotte with the link to the online piece.

> Update to the attached – it happened! I agreed a deal this afternoon. Hope it's not vulgar to confirm the reports in the paper are all true! Drink on Monday, or sooner if you're in town, on me to say thank you for all of your help and advice?! Mia xxx

I try to imagine how she must be feeling out there, watching her plan come off so spectacularly, but also knowing it's *her* book that is causing all of this fuss. Does she even care she's getting none of the glory? I doubt it somehow. I get the feeling Charlotte isn't bothered about being liked. This is just a straightforward business transaction for her. How trusting is she, though? She has no proof she gave it to me… What if I were to make off with everything? I would never do that of course – but I could.

Although again, I bet Charlotte has thought of that and somehow has it covered. In fact, I don't think she's the sort of person I'd ever want to try and cheat. She's too clever for that. She'd always be one step ahead. You'd steal the suitcase full of money, go on the run and wake up in some motel room somewhere to find her standing at the foot of your bed, gun pointing right at you.

Basically, you never steal the suitcase of money. Everyone knows that. It always ends with bad blood.

CHAPTER ELEVEN

CHARLOTTE

Teddy has finally fallen asleep, despite the bright lights, the beeps, talking and crying babies around us. I stroke my son's head, shhhing him gently as he whimpers, while I watch the three female doctors at their station in the middle of the paediatric ward discussing their cases. *Please be deciding to let us go home soon.* I look down at my poor, exhausted boy clutching my hand tightly, and with my free one, I try Tris again. His phone is still switched off. I ring his work mobile. It goes to voicemail, just like last time… so I call the London office switchboard. 'Hi,' I say quietly as Teddy stirs alongside me, 'could you try Seth Tristan's line, please? Or one of his colleagues? It's his wife, again, Charlotte Tristan. No, I still haven't been able to get hold of him. He definitely hasn't been back in the office since he left at half past six, then? No? OK – thank you. Yes, if he does that would be great.'

I hang up and exhale heavily, eyes closed. Where are you, Tris? I have been calling and calling since we arrived at A&E nearly four hours ago. I have left messages everywhere. Your four-year-old son is being treated for a paracetamol overdose – that sounds scary enough to want to know exactly what has happened, surely? Especially when you were the fucking idiot who left the lid off the bottle, for him to find in the first place.

I consider this situation in reverse – him calling *me* to say that one of our children has been brought into hospital in an emergency; that I need to come now. I can't imagine a scenario in which he wouldn't be able to reach me – unless perhaps my phone was stolen, I suppose – but Tris has *two* phones and numerous office lines. By now, if I were him, I would be running over broken glass, barefoot if necessary, calling for updates constantly on my way… yet I have not seen or heard a thing from my husband since he left the house at half past five this morning. As usual he's nowhere near Sheffield, seeing as he definitely left the London office earlier this evening, but nonetheless, it is now nearly eleven p.m., and he appears to have vanished into thin air. It is also completely unlike him to have his phone actually switched off – he never does that.

There is, of course, a possible, rational explanation. He might really be driving to Wales for the stag do, which is why he hasn't picked up yet. His battery could also have died while he was driving.

But it's a stretch. I stroke Teddy's head, lean down and kiss our son lightly. I'm finding it increasingly hard to believe not a single message about Teddy has reached Tris. So, why isn't he at least calling me? Why isn't he here?

I do another restless sweep of all of my accounts, including my email – Mia hasn't mailed today with news, so there won't be any until Monday now, which means his disappearance can't be anything to do with her or any of *that*. I briefly consider his threat of wanting us to talk 'properly'. Could he have managed to push himself over the edge? Decided to just leave anyway? I doubt it. We agreed that we'd—

A baby in the bay opposite starts to cry with the wheezy, broken crackles of a very ill child and, immediately distracted, I can't help but look up at the pitiful sound. One of the two doctors now examining it has begun some sort of procedure that seems to involve the baby's painfully vulnerable spine. The white-faced young father is looking on helplessly, hands on his wife's shoulders as she holds their child protectively in her arms, fighting her every instinct and trustingly letting someone do something that is obviously hurting her child, while trying to make it bearable for them all with desperate songs and loving whispers.

The sight brings tears to my horrified eyes. I don't want to intrude, but neither can I seem to look away from the little family. I know exactly what that woman is thinking right now; that she would sell her soul, do whatever deal with God that it takes, as long as her child is OK. A nurse sees me staring transfixed, kindly stands up and pulls our curtain across.

Relieved, I wipe my eyes and exhale slowly... as my mobile starts to ring in my hand, making me jump – but it's not him, it's my mother.

'Darling! We're still in Ludlow at Jerry and Sarah's and I've found all of your messages on my phone! You're in hospital with Teddy? What's happened?'

I have recounted what Teddy did so many times tonight – to various very nice nurses and doctors – I now repeat it on autopilot for mum. 'He drank a load of Calpol at bedtime. I was running his bath; Clara is at her friend's for a sleepover tonight so he was on his own in his bedroom, otherwise she would have seen what he was doing and stopped him, I know she would. I came in and he was swigging it from the bottle. Tris had given him some in the night because Ted was coughing again, but he didn't put the lid back on properly. Teddy found it and thought he'd have some medicine before bed. Because I couldn't be sure if it was a new bottle or not and I couldn't get hold of Tris to find out – so I didn't know how much he had – I had to bring Teddy into A&E. We're on the paediatric ward now while they keep us under observation.'

'Oh, that poor little boy!' Mum says. 'He's going to be all right though? Is Tris with you now?'

'Not yet. He was supposed to be in Sheffield today, now he might be on his way to Wales, but I'm almost certain he's in

London – I'm just not entirely sure yet.' I pause and gather my thoughts. 'In answer to your question about Teddy, yes. He's OK. He's sleeping. I'm hoping they're going to let us go soon.' I slide away from Teddy carefully and stand up. The baby has stopped crying, so I peep around the curtain to see if a doctor or nurse is free now. I really want to get us home.

'You must be exhausted as well. Thank goodness Clara was at a friend's and you didn't have to drag her out too,' Mum continues. 'I'm SO sorry I'm right at the other end of the country. Even if I left now – and I've had a drink and so has Dad – I wouldn't be there until half two at the very earliest given it's nearly eleven. What about Flo? Have you phoned her?'

'Yes. She's on her way to our house.'

'Well that's a relief.'

'I think she's going to stay the night.' I can't see anyone and so quickly head back to Teddy. I don't want him rolling off the side of the high bed. 'I better go, Mum, if that's OK. I haven't got much battery and I want to keep it in case Tris calls.'

'Of course, big hugs all round. Tell Teddy Nona loves him!'

I barely hear her, hanging up as one of the doctors suddenly reappears around the curtain – a sensible Mum-type. I wonder who is with *her* children while she's in here, looking after us.

'Hello!' She looks at Teddy, still flat out. 'He's had enough then,' she says sympathetically, 'and you have too, I expect.' She smiles at me. 'Want to take him home?'

'Yes, please,' I say quickly. 'That would be great. He's OK then?'

'Everything has come back completely normal – and I'm happy with his obs. Of course, if anything changes or you're worried, come back, and you did absolutely the right thing in bringing him in – but he needs his own bed now, I think. As do you.'

Teddy is so tired, he barely stirs as I quickly put his coat on – the poor little baby opposite has started crying again and I just want to leave, I can't bear it – before lifting my son into my arms. It takes a huge effort to get him into a position where I can carry him *and* my handbag, he's grown so much these last few weeks alone, plus the bag of books, spare clothes, water and snacks I grabbed in panic when we dashed from the house earlier. He's like a dead weight and I stagger through the double doors barely able to see over his shoulder as we pass the now-heaving A&E. I hear someone call out and hurry on, thinking it's probably some drunken fracas I don't want Teddy to wake up and witness, but then I feel a hand on my back and spin round to see Noel, one of the school dads, frowning down at me in concern.

'Hello! You look like you're about to collapse.' He grabs at my handbag, slipping off my shoulder. 'Let me help. You here on your own?'

I nod, too out of breath to speak.

'Hang on.' He turns back to the waiting room. 'Max?'

A boy in his late teens looks up from his phone, other hand aloft, elbow propped on the seat rest, as a trickle of blood runs down from his thumb into the tea towel loosely swathed around his wrist.

'I'm just going to help Charlotte. I'll be right back, OK?'

He nods and returns to his screen.

'My son Max. From my first marriage. I don't think you've met him before. Anyway – sorry. Now's not the time. So you're done? Heading back to the car?' Noel thumbs a gesture in the direction of the car park.

'Yes,' I gasp, as Teddy slips slightly lower still and I have to bend my knees, my biceps already screaming, ready to shunt him back up again. 'He's so heavy!'

'Here, give him to me.' Noel reaches out and takes Teddy, lifting him effortlessly into rugby-strong arms. Teddy immediately rests his head on Noel's shoulder, still fast asleep. 'Poor little bloke, what's he in for?' Noel asks as we start to walk down the brightly lit corridor.

'He found an open Calpol bottle. I couldn't be sure how much he drank, so I brought him in. *I* didn't leave the lid off, I just want to say.'

'Ah,' Noel says and diplomatically doesn't comment further. 'But he's OK now then?'

'Yes, he's fine. What's up with your son?'

'Beer injury. The whole neck of the bottle shattered in the hand he was holding it steady with while he popped the cap off – sliced his thumb open. Total freak accident. It's not his messaging hand and swiping thumb though, so thankful for small mercies eh?' He rolls his eyes, and I smile. '*I'll* no doubt get it in the neck when he goes home to his mum's on Sunday though,' he adds lightly.

It's my turn not to say anything as we emerge into the cold night air. At the change in temperature, Teddy shivers and huddles into Noel more closely.

'This is me here.' I point at the car. 'Thank you so much.'

'You got lucky, getting a space so close – we're about ten miles away. You open the door and I'll pop him in.'

I watch as he carefully puts Teddy in his car seat, pulling the belt across gently so as not to disturb him. Tris should be doing this. Noel straightens up but his smile fades when he sees I'm crying.

'I'm so sorry!' I say, embarrassed. 'Please, just ignore me. Long evening – I'm really tired.' But the truth is, I'm suddenly so angry with Tris for doing this to us, that the tears are as good as burning my skin.

I expect Noel to react like most men: woman-who-I-don't-know-that-well-crying! Mayday, Mayday! But he actually gives me a hug. It's really sweet of him – I think – except finding myself in the warmth of a familiar man's arms… only not my husband's… just makes everything worse. It's like the dream I have sometimes: I'm still with Daniel. It's so vivid I can remember exactly what it felt like to have him touch me. Only we're now married. He's acting like everything's normal but I know, *I know* there's someone else… someone else I'm supposed to be with… then I wake up feeling sick with relief to find Tris alongside me. Or at least, that's what used to happen.

My head starts to swim and I pull back. I want Noel to let me go. 'Thank you,' I mumble, my brain finally grinding into gear. 'It was just very frightening not knowing how much Teddy had drunk. Anyway, I'll let you get back to your son.'

'You've got some help at home?' he asks, obviously trying to decide if he ought to let me drive off. 'Tris is there?'

'Yes,' I lie. 'He'll be back from work by now.'

'Oh, OK.' Noel gives me a thumbs up. 'Sorry us Dads are so rubbish. We mean well, I promise.'

I laugh – it's a horribly fake sound. 'We know! Don't worry! Cheers, Noel, you're a star. Say hi to Kerry for me, won't you?'

Teddy is snoring as I start the car and reverse out of the spot. I glance in my rear-view mirror and wave, as Noel turns and walks back into A&E.

Where is my husband?

He should be here.

CHAPTER TWELVE

MIA

I manage somehow to get through the show, but when I dash to my phone once the curtain is down, there's not a single message. I try him again, but it's just his work voicemail. In the pub, I double-check everything obsessively: texts, WhatsApp – even email… but there's nothing from him. All I discover is that the mail I sent to Charlotte earlier didn't actually send, so I re-send it. I hope she hasn't already seen the news and is pissed off I didn't tell her myself. I wouldn't blame her for being annoyed though, it does look slack. She would *never* be so disorganised.

Everyone, including Theo, wants to buy me a drink. I try really hard to insist I don't want a hangover for the last shows tomorrow, but they keep pushing and pushing. My refusal starts to look churlish, so I give in and I promise myself I will stop after one. It will honestly and truthfully be *one* – but Theo buys a double, to prove how generous he is *really*, and it does start to relax me. I feel my tension about Kirsty easing away and after that it's the same old stupid pattern. I end up knocking back several doubles far too fast. It's on the brink of turning really messy, I'm starting to think to hell with it, let's stay out – before I decide suddenly that I want to go home after all. I want Seth. Where is he?

I weave back to the station in the hammering rain, my umbrella dipping and diving all over the place as I try to hold it up, dimly aware that people are staring at me, so I try to walk in a straight line down the wet pavements, swinging my hips carelessly like I'm just fascinating, actually. Sophisticated. Hot. NOT three sheets to the already blowing wind. I should have got a cab, it's bloody horrible out here.

At the station I'm raging hungry all of a sudden – as well as cold and wet – so I buy some chocolate on the platform and eat it while I leave Seth a voice message telling him it's half past eleven, I'm on my way home and he should come round to the flat if he's able to, I want to see him… It's been an insane day and I'm starting to feel really weird. I want Seth's arms around me, where I feel safe, protected – normal. I look up to see a bloke watching me, half smiling – and scowl back at him. I have *not* just made a booty call, thank you very much. Get back to your phone and mind your own. I love Seth and he loves me. I deliberately choose a different carriage to the perv. Safety first.

At the other end, I stagger up my road against the rain, having given up on my umbrella because it keeps folding in on itself. I just drop it, blown out backwards – and it skitters down the pavement into the gutter. I don't care anymore – I'm busting for a wee… but I hesitate as I round the corner of the drive. The house is completely dark and a bit creepy-looking as I zigzag over the gravel up to my front door. I'd forgotten Julia upstairs is away this weekend. I don't like it when I get home and *all* of the lights are off. I get in, peel the wet clothes from my body and towel-dry my hair, having put some music on to banish the quiet. I have LOVED Fisher's 'Losing It' since I saw him at Coachella even though it's everywhere now and cheesy as hell. I wish I'd stayed out, after all… But I've done so well recently. I so don't want to mess things up just as it's starting to get really good. I decide to try my new dress on instead.

'Mia Justice, author, relaxes at home and reflects on a life-changing year,' I whisper to my reflection in the wardrobe door, stumbling slightly as I twirl and the sparkles catch the light – the track is starting to build and I lift my arms up above my head, but the joy has gone. Just as suddenly, I stop and sink down onto the bed, anxious, afraid – and really stressed. Where is Seth? No! I should go out. I'm not going to sit around waiting for him like some little good girl. I could go back into town and find the others? I slip a strap from my shoulder to get changed – but then, this is not like him.

I jump up and yank open the bedside table drawer, pulling out a packet of fags. I need to calm down. A ciggie is better than doing something else. I'll just have this and decide what to do. I start the track again, get up and weave through to the living space, past the sofa and throw open the bifolds, mindful of my promise to Mum and Dad not to smoke in the flat. It's stopped raining but it's really wet out on the decking and I've got bare feet. I light up and hover on the threshold instead, blowing anxious clouds into the garden that lies beyond, shivering in the cold and absently nodding my head to the beat of the music. Seth doesn't just not call. He doesn't disappear. Something is wrong, I know it. I inhale deeply and try not to panic as I stare at the bushes and trees in the darkness, casting odd shadows while various scenarios begin to creep into my head. Seth ill, or hurt – alone and no one having realised. I picture him lying on the floor of his flat, his mobile having fallen from his fingers as he fell, having blacked out from a stroke, tumour or heart attack… or in a pool of blood having been attacked as he unwittingly disturbed a burglary. I stub the rest of the fag out on the wall and flick the butt onto the grass beyond. Why didn't I think of this before? I must go to his flat immediately! There's no time to waste! I am about to shut the bifold when the front door buzzer goes. I can just about hear it over the music. I hurry into the hall and peer through the peephole only to see the back of Seth's head. Oh, thank you, God! The relief is so huge I feel sick and giddy as I fling open the door.

'Sorry about the noise. I'll turn it off – you're here! I've been so frightened!' But as he turns round the sound dies on my lips. He looks terrible. His shirt is slightly untucked and despite the icy night air, I can smell the warm sweet/sour stickiness of stale booze on his breath and skin. He has also clearly been crying.

'What's happened?' Appalled, I reach out to take his arm but he yanks back, away from me.

'"What's happened"?' he repeats staring at me. 'You really just said that? You little bitch!'

I recoil in shock.

'You thought I wouldn't notice? How stupid do you think I am?' He pushes in through the door and slams it roughly behind him. 'Except I fucking did trust you! I believed you! And all the time – *all* the time you must have been laughing at me. You warned me, didn't you, at the station? Was it just an act then? You said you loved me!'

With that last shouted accusation he suddenly moves across the space with a speed I'm not expecting, grabbing my face around my chin and shoving me backwards like we're doing some sort of violent tango, until I thump roughly up against the wall. He pushes my head back, hard.

'Ow! Seth stop it!' I cry, terrified. 'You're hurting me! What are you doing? It's me! Mia! I love you – I would never hurt you! Let me go, please!'

'You don't LOVE me! You LIED TO ME!' Tears are streaming down his face, he looks deranged, a stranger – no hint of the gentle man I love. 'You LIED and you stole it from me! LIAR!' His face contorts; the harder he pushes the angrier he becomes, or maybe it's the other way round.

It all happens very fast. The music is building again, about to drop, I'm not sure if his hand slips because he's drunk, or he means it to – but suddenly he isn't pushing on my jaw, it's my throat. It's extraordinarily painful and I can't breathe properly. I start to writhe against the wall. My hands flutter up like butterflies, pulling at his fingers in panic.

I'm going to die.

He's going to kill me.

CHAPTER THIRTEEN

CHARLOTTE

'Well done. You got him down then?' Flo looks up as I come into the sitting room.

'Yes, he barely woke. All that paracetamol. Thanks so much for coming. I hope I haven't ruined your night?'

She waves a hand. 'I wasn't doing anything, don't worry.'

'You didn't have plans with Harry?'

She shakes her head and smiles bravely. 'Over. Done. So,' she sits forward on the sofa and becomes business-like, 'do we know exactly where Tris is yet?'

'Nope.' I move over to the fireplace.

'Still nothing?' My sister looks momentarily furious. 'Even if he was driving to Wales he'd have arrived by now, surely?'

I sigh helplessly and check my phone again. No WhatsApp, no texts, no voicemail, no – hang on. What on earth is this? I straighten up quickly. An email from Mia? When did it arrive? Quarter to eleven – just as I was leaving the hospital.

'Sorry – one second.' I hold up a hand and scan the contents quickly, as well as the article at the attached link. My mouth falls open. It's happened and it's *already* been in the papers? How? My heart seizes. Has Tris seen this? He must have. *That's* what this is about. Either he's sitting in a bar somewhere, shocked and panicking, or he's gone to confront Mia. I swallow and look up at Flo, stunned.

'What?' she says warily. 'What's happened?'

'Um…' I hear my voice waver.

'Charlotte?' I can hear a warning tone creep into her voice. 'Tell me!'

A strange excitement ripples through my body. My fingertips actually tingle. I've done it. The sense of calm that settles over me that now there's really no going back is almost liberating. I close my eyes for a moment and it's like standing on the edge of a foreign beach as the sun sets; the last rays shining on my face as the cool breeze of evening begins to blow and lifts my hair in a cloud around me. I feel momentarily exotic… a different person. I take a deep breath and look right at my sister. 'I've done something.'

Flo freezes for a moment and, very slowly, she sits back on the sofa and adopts the position I imagine she uses for clients: legs crossed – but hands in her lap because she's not taking notes. She settles in and then looks right at me. 'Something bad?'

'Um…' I clear my throat. 'You know during your first session with Mia? You were jolted the second she walked in because she looked exactly like a younger me… then this girl you'd never met before sits down and tells you all about her boyfriend, Seth… you see a picture of her hugging your brother-in-law on her screen saver and you realise your new client is sleeping with my husband. You then tell me.' I stop for a moment. I'm starting to feel hot. Less like I'm in cool, white linen on a beach after all. I wish I had a glass of water or something. 'You'll remember I asked you to tell me what theatre she was in, so I could go and see her for myself? Make sure it was really her?'

'Of course I do,' she says slowly. 'I think you need to stop buying time and get to the point. What have you done?'

'I promised I wouldn't speak to her, but you were right. I actually spoke to her quite a lot.'

'I knew it!' Flo springs up and marches to the window before swinging back and jabbing an accusative finger at me. 'I *knew* you were lying. What did you actually discuss – and the truth, this time.'

'I made her an offer. I asked her to pretend to be me.'

Flo draws back in confusion. 'What do you mean?'

'I told her although I've got a really good book to submit to publishers, they don't want to buy into me personally because I'm too past it. I explained I've come up with a way round that and remembered her from Scotland. We've agreed a secret arrangement that she'll be the public face of my next book – she's young, beautiful, with enough of a profile to get them all excited – and we're going to split the money fifty/fifty. You're now the only other person who knows.'

'What would you do that for?' Flo is astonished. She stares at me, open-mouthed, sways slightly on the spot, then placing her fingers on her temples, before closing her eyes. 'I'm assuming you didn't mention to Mia that you're married to her boyfriend?'

'Obviously.'

'And you clearly didn't come home and say to Tris, "I've just cut a deal with your bit on the side". Seriously, what the hell were you thinking, Charlotte? Why would you do something so completely bizarre?'

'Mia agreed a million-pound deal for the book this afternoon.'

Flo's eyes snap open and she looks at me in shock.

'It's also going to be turned into a movie,' I continue.

'OK, that's a lot of money,' Flo says slowly. 'But—'

'The news was in the *Evening Standard*,' I interrupt. 'Tris will have read about it by now, I'm sure.'

'But if he doesn't know *you're* involved won't Tris just think his girlfriend has sold a book for a lot of money today and be pretty pleased?' She moves back over to the sofa, sits down suddenly and stares into space. 'This is so messed-up – I honestly don't know where to start.'

'Well,' I exhale. 'I haven't exactly told you the whole story yet.'

'It gets worse?' Flo whispers, aghast.

I bite my lip so hard I can taste blood. 'So, here's the thing. When you first told me Tris was sleeping with someone I obviously did a bit of digging around.' My voice wavers – she's going to be horrified – but I plough on regardless. 'Weirdly that bit was *exactly* like when I found that message on Daniel's phone all those years ago. I wanted to know everything. You can't help yourself. You need every tiny detail, no matter how much it hurts. Tris doesn't have any social media though – as you know – and there was nothing on his phone. I checked Mia's social media too and there was no mention of Tris that I could see. He's obviously asked her not to post publicly about him. I had a look on his laptop, to see if he'd been emailing her. Which is when I found out he's been writing a book.'

Flo jerks her head back in surprise. 'I'm sorry? What sort of book?'

I'm now starting to feel cold and shivery. 'The sort of book I write. Thrillers. An almost complete book about a man who is a spy, leading a double life,' I laugh and suddenly the bloody tears come back again. It's very annoying – 'who gets a video message from *himself* – on a WhatsApp – telling him he has to leave his family immediately because his cover has been blown. His whole life might be a lie. Are they even his family? He must go on the run… Basically my husband has written a book about giving himself permission to leave us. No doubt taking his inspiration from the double life he's currently leading.'

'Oh my god,' breathes Flo. 'Yeah – it doesn't take Freud to work that one out.'

'Not really, no!' I laugh again, looking up while I blot the tears with my hand. 'You know all that time he was tapping away on the laptop – even on holiday? That's obviously what he was doing. He was away in his own little world. I imagine he did a lot of it on trains and in hotel rooms, probably long before Mia appeared on the scene. In fact, ironically I don't see how he could have had time for anything else while he was writing it. Maybe that's why they started up. His pretty much finishing the book left a space in his life. Irritatingly, it's also good. Well – the idea is. The writing was patchy, baggy and nowhere near pacey enough – but since I copied it, edited it, made the main character a woman and rewrote the ending, it's in very good shape.' I exhale sharply. 'In fact, it's the book Mia sold for a million quid this afternoon.'

Flo audibly gasps. 'You just sold his own book from under him, and you got the girl he's sleeping with to do it?'

'Yes.' I hold my head up high.

Flo stands up – walks to the window, turns her back on me and stares at the closed curtains. She laughs but without seeing her face I can't tell if she's impressed or incredulous. 'It's safe to say you want revenge then?'

'I don't want to hurt Mia,' I say immediately. 'I don't blame her at all.'

'Oh please,' Flo says. 'I don't buy that for a single moment.'

'I don't care if you do or not,' I reply bluntly. 'I know I could break her if I want to, but she's a *child*,' I remind Flo. 'Barely in her mid-twenties. She doesn't even know he's married. She's just a sweet girl wasting the best years of her life on my pathetic, weak and selfish husband… but can you deduce from that I want to hurt *him*? Yes, you can… as far as he's concerned, I absolutely and totally want revenge.'

Flo swallows. 'I get wanting to hurt him, but the way you've handled this isn't rational. You do know that, right? Most people who found out that their husband was having an affair would either choose to keep quiet or confront him.'

'OK. I *could* have just had it out with him and said, "by the way I know you've not been in Sheffield a single fucking time you've said, but are actually having an affair", except where would that lead?' I gesture helplessly 'He leaves/I chuck him out and he goes to her… or apologises and stays here for the sake of the kids. Well neither of those scenarios work for me and they mean he gets no punishment at all.'

'*Punishment?*' repeats Flo.

I am now properly shaking. This anger which has been growing beneath my skin like a disease for the last two weeks is finally bursting through. 'Yes. Punishment. I mean a *spy*? Come on!' My voice becomes louder, and Flo reminds me Teddy is asleep by turning and wordlessly placing a finger on her lips before pointing to the ceiling above. Still simmering, I fall quiet and we stare at each other in silence for a moment.

'If it weren't so tragic, it would be funny,' I say eventually. 'He actually wrote a book about leaving us.' I turn away from Flo. 'All I want to do is protect Clara and Teddy – and Mia – from any more hurt.'

'How is this protecting them?' asks Flo quietly.

I fold my arms. 'Because my plan is going to go one of two ways; I've thought about this very carefully. Tris is out there right now, having realised Mia has sold his book. He'll have recognised it from the description in the papers. What would he do next – what would *anyone* in his shoes do next? He'll go and confront her, ask her why and how the hell she stole his book?' I clear my throat. 'She's then going to say she didn't, another author – me – gave it to her. She'll tell him about our arrangement, at which point Tris is going to realise that I know *everything*.' I hold Flo's gaze, furious again. 'I have held him to account. He then either has to come clean and admit to Mia that actually he's MARRIED to me and it's *his* book – can't see him going for that option, can you? – or, he's going to keep very quiet about me, say he must have made a mistake and have to slink back home – tail between his legs – aware that I know his horrible secret and I've called him on it.'

'Hang on –I thought you just said you don't want him to come home to you?'

I turn and look at my reflection in the mantelpiece mirror. I look old. Tired. 'I'm not going to let him stay but I want him to end it with Mia. He doesn't have to tell her why – in fact it would be kinder if he didn't. She'll be upset, but she'll be better off without him, and hopefully, the half a million quid she's going to get from the book sale will help ease the pain a bit. It might even end up being double or triple that by the time all of the deals have been done.' I shrug. 'She won't ever need to know he's married to me…' I turn back to face my sister. 'Once he's ended it with her, I will tell him to leave.'

'So now you want to end your marriage?' Flo says. 'Because two weeks ago you told me that you didn't want anything to change. You were wanting to go for the keeping quiet option.'

'That was when I'd *just* found out he was cheating on me. I was frightened… and of course I don't want Clara and Teddy's life to implode. They love Tris. But now I've had time to think, I'm convinced him having a second family with some girl half his age – which will inevitably happen if he stays with Mia – would devastate them, *destroy* the people they're meant to be.' My voice is ominously quiet now. 'He can't afford a second family, in any case.'

'Not now you've split his million quid in half, no.'

'He would never have got that much for it himself. Not without my editorial input and Mia's profile and looks. All he had was a good idea. Anyone can have one of them. He should be thankful I brokered the deal I have. I think it's a very practical revenge.'

'But stopping him from having a second family with Mia doesn't prevent him having another family forever. If it's not her, the likelihood is it'll be someone else eventually, if you're going to tell him to leave?'

I say nothing.

'The point I'm trying to make is that I don't think you can try and justify what you've done with rational explanations, because there aren't any. You just want to hurt him.'

I hesitate. 'Yeah, OK. I do. You're right—'

'But—'

'Because I'll be the first to admit things have fallen by the wayside with me and Tris, relationship-wise.' I cut across her. 'I'll be honest – I don't prioritise him. I've become too "communal" within the family since we had Clara and Teddy. I should have made more time for him. And yeah, men need sex… but do *not* sleep with someone half my fucking age again and again – because there's no one-night leg to stand on here – and THEN tell me we've got a problem. Be a decent man! Tell me you're unhappy *before* you line up someone else and a new life. End it WITHOUT cheating on me first and making everything a horrible, complicated mess that makes me want to hurt you… because I tell you this: I *will* protect the kids from the humiliation of having to deal with knowing their father slept with someone else!' I cross the room and sit down heavily on the sofa.

'But that's just doing a Mum. You're going to just not tell them? Bottle everything up?' Flo says quietly. 'Because that's how we do things in our family, right? We don't talk about stuff like normal people do. In fact, you usually just write about the things that hurt you.'

'Do I understand why Mum didn't say anything to us now, you mean? Yeah – maybe I do.' I twist suddenly and look at our wedding photo, sitting on the side table by the lamp. I am so happy; I look ethereal. Tris looks proud and delighted. I had no doubts whatsoever about marrying him and I meant every word of my vows. I thought we were invincible. Open to the stresses and strains of everyday life, of course; arguments about money, the children, bad moods, but never the risk of other people.

'Look at us!' I point at it. 'Look how in love we are! How can the man I share two such amazing children with, and have a nice life with, want to do this to me and them? It's the lack of kindness that I'm finding so devastating… that and how can he be so fucking stupid?'

'I don't know,' Flo says softly. 'I'm devastated too. I didn't think he'd ever do something like this.'

'But you know, it's *because* he is the father of my children that I want him to leave,' I insist, wiping my eyes and now-snotty nose. 'No one could have hurt me more than this. I could have coped with a one-night thing – but not this. I mean look at me! I've already lost a load of weight overnight from pure stress. I've dyed my hair and cut in the most stupidly unflattering fringe I've ever had. Could I be more of a clichéd middle-aged woman finding out her husband's sleeping around?'

Flo doesn't say anything. Just stares at the floor miserably, her arms wrapped round herself.

I reach in my pocket for a tissue. 'You want to know what *he's* been doing while I've been going out of my mind with stress since you told me about his affair? Staying in Putney while telling me he's in Sheffield on business. Ask me how I know this.' I blow my nose.

'Go on,' she says quietly, sitting down on the sofa opposite me again.

'I hid a mobile phone in the boot of the car, in the spare wheel. Using Find My Phone, I can see exactly where the car goes. It's been going to the same street in Putney – where his uni friend Jim lives – for several days at a time for the last two weeks. And before you ask, I've already tried to see where it is right now. I looked at the hospital. The phone is switched off. So either Tris has found it or the battery has died. Anyway, I spoke to Jim about a week and a half ago and said I didn't want to make trouble, I didn't want him to tell Tris I'd spoken to him, but I just wanted to say thank you for supporting him at this difficult time. I was deliberately oblique, but Jim immediately said he was happy to help and Tris could stay as long as he wanted while we "work out our problems". So reading between the lines, Tris has told Jim we're having issues and is staying there – having a lovely little London life for several days a week while he's meant to be in Sheffield – then coming home to be Daddy when he feels like it. He's been nowhere near Sheffield. I don't think there is any project, or client. He's made it all up.'

Flo shakes her head and closes her eyes. 'I don't want you to think I condone his behaviour in any way, it's disgusting.' She looks straight at me. 'And like I've said to you before, I can see it's complicated by how Daniel and Dad behaved all those years ago, but—'

'No, you can stop right there.' I hold a hand up. 'What Dan did and how it made me feel doesn't even come close to this. I was twenty-something and my fiancé cheated on me. It was nothing more than the fear of losing your first love, and my becoming obsessed with *her*. It wasn't a *marriage*. I've always believed, no matter what, Tris loves me – and Clara and Teddy – too much to risk losing us.' I shrug. 'I was obviously wrong and that kills me. He's broken it all. The Dad stuff… I don't know, I can't even go there right now, to be honest, and of course, when Tris leaves I'll do a better job than Mum did of explaining everything; but right now, all I feel is an immense *rage* and I freely admit I want to hurt him as much as he's hurt me, plus I'll be damned if he gets to come out of this with a new girlfriend and a shiny new book based on what he's done. You're right – maybe he will go on to find someone else after all of this, but it won't be Mia because she's too nice for that. She genuinely doesn't deserve him.'

Flo gets up and comes to sit right next to me. 'I get that you want to regain the sense of control that he's taken away from you. I understand completely why you want to try and influence what happens next, but Charlotte, this is not the way to do it. This… plan of yours.' She flounders and throws her hands up, helplessly.

'I keep telling you that people don't act in predictable ways in high stress situations, often they surprise even themselves,' she leans forward and takes my hand, 'but you keep not listening to me. You say Tris is going to go round and confront Mia. You're probably right, but there are a million different possible outcomes after that than just the two you've considered. You're acting like you've worked out their character motivation and the next bit of the plot.'

'No. That's not what I'm doing *at all*.' I take my hand back. 'And you're wrong. I know Tris.'

'But your outcomes rely on the assumption that he doesn't really care about Mia; understandably, because that's what you want to believe. Of course, I hope you're right, but what if you're not? What if he loves her and thinking she's stolen this book from him breaks his heart? What if that makes him angry… or suppose he breaks up with her then and there and *she* goes crazy with grief, because *she* loves *him*…' A note of frustration creeps into my sister's voice. 'What if he confesses everything, tells her who you really are and she feels like the *two* of you have tricked her? You see?' Flo waits for me to speak, but I don't. I can't.

'Even if you're right about Tris, you don't know *her*. Remember what else I told you? People in therapy are vulnerable – and unstable.' Flo sighs worriedly and looks at her watch. 'You haven't heard from him all day? Even though you've left him messages saying that Teddy has been in hospital? He just hasn't responded?'

'The last I saw of him was this morning when he left for work,' I admit. 'I wasn't worried until Mia's email arrived, telling me the news is out, but now I know it is…' I rub my forehead, trying to think, my fingers pressing into my skin so hard it hurts. 'His phone is also switched off.'

Flo's eyebrows shoot up. 'That's weird. Why would he do that?'

'When I was doing some research for my last book I told Tris about how most rookie criminals in real life are caught out by the tracking on their mobile phone. He knows that if it's on, it will connect with a nearby mast and the police will be able to see where you are, or where you've been.' I briefly glance back at our wedding photo, then look down at my hands and the engagement ring that is now too heavy on my much thinner finger. The diamond keeps slipping round, out of sight, leaving only the plain band on view. 'I told him the only way to prevent being tracked is to switch your phone off but the only people who do that have something to hide.'

Flo looks at me wide-eyed. 'I think we need to phone them. The police, I mean.'

I laugh. 'Don't be ridiculous! They won't do anything! It's all rubbish, the stuff you see on TV. In fact, *do* call them now. Call the number for our local police station, because you can't call 999 – it's not an emergency. See if they even pick up. I bet you they don't.' I hold out my phone. 'And if they do, good luck in telling them you're looking for a bloke late back from work who hasn't even been missing for twenty-four hours yet. They don't have the resources to investigate actual crimes, never mind domestic situations like this.'

'I really don't think you appreciate quite how serious this situation you've created could be,' Flo says slowly. 'Mia is vulnerable, and Tris is potentially devastated. Can you not see what you might have done?'

The next laugh catches at the back of my throat. 'What *I've* done?'

'How can you not be anxious? I'm terrified!'

I sit back on the sofa and reach suddenly for my phone. Flo inhales sharply and waits as I hold it to my ear.

'Hello, Jim? It's Charlotte.' I sit up taller as he answers, and Flo breathes out. 'I'm sorry to disturb you and I know this is going to put you in an awkward position, but I need your help. Teddy wound up in A&E tonight. I've been trying and trying to get hold off Tris, but I've had no luck, which is really unlike him. He did tell me he was going to Wales tonight and that might explain why I haven't been able to get hold of him, but I thought I'd just check if you knew anything to the contrary, first? I know he left work at about half six, but after that he… oh… so the car's outside your place right now?' I can't look at Flo. 'OK,' I hesitate. 'Well, I guess he can't be in Wales then. You didn't see him tonight though?… No, but you think he's been back because his work phone, laptop and suitcase are all in the spare room.' I do glance at Flo now. She shakes her head and mutters 'shit' under her breath, before getting up and turning her back on me.

'OK. Well…' I exhale, unsure what to say next. 'If he does turn up, can you ask him to call me urgently? Thank you. Yes, he's fine now – we're home, but obviously Tris should know. Thank you. I will. You too.'

I hang up. Flo doesn't turn round or say a thing.

'Perhaps you better give me Mia's address and I'll go there myself – make sure nothing has happened,' I say eventually.

She spins round. 'You're kidding, right? There is no way I'm giving you her address!' She stares at me, stunned. 'You are so… quietly manipulative.'

'*What?*' Confused and angry again, I throw my hands wide. 'How the hell is my saying I will go and make sure Mia's OK being manipulative? I'm *agreeing* with you!'

Flo puts her hands on the side of her head. 'I can't make sense of all of this. I should never have told you.'

'Well you did,' I say simply. 'And you're right. Given everything, it's concerning that Tris hasn't been in touch… but we really can't phone the police. For a kick off, what are you going to say to anyone who asks how I found out about their affair in the first place?'

She pales. 'So now you're threatening *me?*'

'Of course not! What's the matter with you?' I look at her, incredulously.

'You're angry with me for telling you about Tris. I get it. Shoot the messenger, but we need to—'

'I'm trying to protect you,' I say through clenched teeth, 'and Mia and Teddy and Clara.'

Flo swallows, covers her mouth with her hand, and rushes out of the room.

I jump up and follow her out to the kitchen where she is shakily holding a glass underneath the streaming cold tap.

'You need to get a grip,' I instruct her. 'Put it down and look at me for a moment.' I take the tumbler from her and set it on the side, before turning off the water. 'I would never, ever do anything that would put you at risk, or threaten you. You *must* know I'm not that person? Surely? I know you do!'

'I don't know what to believe!' she blurts, her arms wrapped defensively round her. 'This is all slipping out of control.'

'No, it isn't. Mum's right. You can be very melodramatic sometimes.'

She gasps, but I hold a hand up. 'I am very angry with Tris. I freely admit that – but yes, he should have called by now given the messages I've left him about Teddy. It's out of character for him not to have been in contact under those circumstances and I think you're right to be concerned. So give me Mia's address. I'll go to the flat and make sure everything is OK. That's it. No big panic.'

Flo lets her head hang miserably. 'I *can't* tell you where she lives! It's bad enough that I told you anything at all. When it comes out, what I've done…' She spins round again, grabs the glass, yanks the tap back on and fills it unsteadily before taking too big a gulp. The water splashes over her chin.

I pass her a tea towel. 'Flo, please calm down. No one is ever going to find out that you told me about their relationship. In fact, if anyone asks you… and I mean *anyone*, you say you knew about the affair, but you disclosed nothing to me; patient confidentiality. You deny telling me anything about Mia, you deny telling me

where she lives. No one can prove you told me a thing. Florence!'
I full-name her sharply, to root her back to me as a single tear
escapes from her eye and runs down her cheek.

'Yes, I'm listening,' she whispers.

'Leave the explanations to me. In fact, the less you know, the
better. I shouldn't have told you about selling his book. That
was a mistake.' I tut aloud, angry with myself. 'From here on
in, you know nothing about any book. You have no idea that I
contacted Mia to be my debut. Repeat it back to me, you said
nothing about—'

She shakes her head. 'No. I don't need to rehearse anything.
I get it. But what do I say about tonight? That we didn't discuss
anything other than you not knowing where Tris was? You were
pissed off but used to him doing this sort of thing?'

'That's perfect. Say exactly that. Now, Mia's address. Do you
have it on your computer?'

'No. In case it gets stolen. I keep my client records on paper in a
box file at home, separate to their session notes. I have their email,
GP address, their address and list of meds – if it's appropriate.'

'Good.' I nod, and pause while I think. 'Then I think you
should go home tonight. You look tired and I'm fine here. But
can you come back first thing tomorrow morning? It's just I have
a meeting I've set up – and no one to look after the kids. I won't
be long. I may not need to go – Tris might be home by then. But
in case he's not, would you be prepared to come and sit with them
if I need you to?' I look at her pointedly and wait.

'OK, I'll do it,' she agrees eventually. 'I'll go home now and
come back tomorrow morning, but only if need be.'

I reach out and place a steadying hand on her arm. 'This is all
going to be all right – don't panic.'

CHAPTER FOURTEEN

MIA

My chin is aching and my neck is stiff. I'm juddering violently as I open my eyes and… lying on the hard floor? It's now very quiet. I move my head and a thousand needles push into the same spot on my forehead. I'm on my tummy, but when I try, I don't appear to have enough in me to push myself up onto my hands and knees. My muscles are sore, my arms weak. Instead I turn on my side and touch where it hurts. It's sticky. Why is there something sticky on my head? I wipe my fingers across my chest. My mouth feels lined with tissue paper. I need water.

My eyes begin to readjust in the dark and I start to see him, his outline. A hooded man is crouched down, several feet away from me. I think he's saying prayers. I hear him whispering to God.

I go very still. I mustn't move. He keeps muttering, and I try not to breathe, but instinct tells me it's not working. I am filled with the total certainty that, while he is not looking over at me, he knows I'm here. He senses me. He's going to move towards me. His legs twitch and I panic. I have to do something! I grope around in the dark for something to throw at him. Get away from me! He flinches and melts back down, but he doesn't leave completely. Just hunches over, returning to his incantations, waiting like a crow – until I fall asleep and he can bob over and peck at me until he picks down to my very bones – I know it.

I shan't let him. I can't let myself become so weak I have no fight left in me at all. I stand up, bravely. I will rush away. I *must*, but my legs appear too light for the task; I am made of air and can't control where I go. The direction of the walls changes and somehow I am on the floor again, my hands reaching out to whatever flat surface is under my fingers. It's not clear what is up, or down. Random objects appear in my field of vision and I try to grab at them to anchor me, but they come free and I lose my grip and footing. It's too much. I have to stop and rest even though I know he is still there. I hear him whispering my name and it makes my skin crawl.

I take some breaths and when I get up again I'm somehow in a pine forest and I'm cold. There is a door in the side of a tree, I open it and discover it's bulging full of beautiful dresses; a secret store – just like in the costume shop with its unpromising black front door in the small parade of dingy shops. My father took me there as a child. They also sold jokes. Buzzers my brother would hide in the palm of his hand, sweet cigarettes, fake blood, but I only had eyes for the elaborate Venetian masks hanging on the walls adorned with sequins and multicoloured feathers. I reach out and stroke the silk skirts and I can *see* the red velvet curtain at the back of the shop as clearly as if it is in front of me: the seamstress room. They made pantomime costumes in the rooms behind that curtain, all year round. Rails and rails of full-length dresses with *puffed sleeves, Anne Shirley.* Knickerbockers and frock coats lined with sky blue silk, sashes of scarlet. Cinderella's wedding gown, Snow White's stiff-collared, jewel-encrusted cape. That will do. I reach up. I will slip it on to keep warm. I pull at it and it falls to me, but I have a job getting it to stay round my shoulders. I need to leave this place now. I try the door again and this time it opens into a much wider, open space. I clutch at my cape, step through and look up, but it seems snowflakes are swirling in the air… drifting down, silently, settling softly on my bare skin and eyelashes. It becomes heavier, weighing down my hair. My feet hurt. This is no good. This door is no good. I need another one. I can't see anything here. Wasn't there meant to be the soft steady light of the lamp to guide me? That was the best bit when I watched *Narnia* with Kirsty at the cinema. The soft stillness of undisturbed snow – like a blanket.

Kirsty. I was trying to call her. *Kirsty! Answer me!*

The only person listening is him, still in the corner. I don't like it. I should leave but I am so tired… I must *not* close my eyes. He will come. He is waiting there, his wings tucked under.

Mum? Dad? Kirsty!

I need you.

CHAPTER FIFTEEN

CHARLOTTE

Driving into Blackheath at 8.30 a.m. the following morning I'm whispering exactly the same assurances I gave Flo, under my breath. *Don't panic. Don't panic.* It's so cold I am shivering, even though the fan is blasting hot air out over my fingers and the windscreen is misting over. The bright sunlight keeps catching it, rendering me almost completely blind as I hold my hand up in front of my face in a desperate attempt to stay on the road without sharply braking. By the time my phone tells me I have almost reached the 'destination' Flo emotionlessly gave me just before I left, my nerves are shot to pieces. I don't actually know what the hell I'm doing. This was not part of the plan. I honestly thought he'd come home last night, or that I would at least hear from him, but nothing. So now what? Am I going to knock on the door and confront him if he's there? I have no idea.

I'm even more thrown when I turn into a peaceful, tree-lined street, no more than a few hundred yards from the village itself. This can't be right – the houses are huge, white-fronted Georgian affairs, set back from the road and approached via wide, gravel drives. A flat in one of these would give little change from three quarters of a million quid, surely? I pull up outside number 6, parking on the pavement, and walk tentatively up the drive, on which – unlike the houses either side – there sit no cars. My heart starts to thump. What am I going to say to Mia if he's *not* here? How will I explain turning up like this at half-eight on a Saturday morning when I'm not even meant to know where she lives? And yet my feet continue to propel me towards the two handsome, red doors in front of me. I climb seven stone steps and pause. There are two old-fashioned push bells; the round, marble effect ones – marked A and B. At some point in this gracious house's history, it has been converted into an upstairs and downstairs flat, each with its own private entrance. I have no clue which of the two belongs to Mia.

I walk back down and try to peer in through the large, sash windows to my left, but not only are they several feet above ground height, the full-length white shutters behind the glass are firmly closed. It's the same story with the smaller, basement windows below. I return to the door and impulsively press both bells, simultaneously. I can feel my heartbeat squishing in my ears, taking over my chest completely… and nothing happens. Neither door swings open. So I try again. I practically lean on them. They're definitely working because I can hear them buzzing imperiously behind the doors.

All this, and she's not even in? I laugh in disbelief – press on the bell again… and suddenly door A swings right open.

Mia stands there in a gloomy hall, bizarrely in an ankle-length sparkly evening dress, like a hostess ready to welcome me to pre-dinner drinks rather than breakfast; only the skirt is ripped – in the manner of a stage costume designed deliberately to denote she has been marooned on a shipwreck island. As she wavers dangerously on the spot, she clutches her wildly tousled long hair to her neck, head on one side, somehow almost coquettishly, like she's in a shampoo advert. She has black eye make-up smudged down one side of her face and a daub of what looks like dry blood across her white-blue, bare shoulder. There is a large, gooey, open cut on her forehead. She stares at me, confused, as if not really sure what to do with this pose she finds herself in.

Any explanation I might have needed to come up with on the spot dies on my lips. 'Mia?' I say, astonished. 'What's wrong? You look—' but before I can finish, she drifts slightly to her left.

I look down the length of the hall and through a doorway that seems to lead into a sitting room. I can see the back of a sofa and a large set of oversized doors, open to the elements, and a garden beyond, the bare trees against the bright clear sky as a cream curtain flaps in the wind. My gaze shifts downward and the breath audibly sucks into my lungs to see a male body lying on the floor facing away from me. The torso is obscured by the sofa, but he is naked from the waist down; his bare arse and legs – trousers bunched around the ankles – are clearly visible. His shoes are bent back awkwardly behind him, as if someone tied his laces together and he's fallen with his feet bound. They are my husband's new shoes. I went online and was flabbergasted by how much they cost. We had terse words about these shoes. He is not moving.

My immediate reaction is to step in, but as my foot lifts, I realise, just in time, that this is almost certainly a crime scene. Starting to feel light-headed, I urgently scan the rest of the darker, tastefully white, private entrance lobby, from the doorstep – taking in smears of blood, low down, by the skirting – and another mark higher up on the wall, by the light switch. Other belongings lie on the ground: a photo frame face down, a thin metal lamp still plugged in, but on its side. A knocked-over vase of dead flowers has spilt water and yellowed stems over the floor. I instantly imagine Tris sweeping the items off the sideboard – like they do in the movies – and lifting Mia up to passionately fuck her… but if that was what happened here, something has most definitely gone *very* wrong. I simply don't know what to do. There is a quiet ghastliness to the sight of a body in real life that I would never have been able to appreciate without witnessing it for real. I have to do something. I can't just walk away now. I'll have been seen driving here by a million CCTV cameras.

Every word of warning that Flo gave me last night whispers through my mind as I stare at my husband and try to think. This is bad. This is really, really bad. THINK, CHARLOTTE! Mia is staggering around on the spot like she's drunk. I can't work out if she's high, in shock, injured – I have no idea. I stare at her wordlessly. What on earth has happened here?

'Mia!' I say urgently, beckoning her towards me. 'I've come for our meeting, you remember? The one we set up to talk about the book?' She turns her head and looks glassily in the direction of my voice, but instead walks to the wall, leans her back against it and slides down to a sitting position, her hands covering her mouth.

'Mia – what's happened? Can you tell me?' I say loudly. I would go in, I think? If I'd just arrived for a meeting and found someone on the floor. I'd go in and look at them. Maybe I only know it's Tris because I'm expecting it to be. They might ask me why I *didn't* go in? How I was so sure it was my husband from the doorway? Was I worried I might be implicating myself by walking in? What did I have to hide? That might actually be what trips me up. I step over the threshold tentatively. 'Mia? Are you hurt?' I put my hand on her shoulder and flinch. Her skin is cool marble. The whole place is freezing. 'Mia, who is that man, on the floor?' I say loudly. She's shivering and doesn't look at me. She still has her hands over her mouth, and I don't want to touch her. 'Can you answer me, Mia?'

She blinks and tries to focus, then closes her eyes.

I walk into the living room slowly, my heels tapping on the wooden floor, and round the edge of the sofa – uttering a half scream as I look down. I don't actually think I fake it – I'm pretty sure it's real. His face is looking out of the open door, but his head is also partially under the sofa, as if he's tried to climb beneath it. His skin is bone white and mask-like. His eyes are closed. 'This is my husband!' I breathe – then call out to Mia, my voice shaky. 'What is my *husband* doing, lying on your floor?'

That would be what I'd say, wouldn't it?

'Tris! Can you hear me?' I kneel down next to him, speaking loudly. Am I meant to move him? Put him in the recovery position? Or not touch him – I can't remember! 'Can you hear me, Tris?'

He doesn't move. He's dead? He's *dead*? My hands are trembling as I reach out and place a finger on his neck. I wait, only registering the sound of birds in the garden. No pulse. I place my fingers under his nose, but the wind blowing in through the open doors makes it impossible for me to tell if he's breathing or not. I get up quickly and yank the heavy doors shut, closing off all outside sound completely, before rushing back to Tris. I can't feel a thing!

Jumping up as I start to fumble in my pockets for my phone, I return to Mia in the hallway. She's still slumped in the gloom in a sitting position against the wall, her eyes rolling in her head. She closes them again while mumbling something unintelligible about flies through her fingers. Have they taken something? Is that what's happened here?

'Mia! Listen to me!' I crouch down beside her as her head lolls forward. 'I need to phone an ambulance now, so I have to know what's happened. Concentrate, Mia. Can you tell me?' I jump up to put the light on, then push her upright again by her shoulders.

She lifts her head and as her hair falls back I gasp at my first proper sight of vivid red marks on her throat.

'What happened to your neck, Mia?'

She lifts her hands up and places them on her skin, covering the red marks as she mimes being throttled. 'Attacked.'

'My husband tried to strangle you?' I twist back in horror to look at Tris, still lying there.

She shakes her head and tears start to leak from her eyes. 'Seth. My boyfriend. Says I stole it and…'

My eyes widen with fear. 'You stole what?'

She turns and we both look down the line of sight at Tris's half-naked body. She frowns, confused, as if she can't understand what he's doing there, before lifting a heavy hand to point him out to me – only to let it drop again uselessly by her side, palm up. It's covered in blood.

I jerk back away from her in shock: what has she done? What has happened here? But she draws her knees up, rests her elbows on them and lets her head fall into her hands, covering the cut – and her hands, in more blood – as she closes her eyes.

He attacked her. I scramble back over to Tris. He was physically violent towards her and he's half-naked. I don't know how to make any sense of this.

I swallow as I dial 999. My voice sounds jagged as I try to keep it even while I focus. 'Police and ambulance, please. My husband is lying on the floor and he's not conscious. I don't think he's breathing and he doesn't have a pulse. I don't know what's happened but he's very cold to touch. There's another girl here who is more alert than him; she's spoken to me but she's very cold as well and there are blood smears everywhere. What? Oh yes – where are we? The address is on my phone, hang on.' I almost drop the phone as I look on maps. 'Hello? Are you still there?' I manage eventually to give the call handler the address. 'Er yes, OK.' I reach out and put my fingers under his nose again. 'No, I can't.' I fumble for his wrist this time. 'No. There isn't. He's on his side. I'd have to move him onto his back. Is that OK? Hang on.' I put the phone down, shove the sofa clear – and see the blood. 'Oh shit!' I fumble for the phone again. 'There's blood on the floor!' I look up. Mia is still slumped against the wall. 'No, I'm not in any danger.' I look at the back of his head. His dark hair is sticky and clumped. 'I can't tell, but he's got a head injury of some sort. Do I still move him? OK. You'll stay there, won't you?'

I roll Tris onto his back, place my fingers on his forehead, my other hand on his chin and tilt his head back. His mouth opens.

I watch for any rise and fall of his chest. I can't see anything. I place my hands over his breastbone and I start compressions. He tried to strangle her? To *assault* her? The more I push the more frightened and shocked I become. I look down at my husband's lifeless face and I hear myself cry out loud. I push harder and I know what I'm feeling is pure rage while simultaneously trying to save his life, then somehow I'm *hitting* his chest. I stop suddenly and sit back, panting with exertion. I stare at him for a second until I realise I can hear sirens and, shocked into action, I start compressions again.

'Help!' I shout. 'Someone help me! We're in here! Help me! Please!' Shapes appear in the doorway, people who pull me away and start working on him then and there on the floor, in front of me. I step back, starting to shake violently. More sirens. Police. Blue lights. It seems Flo is right after all – it is just like it is on TV, in fact.

They get Tris into the back of an ambulance as another appears and takes over Mia's care. She doesn't appear to be moving either. This is actually happening. I close my eyes briefly and see only Clara and Teddy. My beautiful children.

I'm going to have to phone Flo, tell her I need her to stay with Teddy and be there for when Clara is dropped off.

'What's happening?' She doesn't even bother with hello.

'Don't panic.' It's all I seem able to say to her at the moment. 'I'm at Mia's flat and there's a situation. *Tris* is here.'

'Oh my god! Charlotte!'

'I know,' I interrupt her quickly before she can say anything incriminating, something that could be listened back to at a later date. 'I can't quite believe it either. I think I'm going to need to go to the hospital with him.'

'Hospital? He's been hurt?'

'I'm not sure what's happened.' I turn back and watch them working on him in the back of the ambulance, and wipe my free hand on my trousers where I touched his skin. I want to wash my hands. 'He wasn't breathing when I found him.'

My little sister utters a strange, breathy cry, a sort of whimper of fear.

'Flo – stay calm. Can you do that? Stay with the kids and tell them I'll be back later. Can you say I've gone shopping or something, please?'

'Yes,' she manages eventually. 'What has?—'

'I need to go now, the police want to talk to me, but I'll be in touch.' I hang up immediately as a uniformed officer approaches. I manage to confirm Tris's full name, and my own.

'And do you know who the woman is?' He gestures in the direction of the ambulance Mia is being stretchered into.

'Yes, her name is Mia Justice. This is her flat. She's a work associate of mine.' I take a deep breath. 'I wasn't aware that she also seems to know my husband.'

He looks up quickly from his small screen, but doesn't react further than that. 'Thank you.'

I hear a call from the ambulance. 'OK, we're ready! Now, please!'

The policeman turns to me. 'Do you want to go with your husband to the hospital?'

I would say yes, wouldn't I? I don't know anymore. I twist to look in the back of the ambulance; I walk towards it automatically and the paramedic standing next to Tris beckons me up.

'We're ready to transfer. Don't be alarmed at the tube you can see in his mouth – that's just to keep his airway open. The silver blanket is to try and warm him up. He's hypothermic.'

My breath catches. But he's *alive*?

'That was some excellent CPR you did.'

'I hit his chest,' I blurt. 'Really hard.'

'That's OK,' the paramedic reassures me. 'It's better that than too light. You did really well.'

I can't look at him, or Tris. I turn my head away towards the drive, now swarming with police, busily sealing off the flat. A middle-aged, short, balding man in plain clothes and an overcoat is talking to the officer who just took my details. He turns and looks directly at me. Our eyes meet for a moment before the ambulance doors are slammed shut and the paramedic starts to explain that when we arrive at the hospital they have something called a Bair Hugger blanket – a device like a sort of soft plastic suit they pump with heated air to raise to body temperature externally, but that they might also warm Tris up with warm intravenous fluids. The words wash over me as I try, instead, to concentrate on what the inside of the ambulance looks like, the sounds – how it makes me jump as the siren comes on intermittently. It'll be useful one day when all of this is over…

I force myself to look at my husband. He has been successfully living two lives – I have no idea how he even found the time to write a book – and yet now he's barely one whole person. I am frightened. I have lost control of this story. I don't like it when something takes on a life of its own – becomes unruly, unpredictable – and I don't know what to do to fix it.

'Is he going to be all right?' I ask suddenly, and the paramedic smiles kindly at me.

'He's still very ill but he'll be in the best place, in under a minute. We're nearly there.'

He's not giving me a direct answer. Making me no promises. Sure enough Tris is whisked off immediately at the hospital, but the police are already there too. Mia's ambulance has arrived and I see her stretchered in once I've climbed out and am standing unsure if I am supposed to follow in through the ambulance entrance into A&E. Several uniformed officers walk in and disappear beyond two double swing doors, just as a nurse appears by my side.

'Mrs Tristan? Would you come with me?'

I follow her silently down some corridors until we arrive at a small, separate relatives' room.

'Can I get you a drink?' she says. 'Tea? Coffee? Hot chocolate?'

Before I can answer, the man from outside the flat who was talking to the police sticks his head round. 'Mrs Tristan? Hello. I'm DI Travers!' He looks like a briskly enthusiastic train conductor. I wouldn't be at all surprised if he asked me for my ticket then gave me information about my destination I never asked for in the first place. 'I wonder if you can spare me a moment?'

*

'No – I wasn't angry, just concerned when Tris didn't contact me last night. I'd left him numerous messages and it's not like him to not respond, but I just assumed he was making his way up to Wales for the stag do he'd mentioned attending after all. My husband's arrangements are often fluid.' I force a smile. 'Our son was also fine in the end, so my plan was to try and reach him this morning, after my meeting with Mia. Given she'd just agreed a seven-figure deal, we had some talking to do.'

'I can see that,' DI Travers agrees. 'But you arrived to find your husband lying semi-naked on the floor of the hallway, unconscious.'

'Yes.'

'You weren't aware of any relationship between your husband and Ms Justice? Up until that point?'

'Would you willingly give half a million pounds to the man your wife was sleeping with?'

DI Travers ponders that. 'I can't say I would.'

'I was deeply shocked to discover him there,' I say quickly. 'I referred to him as my husband in front of Mia – and she corrected me, identifying him as "Seth" and "my boyfriend".'

'She was clear about that?'

'Very. She was, as I said earlier, in a state of mental confusion when I arrived and her appearance was dishevelled, but yes, she was clear that Seth was "her boyfriend". She seemed to have no idea he's married.'

'Just to clarify, you said her dress appeared ripped?' DI Travers leans slightly towards me. He's not so jolly now he's rolled up his sleeves to get a look at the engine. What I mistook for an inappropriate lack of empathy is simply a man who enjoys his job – eager to get started.

I hesitate. 'You're right to pull me up on that. I'm afraid I wouldn't be able to confirm if that was "accidentally ripped" by catching it on something or "deliberately ripped" by someone. I don't want to speculate or appear to be implying something isn't the case.'

The DI nods gravely. 'I understand completely.'

I sincerely hope you don't. I take a sip of the watery hot chocolate. The thin, hospital paper cup is burning my hand. 'She looked like she'd had a particularly heavy night out and just woken up, and at first I thought she was drunk, but she had a cut to her forehead, blood on her shoulder and when I touched her, she was very cold. I quickly realised what I had assumed was her being drunk could also be mental confusion. She didn't seem to know what had happened or what she was saying.'

'But she *did* speak to you, and in addition to identifying "Seth" as her "boyfriend", the other word you clearly made out was "attacked". What did you make of that?'

I exhale. 'She placed her hands on her neck and mimed being strangled. She had visible red marks. I took it to mean my husband had attacked her.'

'Is he a violent man?'

'No,' I say truthfully. 'I've never known Tris be physically or sexually violent. He has never threatened me or our children in any way. I've never seen him involved in a fight of any kind. He can be a bit belligerent when drunk, but nothing that has ever given me any cause for concern.' My hand starts to shake as I speak and to my enormous surprise I am suddenly crying. Tears are flooding down my face. I have to move to set the cup down.

'I'm sorry!' I gasp, trying to stem the flow with the heels of my hands.

'Please don't apologise. You've had a very traumatic experience.' He waits for me to compose myself. 'I can organise someone for you to talk to, if you would like?'

'No, thank you,' I breathe. 'Things haven't been great between me and my husband recently. For example, I know he's been staying with a friend of his in Putney while telling me he's in Sheffield. He has a demanding job and is the major breadwinner in our relationship. I thought he was having a bit of a midlife crisis and needed some space. I never thought for one moment he'd cheat on me. He knows that'd be my red line—'

'"Red line" meaning?…' DI Travers interrupts.

'It would end our marriage. But—'

'So he knows he would have a lot to lose if you were to find out about his extramarital relationship?'

'Yes.'

'Can I ask when you told your husband about your publishing arrangement with Mia Justice?'

I force myself to focus. 'I haven't. He already thinks my writing is a waste of time and that I ought to give it up; I didn't want to give him any more ammunition by admitting to taking such drastic action unless it actually came good. I didn't *know* it had happened until late last night. It was reported in the *Evening Standard*, I believe, but I didn't see that. Mia emailed the link to me, but I didn't pick it up until I'd come back from A&E in Pembury with my son.'

'I see.' He nods. 'But he knew about the book itself? Is it a distinctive plot? One he might have recognised from the newspaper report?'

'Yes, he knew about the book and yes, he would have recognised the plot.' Not a lie. All true.

'So he would have deduced some sort of connection between you and Ms Justice?'

'Yes. That's possible.'

'And worried, he might have gone to her property last night to end their affair, perhaps? Fearing this connection? Or gone to ask her how she appeared to have sold *your* book?'

I shrug. 'I have absolutely no idea.'

'But while he was there – he sustained an injury. He was hit on the head with some force. You didn't think perhaps Ms Justice could have meant that she attacked *him*?'

'At the time she said that, I didn't think so, no, because I wasn't aware of his head injury, but I could see she *was* hurt. I really wouldn't like to speculate on what she may or may not have meant.'

'I appreciate your efforts to present the facts to me so accurately and objectively. Lots of people in your situation wouldn't be so fair, I don't think,' he says gravely.

I start and look at him, worried. Have I made a mistake? Am I appearing too emotionless? Cold? Is this alerting him to something? But mercifully he stands up. We're done.

'One last thing, Mrs Tristan.'

I tense warily. I've seen them do this before on *Unforgotten*. Wait right until the end of the interview when everyone has relaxed, *then* come back with the killer blow question, catching everyone off guard. It's a nice technique. I noticed it too, DI Travers.

'Just a total coincidence you chose Mia, I suppose?' He smiles at me amiably as he reaches the door. Back to jolly inspector. Tickets, please!

So far I haven't successfully protected anyone at all. I picture Mia stood there in her beautiful, ruined dress with her cut forehead. I see her small, tear-stained face in the bar telling me earnestly that she could play late teens through to mid-thirties. I hear Flo telling me I promised not to speak to Mia.

'No, it wasn't random at all,' I say truthfully. 'I first met Mia in August last year at a festival in Edinburgh. I signed a book for her; we spoke briefly. I was struck by how she looks a little bit like me and I found myself wishing *I* was back at the start of my career, like she is, only with the knowledge and skill set it's taken me the last ten years to hone; what a combination that could be. That's when the idea occurred to me.' I shrug. 'Once I had a manuscript I was happy with and I'd watched her in a play and knew she was a good enough actress to pull it off, I approached her. You make your own luck, DI Travers. Unfortunately, it appears I wasn't the only one who noticed her in Edinburgh. My husband did too.'

*

By late afternoon Tris has started to come round from the sedation he's been placed under so that the doctors can control all parameters while they rewarm and 'rest' him. He's pulling at his airway support, so it's decided to remove it while keeping him in ITU as a precaution, to make sure he can maintain breathing on his own. The doctors are amazing and a particularly nice one – a young man who weirdly makes me think of a grown-up version of Teddy, with his unruly curls and earnest frown of concentration – explains carefully that although Tris has been warmed up, he's still being treated with fluids and medication to reverse his alcohol and chemical imbalances.

'He'd had quite a few drinks,' he scratches his head awkwardly, 'so was already dehydrated, then add in the hypothermia and a long lie on the floor, your muscles start to react and the chemicals in your body can have a breakdown, but the good news is obviously his CT scan was clear and there's no bleed internally from his head injury. Basically we're going in the right direction and we're making preparations to move him from ITU to another ward, but it's slightly complicated by um, the situation.' He glances at the two uniformed policemen sat alongside us, outside Tris's room, on duty. 'We'll keep you updated though.'

'Thank you.' I turn to the two officers. 'I'm assuming it's still OK for me to go back in and sit with him now that he's come round and is starting to talk?'

'Yeah, it's fine,' says one of them. He looks so young too. 'Just, if you could avoid discussing the case with him? Thanks.'

I nod and as I close the clear door behind me, I see them both return to their phones, boredly. A nurse is busily checking one of the drips going into Tris's arm.

'I'm sorry, this keeps going off. I don't think it's the bag, but we'll change it anyway. I wonder if we might also site a new line?' She inspects the cannula going into the back of his hand. 'It's looking a *little* red and sore. It might have tissued. I'll go and get the bits and pieces.'

She leaves the room, and I sit down next to the bed. Tris turns his head very slightly on the pillow and opens his eyes.

'Hello.' His voice is very soft and low.

'Don't try to talk. Your mouth must be sore.'

He closes his eyes. 'What do you know?'

'You mean about Mia?' I say lightly. 'Everything.'

I watch him wince. We sit there in silence. Just the regular beeps of machines. I glance out of the window – the sun is setting on a bright, Saturday afternoon. We would normally have taken the kids swimming and after lunch back at home, perhaps we would have gone for a kick-the-autumn-leaves walk at Knowle followed by a hot chocolate. By now I'd be about to start tea. My phone bleeps with a text from Flo.

All OK here – don't worry. Mum and Dad have just arrived. Let me know when you want me to come to you Xxx

I look up at the back of the policemen's heads through the glass – still on their phones.

'She says you hurt her.' I say quietly. 'Tried to strangle her.'

He shakes his head silently, eyes still closed.

'Tris, I was there. She told me herself. I saw the bruises on her neck.'

His eyes open slowly and he looks right at me. 'You? At the flat?'

'I found you half-naked on the floor,' I continue. 'Were you having sex with her or trying to assault her?'

He tries to sit up. 'Neither!'

'Don't try and move like that,' I put a hand out, 'you'll block the drip – it's been going off for ages as it is. Lie down.'

One of the policemen briefly turns round. I give him the thumbs up and he turns away again.

Tris collapses back. 'Someone is trying to make it look bad.' He coughs. 'Mia.'

'Mia?' I say incredulously. 'You're saying Mia has – set you up?'

He lifts both hands from the bed, briefly, in helpless gesture. 'Told her it was over. She went for me. Tried to hold her back. She kneed me, grabbed a light. Hit me – I was doubled over.' He coughs again and I pass him the cup of water on the side table. He takes some small sips as I hold it to his mouth, before placing it carefully back down.

'Do you love her, Tris?' I ask suddenly.

He shakes his head. 'I love you and the kids.' His voice cracks and tears begin to leak down through his laughter lines. 'You and the kids.' His hand reaches for me, but I can't bring myself to touch him. 'Forgive me. Please.'

I watch him start to cough again, and again automatically pass him the water. I try to imagine what he has just told me; Mia, crazed, rushing towards him, screaming. She told me herself she had a breakdown over a former boyfriend. And as Flo warned me, people do unpredictable things in high stress situations.

Perhaps, *perhaps* I could believe that he didn't hurt her, but restrained her, because I have never, ever known him be violent. Unpleasant, yes, violent no. But do I buy that Mia panicked and stripped him to make it look like an assault? It's not impossible. She's an actress – perhaps she wasn't in the state of confusion I believed her to be in when I arrived. Maybe it all happened exactly like he just said it did.

Except who believes the already proven liar?

'The thing is,' I say slowly, 'there shouldn't have been anything that you needed to go and end in the first place. You know that's my red line. You know how I feel about the damage infidelity does.'

'Don't punish me for what your dad did.'

I half laugh, half cry at that. 'I'm not. This is hurt you've caused all on your own, to all of us. Clara, Teddy, Mia – and me. Do you even want to ask me how Teddy is? If he's OK?'

He looks blank, confused.

I exclaim aloud again. 'So you didn't even bother to check the hundred messages I left for you?' My tears are breaking through my voice now. Just when I think I'm standing on the furthest edge of hurt, another little piece falls away. 'You left the lid off a bottle of Calpol. Teddy drank it. I had to take him to hospital last night.'

He looks horrified.

'He's OK,' I say quickly. 'But you thought it could wait, didn't you? You were distracted.' I can feel everything changing within me like a speeded-up film of clouds moving across the sky; I am becoming relentless. I will spare him nothing. 'I never call you like that unless it's an emergency… but *you* thought your situation was more important. You were angry, you wanted to know why and how Mia stole your book and sold it for a million pounds yesterday.'

He stares at me; I hear an exhalation escape through his dry lips.

'While I was looking for more evidence of your affair, I found your book on your laptop,' I say simply. 'I don't understand why you didn't just tell me what you were working on. I could have helped you.'

I wait but he says nothing.

'What were you going to do?' I'm desperate to know. 'Have a go at selling it and *then* fess up? Did you imagine it was your way out of your "stagnant" life? Number one in forty countries, a whirlwind of book tours, audiences hanging on your every word? You would have been good at that, in fairness, and publishing loves a bad boy even more than a beautiful girl. You could have been their very own Mr Ripley; a smash book based on a *real*-life double life. Were you going to take Mia on the ride with you or dump her too?'

Still he says nothing.

'Or did you not really know what you wanted?' My eyes fill up and I stem the flow of tears with my fingertips. 'Anyway, I reworked it and *I* gave it to Mia. I told her it was my book. We've pretended she's written it – and *we've* sold it. She thought she got the gig after we met in Edinburgh. You remember – you met her briefly there too, didn't you?' I point at him lightly. 'I saw you speaking to her in the doorway. I assume you took an interest at a distance in her career after that, until you "bumped" into her on the station and asked her to coffee?'

His eyes have widened but he holds my gaze.

'Should I be flattered that you went for a brand new version of me, or just devastated? She doesn't know I'm married to you, by the way. She will have had no idea why you were so angry with her last night.'

'I don't believe you,' is all he says. That's it. I wait, but that's the best he can do. Not a man of many words now.

'I'm not sure *I* believe *your* version of last night's events. I don't think you went there to end it. I think you wanted answers. I think you felt betrayed.' There is no anger left. The film has stopped. The clouds have covered the sun. My tears start to fall.

'You've hurt me more than I thought was possible and I want a divorce.' As my mouth says it, I know that's the truth of where we are. 'We can't come back from this. It's broken.'

He is still staring at me. 'You did this? Not her?'

I shake my head. 'In these sorts of stories, it's always the *husband*. You should know that by now.'

He doesn't seem to hear me. 'You sold the book. What have I done? What the fuck have I done?' he whispers, staring up at the ceiling his eyes wide. 'I thought – Mia! Oh my god, I'm so sorry, Mia!'

Oh! The knife shoves in so quickly I don't feel it; it's more like being punched in the gut than fatally injured. This is him loving *me*? By apologising to *her*? The breath leaves my body as I fall backwards from the edge. I watch him disappearing away from me, our life together becoming smaller and smaller.

Machines start to beep. He gasps and a look of fear spreads across his face.

'Tris?' I reach out, but he doesn't answer. 'Tris!' I shout.

One of the policemen turns and stands up, calling to someone and pointing in through the window.

The door bursts open. People are flooding into the room. 'Mrs Tristan? Can you come with me please?'

I am very firmly led away, but not before I see someone beginning chest compressions – all over again.

CHAPTER SIXTEEN

MIA

'Sweetheart, I'm here!'

I open my eyes and blink in the bright light, to see Kirsty sat right next to me, stroking my head. She's been crying. I fumble for her hand and she takes it instantly, squeezing me so hard I exclaim aloud.

'I'm sorry!' she says instantly. 'I didn't mean to hurt you! You were calling for me in your sleep. I just wanted you to know I'm here.' She looks devastated. 'I came as soon as I could and I'm so, so sorry I didn't answer any of your phone calls yesterday. This is all my fault!'

'Don't be stupid! How did you work that out? Of course it's not.' I reach up with my other hand and tuck a bit of stray hair that's fallen forward back behind her ear.

'I should have picked up. You needed me and I wasn't there.'

'I'm not your responsibility. You're allowed to be angry with me. I said some really mean things. I'm sorry too.'

'I love you so much,' she whispers and a tear runs down her face. 'I will never, ever stop loving you, Mia. You hear me? There is nothing you could say to me that could ever change that. Ever. We're all here with you now and we're not going to let anything happen to you, ever again.'

I nod. I don't want to speak because I don't want to start crying myself. Kirsty watches me worriedly.

'So, I brought you some clean clothes.' She opts for practicalities while I catch my breath – letting go of me to reach into a plastic bag on the floor at her feet. 'I've got you a toothbrush and some shower bits as well. Some pyjamas, although Mum says they're going to discharge you soon. That's good!' She straightens up and reaches for my hand again. 'How *is* your neck?' She doesn't shy away. I wouldn't expect any less from her. I wonder if she knows how many times her strength has carried me? 'Still hurting?'

'A bit. It's OK though.'

Her gaze falls to my throat. 'The marks are very red. I can actually see where his fingers were pressing.' I watch her jaw clench.

I don't say anything. Just withdraw my hand and look down at the bed.

'And what about your head, where you were cut. How is that feeling?'

I lift my hand instinctively, forgetting I have a tube going into the back of it. It pulls slightly and I let it drop down onto the sheet again without touching the dressing. 'It's OK. I'm pretty sure I slipped on the rug and hit it on the edge of the radiator. Did Dad tell you it looks like I went into my room and tried to get something warmer to wear from the wardrobe? I put a pair of trousers over my shoulders and went outside in the rain, before deciding that wasn't such a good idea after all, only to come back in?' I try to smile. 'I was pretty confused.' My voice starts to tremble. 'And weirdly,' I cough, in an attempt to steady it again, 'I remember thinking I should get into Dad's car. I thought I was back at the old house, in Brighton.'

'You were trying to escape,' she says softly. 'I think you're amazing. Mum said they found your phone right next to you. How strong are you, that your survival instinct was *still* there?'

'Well yeah, except I didn't actually manage to phone anyone to help me.'

'It doesn't matter,' she insists. 'You're safe now. He's never going to come near you again.' Her voice takes on a low determination that she doesn't try to hide. 'Mia, there's something I need to tell you. After we argued on Thursday I did a search on him. I got his address from Companies House – he recently set up a limited company – and I went there. I saw him come home from work and use a key to get into the house. I saw his children moving around inside. I saw his wife. I didn't ring the bell or confront him or anything, I swear, but I couldn't bring myself to tell you. I wanted to, but I couldn't. I was trying to work out what to do, if I should interfere or not. That's why I didn't answer when you called. If I'd told you, you'd never have let him in last night. I'm so very, very sorry.'

I don't know what to say to that and end up just staring at the sheet on the bed.

'Do you want to talk about what happened? What he did?'

I wipe my eyes and nod at the two policemen sat on the other side of the glass wall. 'They said I'm not allowed to.'

Before Kirsty can respond to that, the door opens and a nurse comes in.

'You're looking a *lot* brighter.' She smiles kindly. 'You've got actual colour in your cheeks again! Clever girl. Excuse me, can I just sneak past you?'

She edges around Kirsty and the huge elephant in the room. None of the medical staff have directly mentioned the police sat outside the door. If only they too could turn out to be one of the many hallucinations I've apparently had in the last twelve hours. I don't even like to ask why they are there. To protect me? Or because *I* hit *him*?

'I'm just going to check your drip, Mia. Ooof! They never give you enough room in these little bays. So, what have we got here…

Very nice. I think we can look at getting this down for you soon! That'll make you more comfy.' She gives my shoulder a quick rub.

'Thank you.' I try to smile.

'I'll just check with the doctors. See what their plans are. I'll pop back in a minute and let you know.'

As soon as she leaves, Kirsty pulls her chair closer again, looks over her shoulder and twists quickly back to me. 'You can tell me – what happened?'

'I'm not allo—'

'No one can hear us. It's just me.'

'Honestly?' I look her right in the eye. 'I don't actually know. I opened the front door and found him crying.'

'About what?'

'I've no idea. I've never seen him like that before. He pushed in, got me up against the wall. He had his hand on my face. He was calling me a liar and saying I don't love him, that I'd *stolen* his love. I told him, of course I love him, then his hand sort of slipped onto my neck. This is going to turn out to be some sort of horrible misunderstanding.'

Kirsty stares at me. 'A *misunderstanding*? Mia, you hit him. You would never have done that unless you were frightened and trying to stop him from hurting you. I can *see* that he hurt you. What happened after his hand was on your neck?'

'I'm not supposed to talk to you about this.' I look up at the ceiling, desperately. 'Please! I don't want to get anyone into more trouble.'

'You won't. I know this is really difficult,' she tries again, 'but he was half-naked when his wife found both of you. Did he try and assault you?'

'No!' I reply immediately. 'He'd never do *that*. I don't know why he was like that. I can't really explain it.'

'"You can't explain it"?' she repeats incredulously. There's a long pause. 'Sweetheart, I'm worried that you might be trying to protect Seth. Please, just tell me the truth!'

'I am!' I insist.

'Then why did you hit him?'

'Please, don't ask me to answer that,' I whisper.

'My darling, whatever you think you had with this man, you didn't. No one that loves you would ever, *ever* try and hurt you, no matter how angry he got.'

'He was drunk,' I interrupt. 'I don't think he knew what he was doing.'

'Oh, come on!' Kirsty says. 'Forget for a minute that he's still married, forget that he's lied to you and his wife. He wanted to hurt you, Mia. This is not a rational, sane, stable man. This is not the man I want for my beautiful little sister.' Her voice cracks. 'This is a man trying to stop his dirty little secret from being discovered. A man panicking… a man I want to kill for daring to lay a single finger on you. There was no misunderstanding. He intended to hurt you and he did. If his wife hadn't found you when she did this morning, I might not even be talking to you now.'

I close my eyes and picture Charlotte looking around her in horror at the scene she discovered. I don't actually remember when we agreed she should come to the flat for a meeting. I very vaguely recall talking about it with her, but I certainly can't pinpoint the specifics. I'm struggling with a lot of details right now. Mostly how Charlotte can also be Seth's wife. It's like someone unexpectedly appearing in a city where they shouldn't be, where you would never normally see them, like in *Inception* when the buildings start crumbling down. Everything is out of context and in the wrong place. I think about us sitting in the Crypt on Tuesday while she told me about her cheating boyfriend inspiring her first book. She must be as devastated as I am. She must hate me.

'Mia?' Kirsty waits until I look at her again. 'I *need* you to protect *yourself* now and tell the police the truth. Tell them what he did and why you hit Seth. Promise me?'

Before I can say anything, a movement catches my eye on the other side of the glass. A balding man has appeared and is talking to the policemen, who are standing up.

'Kirsty,' I say, worriedly. 'Where are Mum and Dad?'

'They just went to grab sandwiches and scare off a couple of journalists. They'll be back in a minute. Why?'

'Something's happening.' I point over her shoulder and she twists to look, just as the door opens and the man comes in with the two officers flanking him.

'Amy Hendricks,' he looks right at me, as Kirsty jumps up, 'I am arresting you on suspicion of the manslaughter of Seth Tristan on Saturday, the 10th of November 2018 at 6 Dolcis Road, Blackheath. You do not have to say anything, but it may harm your defence if you do not mention, when questioned, something which you later rely on in court. Anything you do say may be given in evidence.'

'Manslaughter?' Kirsty repeats in shock. 'He's *died*? But why are you arresting HER? Look at her neck! Look at what he did to her!'

My parents choose this moment to return with a bag of food and takeaway coffees. I close my eyes while all of the voices in the room begin to rise as they all tell each other to calm down and listen. Other people, medical staff, start to flood in.

Seth has died. I try to block them all out. He's dead.

I see him standing outside his office, holding the heart shape over his head, smiling at me as I looked down the road towards him. He loved me, I know he did.

I feel his arms around me, holding me gently to his body in my bed and I start to cry.

I've killed him.

CHAPTER SEVENTEEN

CHARLOTTE

When they tell me they did everything they could, that they worked on Tris for over an hour but, despite their every effort, he has died, I hear the echo of our children's happy laughter ringing in my ears... sudden splashes and shrieks of delight... reflected sunlight on our bare skin. Me warning everyone firmly that you can burn in the water without realising, until you climb out.

I hear him asking me to marry him – feel his lips on mine as we kissed – and I remember waking up all the way through that first night to stare in delighted happiness at the dazzling diamonds on my finger: the ring I'm wearing right now, eleven years later.

They ask if I want to see him. Unable to speak, I shake my head.

We have no answers for each other anymore.

CHAPTER EIGHTEEN

MIA

Once I'm dressed the two officers lead me to the car. I can feel people staring. Someone shouts something – a question, I think – and my heartbeat quickens as I ignore them and focus on the floor. Once we are outside the hospital, I don't know what makes me do it, but I lift my head just in time to see Charlotte walking across the car park towards a woman sitting in the driving seat of a stationary red car. She sees me and hurriedly pulls the visor down, blocking my view, but it's too late. I saw her face and I know who she is. Florence. She counselled me after Maureen became ill, for all of two sessions. She knows Charlotte. That's how Charlotte knew my address.

I climb into the car, my limbs rigid with shock and think about the things that I've disclosed in various counselling sessions. Things I would never want anyone else to know. Deeply private, personal, black-as-night troubles, questions and confessions about things I've done and have happened to me. I wonder what other details Florence might have disclosed, what else she might have told Seth's wife and I feel violated. There's no other word for it.

*

My prints are taken and, mindful of my dad's shouted instruction 'not to say a word' until my solicitor arrives, I stare at the wall of the cell silently while I wait to be taken for interview. I want to switch off my head; I feel jangly and unable to sit comfortably in my own skin. When the solicitor does appear, she reminds me a little bit of Charlotte – the same no-nonsense calm and self-assurance – kind but detached. I wonder what she's left to come and help me today, instead of what she had planned for her weekend. She certainly looks the part: an anonymous black skirt and jacket with a cream silk shell top underneath as she scribbles on her notepad.

'So you hit him because he assaulted you, by which I mean your visible bruising,' she looks at me over the top of her glasses and notes something else down, 'that no doubt matches his hands. Someone slender like you has virtually no superficial fat on a delicate area like the neck. It's beautifully clear, practically a print. And that's a scratch there too,' she points the pen at me, 'so your skin will probably be beneath his fingernails. If it is, they'll have found it.'

I look up at the strip light on the ceiling, but all I see is Seth falling to the floor. I feel my fingers releasing the lamp in shock. He was a husband, a father…

'Do you need a moment?' she says, noting my distress.

'Thank you. I'm OK,' I answer quietly.

'Well, say if you do.' She notes something else down on her pad of paper. 'In a minute, we'll go through into the interview room and DI Travers – the same man who arrested you – will caution you, then ask you some questions that will be tape-recorded. I'll advise you while we're in there and going along. Mia, they're going to ask you why Seth Tristan was half-naked. There's nothing to be gained by protecting Seth's reputation, certainly not at a cost to yourself. Could you tell me what happened?'

I think about sitting opposite Florence in her counselling room, disgorging details about Hugo I would never want anyone to know. I think about Seth telling me it was his turn to have his kids at the weekend, when I guess he was simply at home with his family, in the house my sister watched him walk into on Thursday night. So who even lives in the flat in Putney we had sex at? The one he said was his?

I don't want to trust anyone with anything, ever again.

I should be on stage in the matinee right now, about to take a bow, performance over… the sound of applause. I wonder if everyone will think I was too hung-over to show up and couldn't be bothered now I'm going to be a writing star? I want to be there, pretending to be someone else.

I do not want to think about what happened last night, ever again.

'Mia?' The solicitor looks at me.

I shift in my seat. 'I already told you. He was drunk when he arrived, and upset. I don't know what about. He put his hands on my neck. I was very frightened. I kneed him in the groin and when he let go I ran into the sitting room towards the door that was open into the garden, but he came after me. I grabbed a light and I hit him with it. He fell to the ground. I ran from the room, I slipped and hit my head. I don't remember anything else apart from coming to in the hospital. I have bruising on my neck – I was obviously trying to defend myself when I hit him, which is what you called the unlawful act earlier, right?'

'Correct. There is reasonable doubt, yes.'

'That the unlawful act didn't kill him, you mean? Because he died in hospital?'

She nods. 'I would expect a post mortem to confirm the cause of death is wholly unconnected with the unlawful act, yes.'

I twist away from her and stare at the wall in front of me again, my hands clasped tightly in my lap. 'After they interview me and they've gathered their other evidence, tell me again what happens then?'

'The file is presented to the Crown Prosecution Service who decide if there is enough to charge you with and take this to trial in a court.'

'And if you were reading a file based on what I've told you already, would you charge me?'

'If I were a prosecutor?' she says. 'No, I wouldn't run it. While I think I see where you're coming from, you do need to be aware that when an allegation of a sexual offence has been made, the victim – in this case you – is entitled to anonymity in the press. Nothing could be published which is likely to lead members of the public to identify you. That's also what I mean by protecting yourself. Yes, the information you've given me already is technically "enough" but with *all* of the details, I could apply instantly for reporting restrictions. Your father would like me to shut this down.'

I sigh and close my eyes. Do I want all of this tweeted, Facebooked, Insta'd, documented forever whenever anyone searches for me online? No, of course I don't. Mud sticks. They'd probably lift the same photo of me and Seth I showed to Kirsty, the one of us grinning next to each other. I posted it on Facebook. I don't think it makes any difference that it's on my private page. I'd look like a psycho. *This is me with my married boyfriend before I hit him over the head and he died!*

'He had his hand on my neck and he started to undo his trousers,' I say flatly. 'I knew he was going to try and force me to do something sexually that I didn't want to. I kneed him in the groin and the rest happened exactly as I told you. I don't remember anything between hitting my head and waking up in hospital, and that's the truth.'

It isn't, but I'm not telling her that. I've told her enough already.

CHAPTER NINETEEN

CHARLOTTE

I don't tell Teddy and Clara when I get home. It's too close to bedtime. They are cosily tucked up on the sofa with Dad, cuddled either side of him, watching a movie. Luckily they don't hear me come in because the sight of them, so content, almost breaks me.

I assume they've already eaten as its past six o'clock, but as I walk quickly down the hall, into the steamy, warm kitchen I realise Mum is still cooking spaghetti. Every single pot and pan is in use and I'm immediately anxious that it's so late. Clara and Teddy must be starving. My mother looks up to see me in the doorway, drops the spatula immediately, wipes her hands on my apron and crosses the room in three steps, pulling me into a hug. I am rigid in her arms. 'Sweetheart! Oh Sweetheart!' She says through muffled tears. She lets go just as quickly and takes several deep breaths. 'But we must stop this now, you don't want the children to see you upset.'

'Here—' She reaches to the side and grabs a bottle of wine next to the spaghetti sauce, slinging some roughly into a nearby tumbler. I shake my head but she ignores me and holds the glass out insistently.

'No, Mum. It's on the turn, only really good for cooking now.' I push it away. 'I haven't eaten anything all day either. I'll be sick. Is

this nearly ready? Can I do anything?' I look around me, desperate
to get everything under control.

'No, you can't. It's almost done, I promise.'

I cross the room and sit down at the table redundantly. 'They've
arrested his girlfriend.' I don't know why that's the detail I choose
to tell her.

Mum doesn't say anything, just turns back to the sauce and I
wonder for a moment if I've even said that out loud, as Flo walks
back in. 'Who would you like to stay with you tonight? I can or
Mum and Dad will?'

'You don't want more sheets to wash,' Mum says. 'You stay,
Florrie, you were here last night anyway. Why don't you bring the
children over to us for Sunday lunch tomorrow instead?'

Flo and I stare at each other.

'Mum,' Flo clears her throat. 'Charlotte has just lost her husband.'

'I meant bring the children over after you've told them in the
morning, so that you have something familiar to do which isn't
threatening.' She keeps her back to us and stirs vigorously.

Flo comes over and kneels down in front of me, taking my
hands in hers as she looks up at me earnestly. 'You tell them
however you want to. We'll be with you every step of the way. I'll
do the children's baths and stories. They don't know you were at
the hospital. I told them you went to see a friend today. Can you
cope with being around them, can you fake it, or do you need to
go straight back out, or up to bed?'

Mum laughs. 'Of course she's not going to bed! That's not a
luxury you have as a parent, Florence.'

'Mum!' Flo rounds on her furiously. 'Please!'

'No, she's right. It'll freak them out even more if I do that. I'll
tell them tomorrow.' I wipe my eyes again, get up and walk over
to the sink, splashing cold water on my skin before patting it dry
with a tea towel. I turn, but catch sight of the drying rack over
by the window. Tris's running gear is airing. 'This is all my fault.'

'I think perhaps that—' begins Flo, but Mum rounds on me, holding up a hand. 'No. I'm sorry – but no. These were his choices, Charlotte. Were you there when it all happened last night? No. Were you the one they arrested? No. So are you to blame? No.' Mum looks me straight in the eye. 'Now, you paint that smile on your face. It's time to call those children into tea.' She takes her apron off. 'You can serve. I know you think I always dish them up too much. Clara! Teddy! Teatime!'

They come dashing through and she bends down, arms open, and scoops them up, laughing and covering them in kisses. 'Who is going to sit next to *me*?' She twinkles at them. 'And who is also having Nona's chocolate sauce on ice cream, with marshmallows, for pudding?'

'Me! Me!' They both jump up and down, already thoroughly overexcited.

'Come on then, my darlings!' She rushes them over to the table. 'I think spaghetti might just be my favourite tea too! If you had to pick your three best meals, what would they be?'

It's an impressive performance and it works. The kids sit down and start to chatter away, oblivious to everything else. Flo shakes her head, gets up quietly and leaves the room. Mum ignores her, prattling on, and before the children have even finished telling her what their best meals are, she's already got her phone out and is showing them some video she saw of a cat climbing up a door and letting itself in. I'm not sure if she's doing it for them, or filling her mind up so she doesn't have to think.

I make a start on the dirty pots and pans, scattered all over the side, when the doorbell rings.

'I'll go,' Flo calls out.

'It's OK. I'll get it.' I dry my hands and make my way down the passage approaching the shadowy figure on the doorstep.

'Mrs Tristan?' A young woman smiles sympathetically at me as I open the door. 'I'm from the *Daily*—'

'You're a journalist?' I interrupt in disbelief.

'Yes. Could I ask you about what happened yesterday regarding your husband's?—'

'Shut up!' hisses a voice behind me and Flo steps round me. 'She hasn't even had a chance to tell her *children* yet. You people make me sick.' She slams the door shut, shaking. 'If it goes again,' she turns to me, 'you call me. I'll take care of them.'

*

I flick into autopilot after that and we get through bedtime. Teddy hugs me and kisses me – tells me he will never stop loving me. Clara politely declines any songs. I've just turned her light off and am leaving the room when she whispers: 'Mummy?'

I turn back.

'Is Daddy coming home tomorrow?' She looks at me enquiringly in the dark, her beautiful eyes catching the light I always leave on in the bathroom so they don't get scared if they wake in the night. 'Is he in Sheffield?'

'I'm not sure.' I smile, breaking into a thousand pieces inside. 'I'll find out what's happening in the morning.'

'OK.' She snuggles down contentedly, clutching her cuddly dragon.

I manage not to cry until I'm downstairs, where I close the kitchen door so I'm sure they can't hear me. Mum and Dad stay in the sitting room watching TV, and Flo hugs me. We cry together until, for the time being, I can cry no more.

I'm standing in the side passage stubbing out the remainder of the fag I've just smoked and deciding I must now give up properly, when to my shock I see our car suddenly pass the open back gate. I run down, in time to see Jim climbing out.

'You didn't need to bring it back today,' I say in amazement. 'I'm so sorry. That's not why I messaged you earlier. I just thought

you should know we'd found him, in case you were worried when
he didn't come back.'

'I'm really sorry you had to do so much running around tracking him down. That must have been really stressful. He doesn't
deserve you.' He flushes bright red the second the words are out
of his mouth. 'Anyway, how is he? Still in hospital?' He passes
me the keys.

'Um,' I bite my lip. How do you tell people? 'He died this
afternoon.'

'What?' Jim takes a step back from me and puts his hands on
his head in shock.

'I'm so sorry.'

'Charlotte. I…' he trails off. 'I don't know what to say.'

'He was severely hypothermic when he was found.'

'But it wasn't even that cold last night!'

'It was cold enough. He was right next to an open door and
he'd been drinking. It doesn't take nearly as much of a drop in
the outside temperature as you'd think, apparently, and there were
complications.' I wrap my arms around myself. 'Um, do you want
to come in? Have a drink or something? I don't know…'

'Charlotte?' I hear Flo say behind me. 'Everything OK?'

I twist to look at her. 'Yes, thank you. This is Jim; Jim this is my
sister, Florence. I think you may have met actually? At the wedding?'

'Oh, right.' Flo relaxes again. 'Hi.'

'Hello again.' Jim nods at her politely, obviously unsure if he
should smile or not. 'Listen, I've got his suitcase and laptop bag in
the back.' He gestures helplessly behind him at the car. 'I'll just…
get it out for you.' He moves quickly to the boot and retrieves
them, placing Tris's laptop bag on the case and pulling the handle
up to keep it from slipping off.

'Thank you. Now, that drink?' I offer automatically, turning
to the house.

'No, no.' He holds a hand up. 'I don't want to intrude. I'm going to get the train straight back into town.' He gestures back down the hill, then hesitates and steps forward, drawing me into a brief tight hug. 'I'm so sorry. I honestly don't know what to say to you.'

'I'll be in touch when we know what's happening about the funeral.' These are unreal words. How does my mouth even know how to say them?

'Of course. Goodbye, Florence.' He turns to my sister, and she nods tearfully. He lingers though and it dawns on me there is something else he wants tell me after all, privately.

'I'll be right in,' I say to Flo, who looks between us, realises we want her to leave and tactfully walks back into the house.

I turn back to Jim and, suddenly, I don't want to hear it, whatever it is he's going to disclose. I cut in quickly before he can say another single word. 'I'm so grateful to you for giving Tris and I some space while we were going through our rough patch, and I know he was too. It was really kind of you.'

He looks down at the floor and says quietly: 'He did love you all very much, you know.'

I manage not to say: *by all of us, I assume you mean, me, the kids – and Mia?* It's not Jim's fault for keeping quiet anymore than it's Flo's for telling me. These were our problems. No one else's. Instead I say a simple 'thank you'; grateful, at least, for the sentiment, if not the lie.

*

Up in our bedroom, once Mum and Dad have gone home – Mum was so twitchy it was setting me on edge, while Dad could barely look at me – and Flo has gone to bed, I quietly unpack Tris's suitcase. I automatically throw his dirty clothes in the basket behind me. I remove his washbag and put it on his bedside table, for want of knowing what else to do with it. I take out the book he was reading, his cufflinks and watch case, both empty. They too go on his bedside table. I don't switch on his phone. What would be the point? I am surprised, however, to find his wallet in the case. He went out on Friday night without it? Who does that – unless it's someone wanting to stay anonymous, I suppose. I open it to find his cards, and in the change pocket, his wedding ring.

Feeling numb, I stare at it sitting in the palm of my hand, then cross the room and put it carefully in my jewellery box. I look through the rest of the sections and in the clear plastic window bit, find a picture of him and Mia kissing in a photo booth, where normally I know a picture of the four of us resides. I find our one carelessly tucked inside the flap of his mobile case – where some people put a credit card if they go out – presumably to be swapped over when he was ready to come back home. For display purposes only. Safe to say Jim didn't go through his things first then… or perhaps he did. Who knows? I look at the picture of Tris kissing Mia again. She looks so happy. They both do. I'm sure she has one of the remaining four of the series of pictures, however, so she won't need this one too.

I carry the photograph into our en suite, open the window, and pulling my lighter from my pocket, I set fire to the corner of the tiny image, dropping it in the sink as it starts to burn my fingers. I pick the ashes out and flush the remains down the loo. I don't ever want the kids finding this and at least it's one less reminder for Mia to take care of, later down the line, when one day she opens a bag full of memorabilia and is jolted to see a picture of the man she thought she loved but is relieved to discover has no power over her anymore. She will remember how it felt to love him, but not the feeling itself.

I open up the laptop and look at his book files. He last worked on it on Wednesday. I also click on his notes.

To do:
Show, don't tell what he has learnt. Resolution.

He must go home in last chapter.
See him open the door to the house/their future, and step in. End

I gasp out loud and tears flood my eyes so quickly I have to wipe them away so I can reread what he's written, in disbelief. Even if that was what Tris wanted, the moment he slept with Mia it was never going to be *our* happy ending. He would have known that. These are just words… the end of a made-up story.

So he knows he would have a lot to lose if you were to find out about his extramarital relationship?

You're wrong, DI Travers. He lied to me. He didn't go there to end it. He went there angry, because the person he loved had hurt him and he wanted to hurt her back. Isn't that how it works?

And yet…

He must go home in last chapter.
See him open the door to the house/their future, and step in. End

I read the words again. I hear him saying: 'Charlotte, do you love me?' I picture the look of surprise and pain on his face when I calmly agreed that we should talk about separation. We would have been doing that tomorrow night.

If I hadn't known he was having an affair, if he'd come home from work on Wednesday and told me 'out of the blue' that he simply couldn't bear our lack of intimacy a day longer and wanted to leave me because of it, would I have reacted the same way? No – I would not. I would have been devastated. I would have listened to him. I would have tried to fix it. We might have had sex that night. He might have come back in from the edge, deciding that trading me and the kids for Mia wasn't worth it after all. He might have finished with her and I'd have been none the wiser. We would still be a family. My children would still have a father.

But I did know and look at what I've done.

*

I tell Clara and Teddy after breakfast, Flo sitting on the opposite sofa for support. I explain that sometimes – not often, but sometimes – grown-ups get ill and the doctors can't make them better and that's what's happened to Daddy and he's died. Clara goes very quiet and immediately buries her head in my arm, clutching onto me, frantically. Teddy stares blankly and asks if he can watch a film now?

I get up to put something familiar and comforting on in the background while we talk, but I don't know what to choose, realising suddenly with a jolt quite how many Disney movies start with parents dying. I opt for *Aladdin*. I answer Clara's questions truthfully and honestly, including: 'Yes, Daddy is in Heaven, but I don't know where it is because I've never been there… he's absolutely safe, but no darling, he's not coming back.'

The door goes again, making us jump – another journalist – and Teddy pushes his snack bowl away announcing his tummy hurts.

'That's OK, Teddy. You don't have to eat anything.' Flo takes it away from him gently. 'Come and sit on my lap.'

The doorbell goes again and, unable to stand it, I get up. 'Come on. We're going to Nona's for lunch.'

*

The house is full of music and the comforting smell of a cooking roast when we arrive. Mum has got the dressing-up box down: a treasure trove full of odd hats, jangly beads, scarfs, high heels, white evening gloves that go up to the elbow, fur stoles, clip-on diamante dangly earrings. She begins to make the kids up, laughing delightedly when Teddy pouts at her in bright pink lipstick, and clicks away with her IPhone. I watch them carefully. Clara is laughing too. I'm shocked and worried at this until it dawns on me that, far from being nonplussed, what I've told them is so big and overwhelming they simply can't make sense of it in what is *their* version of devastation.

*

I take a moment to slip out into the garden before we leave, making my way across the soggy tufts of grass, right down to the river. I slide Tris's laptop from under my arm and look around, but it's a cold day. No one is watching me lean over the top of the picket fence and drop it, side on, into the water. All the evidence of him having written the book slips beneath the surface rather elegantly, with barely a splash. I look out over the water and as the cold breeze lifts my hair, I swallow down a nauseating wave of déjà vu. I can hear my mother saying the words to me that I repeated to Clara this morning… *Daddy isn't coming back.*

It was not supposed to happen like this. None of it. My God – it was not supposed to happen like this… the damage…

'Charlotte.'

I whip round at the voice behind me. My father is standing there. For a moment I think he's going to ask me what I'm doing fly-tipping computers over his back fence. He walks down the garden until he's standing alongside me and we're both staring at the water, neither of us saying a word.

'I'm so sorry for your loss,' he says eventually, and my eyes cloud with tears as I nod. I don't trust myself to speak.

'I cannot bear watching Clara and Teddy in there.' He turns his head away from me, so I almost don't catch what he says. 'I look at them and I see you and Flo.'

Shocked, I stare at him. Even during his father-of-the-bride speech on my wedding day he made no mention of my childhood. All of the anecdotes were carefully selected as being post his return. Anger and sadness rushes up within me but I choke it back down, gripping my hand into a tight fist, feeling the nails dig into the palm of my hand until it hurts.

'They will survive, just as Flo and I did.'

'Yes, they will, but they shouldn't have to and neither should you.'

'Ohhhh!' I hear myself give a strange sort of cross between a gasp and moan of pain as my head falls back in disbelief and I stare up at the sky 'Go on then, Dad! Let's hear it. Obviously the day after my husband has died is the perfect timing for this conversation, having kept me waiting for thirty-three years.' I turn to face him.

'It's *because* I can see it in front of me!' Dad has tears streaming down his face. 'I look at those two little children and they've done nothing wrong. Nothing! But I swear this isn't history repeating itself.'

'Really? Then who was the woman I saw you kiss in the car.' I have nothing more to lose. I feel empty. 'The one who told you she loved you?'

He closes his eyes, scrunches them up so tightly. 'My wife.'

I step back from him in shock and confusion.

He turns to face me, frightened. 'I was still married to someone else when I met Mum, although we'd been apart for a while. I left her. She was a violent woman. She used to…' he swallows, 'slap me, pinch me, pull my hair… it sounds like little kid stuff, I know, but… she burnt me once with the back of a hot spoon of all things,' he laughs flatly and pulls up his sleeve to reveal the dark patch of rough skin on his forearm I've noticed a hundred times before but always assumed was a birthmark. 'I feel stupid saying it like this now, but back then there wasn't really very much you could do for things like that. There wasn't anyone I could tell. I did try. I had a mate who was a police officer. He told me to give her a slap back and that'd sort her out. I didn't want to do that – so I left. Just walked out. I shouldn't have, but there you are. She had plenty of money in her own right; I didn't leave her destitute or anything. The house was hers anyway. Her parents bought it for us outright when we married.' He shrugs and breathes out deeply, looking up the river. 'Anyway, I met Mum and I just didn't tell her. We fell in love, we got married and had you two. We were very happy, but yes, you're right,' he says, before I can speak, 'all that time, I was married to someone else too.

'And eventually she came for me. It had been years, I thought it was done, but she appeared in the car park – you and I had gone shopping. I thought I was hallucinating. She just climbed into the car, and I didn't want a scene, I didn't want to frighten you. She told me I was to come back with her or she'd tell everyone what I'd done. I'd have gone to prison for bigamy, Charlotte. I'd have lost my job; we would probably have lost the house because the mortgage was completely in my name. Again, that was just how it was then. I told your mother, and we agreed I should go. It was for the best. We didn't want that woman anywhere near you. She was pure poison. So I left. I still looked after you all – financially I mean – I just wasn't there, and that broke my heart.'

He clears his throat. 'When she died, eight years later, I asked your mother if I could come home and she said yes.' His lip trembles again and fresh tears run down his face. 'I'm not asking for forgiveness, but that's the truth. We obviously never talked about it with anyone. I don't know where it would all stand now, you see… if we're legally married since my first wife died. She didn't leave me anything – I didn't benefit from it in any way; she left the house to a cat rescue charity. Anyway, Mum and I act like it's not a problem, so no one questions anything. No one ever has. Everyone thinks I had an affair and just came home in the end.'

'Mum didn't see it in my diary then?' I say faintly.

'See what?' he says, confused.

'I wrote about the woman kissing you in my diary. I thought Mum had seen it and thrown you out.'

He shakes his head, not understanding the implication of what I'm saying, that this is something I held to my chest for *years*. 'No love, it was nothing like that. There was no anger. Mum loved me. She's always loved me, as I love her.'

I'm so overwhelmed I feel light-headed. I cannot process any more. This is too much. He stares at me, worried, then quickly continues.

'But sweetheart, what I'm trying to say is you've been let down so badly by me and Tris and I'm so very sorry. Just because someone tries their best doesn't mean it's good enough. I want you to know, though, that I am here now. I can't make up for what you, and now they, have lost – but I'll be alongside you every step of the way to help hold you up, if you'll have me?'

I don't say anything. I simply can't and he nods quietly, to acknowledge he understands, before turning on the spot and walking back up to the house.

I stare unseeingly at the river as the wind blows, forming ripples on the surface of the water. *Come on! Come on!* I hear Tris's voice in my head. *It's time to go. Long journey ahead...*

I turn and go to find my children.

CHAPTER TWENTY

MIA

The first phone call comes at 11 a.m. on Monday lunchtime while I'm curled up on Mum and Dad's sofa, staring mindlessly at an old episode of *Friends* on TV:

AGENT!!!

I ignore it.
The phone goes again at lunchtime:

AGENT!!!

'Don't you think you ought to answer that?' Mum nods at it, able to see the screen from the other end of the sofa, where she's sitting reading yesterday's Sunday supplements, my untouched sandwich on a plate between us. 'I know you don't feel like it now, but there's going to come a moment when you'll be grateful for a new project to focus on.'

'I don't know what to say to them.'

'You tell them the truth. You've done nothing wrong, Mia.'

My eyes well up for the millionth time today and the call goes to voicemail again. Mum puts her magazine down and moves over to hug me, as I lean on her and sob, the sleeves of my jumper pulled down over my hands.

The phone starts to ring again.

AGENT!!!

She picks it up and holds it out to me. 'It's obviously important and you can't run away forever.'

I take a deep breath. 'Hello?'

'Mia!' Jack sounds delighted. 'I've tracked you down! I'm sorry – you must be feeling hounded. I called you earlier this morning and Cary is trying to reach you, too, I think. Don't panic, it's all good. We've just concluded your American deal. There was a feeding frenzy, but we have arrived at a neat two million dollars with a *very* nice publisher. Huge congratulations! Our book-to-screen agents also want to talk to you about a couple of producers who want to option the film rights. I'll let them discuss that with you though.'

'I can't make any sense of this,' I whisper.

He laughs then says soberly: 'I know. You're right, it is surreal and this certainly doesn't happen to everyone. Talk to me if this starts to feel a little *too* much.'

'Jack, I was arrested for manslaughter over the weekend.'

There is a stunned silence.

Mum places a gentle hand on my arm for support.

I take a deep breath. 'I was attacked by my boyfriend. Everything went a bit wrong.' I clear my throat and try not to start crying again. 'I'm currently on bail waiting to see if I'm going to be charged.'

Another long silence.

'Jack?' I pause. 'Are you still there?' Has he hung up on me? My heart starts to pound.

'Hello? Hello? Mia? This is such a bad line. I didn't hear a word you said just then.'

I close my eyes. I'm going to have to repeat it all? 'I said that over the weekend I was arrested for manslaughter.'

'Nope – still nothing, I'm afraid,' he says firmly. 'Ah, you're back! Now Cary mentioned that over the weekend you were taken ill.' He speaks pointedly. 'You poor thing.'

I look at the phone in confusion. What?

'You had to miss the last show and will likely be out for the rest of the week, I gather? It's *such* a common reaction to the end of a run. Your body just says enough is enough, doesn't it? I think that's a very wise decision. Shut yourself away for the week, don't talk to anyone and when everything is back to normal, we'll hit the ground running again. Why don't we check in at the end of the week to see where the land lies?'

The penny finally drops. 'I think I really do need to take the rest of this week out to recover, yes.'

'Good,' he says. 'That's settled then. You can't mess around with health. I'll tell Cary and we'll carry on this end, minding the shop. It's going to take a little while to sort contracts, in any case, and I daresay Hollywood isn't going anywhere either. You take care. Proper flu is a nasty business.'

'OK. I'll be in touch.' I hang up and stare at the phone. Finally I turn to Mum. 'I think I've just been told in so many words that the deals will be off if everyone finds out about this. He's going to carry on in the meantime but I've only got about a week.'

'A week?' Mum exhales. 'Well, we travel hopefully.'

I'm not really listening to her. Charlotte will never be able to resell this book now. Not after every publisher has already read it and thinks I wrote it. She must curse the day she laid eyes on me. I lean my head on the side of the sofa and stare into space. This is all such a mess. I curl up a little tighter.

Mum takes the sandwich away, untouched.

*

'Why don't you call the solicitor and ask her the time frame you're looking at?' Mum appears in the doorway a couple of hours later to find I've barely moved. She walks across the room and puts another log on the woodburner that she lit earlier when I couldn't stop shivering. 'Forearmed is forewarned.'

'She told me on Saturday it was a question of waiting until the police have prepared an advice file, or something, and that they would be in touch with me to let me know what happens next, if I'm going to be charged or not.'

'I still think it's worth asking.' She takes the blanket from the other sofa, comes over and puts it round me, tucking my legs in as if I'm an invalid. 'It would be so very unfair if these opportunities were to disappear because of what happened.'

I look up at her, wondering if I should just tell her the truth about the deal with Charlotte: *By the way, Mum – I didn't write the book at all – and now I've fucked it all for Seth's wife, having already fucked her husband.* Instead, I pick up my phone and call the solicitor. 'Can I speak to Penny Osbourne, please?'

Mum looks relieved and sits down on the arm of the sofa to listen.

'Mia. Hello,' Penny is brisk when I'm put through. 'How can I help?'

'I was just wondering how long you think it will be until the police make a decision one way or the other? We didn't really talk specifics on Saturday; I should have asked. I'm sorry.'

'That's fine. Sadly I don't have a concrete answer to give you. The police are still evidence gathering and waiting for items like the post-mortem results. Once that has concluded, they prepare an advice file which is passed to the Crown Prosecution Service for review. That process can take days, sometimes it sits on various desks for months. Just a waiting game now, I'm afraid.'

'Months?' I repeat incredulously. 'It's just I have a work situation that this is going to affect.'

'Well, you're under no legal obligation to tell an employer that you're on bail – unless they specifically ask or a contract requires you to disclose that sort of information.'

Pretty much *exactly* my situation then.

'Do contact me in the meantime if you have any other questions, won't you?' She waits for me to get off her phone. I can hear the suppressed impatience in her voice. I doubt she means to be rude, she just has more important things to do.

'I guess you heard. Worst-case scenario – months,' I tell Mum once I've hung up. 'Could you just give me a minute, if that's all right? This is all feeling a little bit much.'

'Of course. Come through into the kitchen when you're ready. I'll make a cup of tea.'

I am swimming in tea and tears. I know I shouldn't be, but I miss Seth. I have no rational explanation for how or why he was that person I didn't recognise on Friday night. I don't understand. Was he always like that and there were signs I didn't see? Was he waiting until he felt comfortable to show his true colours? I have never had a boyfriend be violent with me, ever – but I've always said that if someone did, it would happen once and we would be over. He hurt my neck. Drunk or not, he hurt me. I was terrified.

I stare out of the window and rub my head with my hand. I am starting to feel uncomfortable in my own skin. This all feels horribly reminiscent of when I had my breakdown, sitting around in the house for days after my biological father's death, while the world carried on as normal, on the other side of the window. Sometimes I would lie in bed for so long, unable to get up, that my shoulders would ache from lying on my side so much. I don't want to go back to that place, ever again. And now to cap it all, my being on bail is going to take away everything that Charlotte has left. She must be going out of her mind with grief and anger. I would have so many questions in her shoes:

How long had it been going on?

Did I know she was his wife when she offered the deal to me?
What really happened on Friday night?

I watch a mother walking slowly down the street, past the window, holding the hand of her small toddler. She waits patiently as he bends to inspect something on the ground, before gently urging him on their way. I exhale then jump guiltily although it's only an alert pinging in on my phone. An email from… I glance at the banner on the screen listlessly…*Charlotte Graves?*

I sit up in shock and fumble to open it.

Meet me in the Crypt again, Friday at 11 a.m. Please?

That's it. Nothing else. But that 'Please?' poleaxes me. It sounds so desperate, so unlike her. So she does have questions. Of course she does. I have plenty of my own.

She must know that I can't, though? It was one of my conditions of bail. I'm not allowed to meet with her. I could be arrested again if I did. I know I owe her, but I just can't. I put the phone back down on the sofa, close my eyes and see Seth inches from my face shouting *LIAR!*

There is a sudden rush of air in the otherwise silent room, and my eyes snap open again. The log that Mum put on the fire has just caught and fierce flames blaze in the grate behind the glass as the wood becomes engulfed, the bark lifting in the intense heat and peeling away from the grain below, like skin.

It dies back down surprisingly quickly and before long it's only quietly glowing – little more than stubs of white ash and charcoal, flaking and wisping away into nothing.

I might have died had Charlotte not found me and called for help. She's asked to see me.

Maybe it's just as simple a choice as that?

*

I don't respond to her email but I don't think about much else. The weather has turned again, rain flattening against the windows daily, as storms blow through – on their way to Europe, according to Dad. I keep my position on the sofa, finally reading and then immediately rereading, Charlotte's book.

It's certainly a page-turner. I have no idea what is going to happen next and I'm quite good at seeing where things are heading normally because I read so many scripts… but I'm not sure I like the heroine very much. Like Jack said, she's detached from her family and children in a way that's unusual for a female character. She basically doesn't feel part of her own life; she's pretty unhappy and bits of it are so brutally honest and raw, it makes me cry, particularly because the underlying theme is clearly trust and betrayal – which just breaks my heart, for both me and Charlotte, really. I can even hear Seth's voice in places – she's obviously borrowed some of his phrases and mannerisms, as I suppose you do when you spend a lot of time with someone and become so familiar with their way of seeing the world it occasionally becomes your own. It's both comforting and deeply disturbing to find him living within the words she's written.

I thought I'd have all of that with him; a life spent together. I was so sure we felt that way about each other. It felt instinctively right. I don't understand how I got it so very badly wrong. He put his hand around my neck… and yet I read the book obsessively, looking for him in every chapter, until I practically know it by heart, as the end of the week creeps ever closer.

*

Mum is surprised but delighted to see me dressed and in the kitchen for breakfast by 8 a.m. on Friday morning, which makes me feel both shabby and jittery for not being honest about the real reason behind my new lease of life.

'Where's Dad?' I ask, glancing at the side to see if his keys are here. They're not. He must be taking the boys to school this morning for Kirsty and Bill. I'm absorbing into the routines of my parents' life with alarming ease. While it's been a welcome release to pass all responsibility to someone else, I can't stay anaesthetised forever. Today will be my baptism of fire.

'He's gone to meet Julia at the flat. We've decided to sell it and you know she's always asked for first refusal to turn it back into one house. In any case, I think with everything that's happened it might be a bit tricky selling it on the open market. It might be a little less exposing if Julia takes it, and I don't think she's the kind of person to be bothered about any of that in the slightest.'

They're going to have to do this because of me. Yet more money I've cost them. 'You don't have to sell it.'

'I want to,' she says simply. 'It has no place in our family's future. It's time to move on. So you're going out?' She stands up and reaches for the cafetière and two mugs, before returning to the table. 'That's good. It's a much nicer morning today. It'll do you good to get a breath of air.' She nods at the freshly washed clouds through the window, scudding across a blue sky, for once.

'I'm only meeting a friend for coffee near Charing Cross this morning, then coming home again.' I look away as I speak and I feel her notice.

'That'll be nice.' She asks me no questions after that, so I tell her no lies. Sometimes it's just easier that way.

*

It's harder than I thought it would be, being back among so many people, having been hiding for five consecutive days. The overland journey is bad enough, but I can feel the energy of people's thoughts and the intent of their body language bouncing off the walls of the tube tunnels when we all descend underground to the platform – and the rush of hot air blowing dirtily through our hair as the train approaches. I don't like the feeling of strangers standing so close to me in the carriage and having to touch the pole with my bare hands to steady myself when we set off makes me actively uncomfortable. I take a tissue from my pocket when I re-emerge above ground at Charing Cross station and wipe my palms repeatedly, but I don't feel clean. *Five days*, that's all it's taken me to arrive back here again at… Nut Job Central. I breathe out and try to steady my mind, but it's all too much: the echo of the tannoy announcing departures, feet striking the floor, voices, shouts, people getting too close, snatches of conversations as they pass. I'm shaking violently and have to lean on the wall outside the station entrance for a moment. It's just a coffee.

Which could get you arrested.

It's just a coffee.

After a few more breaths, I dig my hands deeper into my coat pockets and make my way over to St Martin-in-the-Fields and down the steps to the Crypt.

She's sitting at the same table as last time, and I see her visibly jolt when she looks up and realises I've arrived.

'You came.' She gets to her feet, rolling up the sleeves of the same black polo neck as last time before reaching for her purse. She's lost even more weight. Her wrists look like they might snap. I can see the sinews as she takes out a £5 note. 'What can I get you? Tea? Coffee? A time machine?'

I must look astonished, because she immediately lowers her eyes. 'Sorry,' she says briefly. 'Forgive me. That's not constructive, or funny. Tea or coffee?'

'A cappuccino if it's possible, please.'

I watch her walk to the counter as I take off my coat and hang it over the back of my chair. She stares straight ahead as she waits in the queue, arms folded. She's clearly exhausted. As she would be. Having ordered and paid, she carefully carries my drink back, without spilling any in the saucer, and places it down in front of me.

'How are you?' She sits down.

'Right now? Nervous.' I immediately spill some of my drink on the table as it slips in my grip. 'Oh no! I'm so sorry.'

She grabs a napkin and efficiently wipes it away. 'It was an accident, it doesn't matter at all. And don't be nervous. I'm not going to tell anyone we've met today. It was a big ask. I didn't think you'd come, so thank you.' She reaches into her bag and pulls out a tissue to blow her nose.

'I'm so sorry for your loss,' I say in the uncomfortable conversational pause that results. 'And for Clara and Teddy's loss too.'

She freezes for a moment; her eyes don't leave my face. 'Thank you.' She puts the tissue back in her bag.

'All I knew was that he had two children and was divorced. I'd been seeing him for little more than a couple of months. Had I known he was married, I would, of course, never have begun anything with him.' I blurt it all out, then sit there, unsure what to say next.

'It's all right, Mia. I know he lied to you too. I'm sorry for your loss as well.'

There's another awkward silence. 'Do you want to know what happened on Friday night?' I say tentatively, a little confused. 'Is that what this is about?'

She holds up a hand. 'It's OK. Tris told me everything just before he died.'

The noise of other people's chatter, chairs scraping, cutlery on plates fades away. I'm only aware of the shapes of bodies moving around us.

'He said that you were about to have sex when you changed your mind,' she looks down at the table, 'so he put his hand on your neck and tried to "persuade" you. You understandably took action, which necessitated hitting him forcibly over the head.'

I'm not sure I'm breathing. That's not true. I know, I was there.

She swallows before continuing. 'You may like to know that he very much regretted his actions and was aware that there was no excuse for them, regardless of the fact he was drunk. This is the information I gave to the police in an interview on Monday.'

I just stare at her. I see myself hitting him hard and him falling to the floor. What she has just said makes no sense. 'Seth was furious with me about something when he arrived, like, raging.' I can't think of any other way to describe it. 'Did he tell you why? Or what he thought I'd done?'

She takes a deep breath. 'He'd seen the book announcement in the press. He recognised my plot and thought that you had somehow stolen it from me. He panicked really – he knew we were about to find out about each other, or already had. He was very shocked when I told him about our deal and that we had no idea we were already connected – through him. Where are we with all of that, by the way?'

I blink, thrown. 'The deals you mean? You still want us to work together?'

'I can't afford not to. I have two young children to support. They need the income from the sale of that book. My share of a million quid is money I can't walk away from. I very much hope you don't want to either.'

My heart plummets. She's going to be devastated. 'I'm not sure we have a choice. I'm on bail until the police tell me they're taking no further action. I told Jack on Monday when he rang to tell me it's sold in the States for two million dollars—'

'Shit!' Charlotte breathes in disbelief.

'But,' I hold up my hands, 'he basically told me the deals will be off if the editors know about the charge.'

'What?' She is devastated. 'I told the police on Monday what he admitted to me. You had marks all over your neck. I saw them. This wasn't your fault!'

Ah – now I get it. This is what's behind Seth's 'confession'. He said no such thing; she has lied to the police.

'When you take on an acting job, you have to sign a contract that says you won't do anything that will embarrass the studio publicly – that includes allegations of offensive behaviour,' I tell her. 'They've always been there, but post #MeToo they're huge. I'm guessing book contracts are going the same way and I'm pretty sure "offensive behaviour" includes being charged with manslaughter. My solicitor told me on Monday that this case could take months to conclude. I'm meant to call Jack this afternoon and give him an update.'

Charlotte looks up at the ceiling and I'm stunned to see that she is trying not to cry. I don't know why that's such a surprise, she's just lost her husband and her children have lost their father, now this. I can't imagine what his children are going through. Seth talked so proudly about his kids. I had always assumed they would come to play a huge part in my life too, that I would help look after them. I was very ready for the reality of that responsibility. I was excited to meet them.

'*I* won't walk away from the deals, I promise you,' I tell her truthfully. 'But I just don't know that it's all going to happen now. I'm so very sorry, Charlotte. I'll keep everyone hanging on as long as I possibly can. I promise. I read it, by the way.' I wait for her to look at me. 'Several times. It's a really great book – I can see why they all want it.'

She exclaims and wipes her eyes. 'Thank you,' she whispers.

I take a deep breath. 'Charlotte, who is Florence to you? How do you know her?'

She jerks back away from me like I've struck her face.

'I saw her waiting for you in the car at the hospital. That's how you found out where I live, isn't it? Florence told you.'

I watch her gape at me, like a fish out of water, struggling for air. 'She's my little sister.'

Her *sister*? I feel faint and start to tremble again. She notices and reaches an urgent hand out across the table, placing it over mine. I flinch at her touch but she's right to try and anchor me. She's still wearing her wedding and engagement rings.

'Yes, she gave me your address when he didn't come home on Friday night. Teddy was ill; it wasn't like *Seth*,' she says his name awkwardly, 'not to call me back in those circumstances. I was frightened. But she didn't tell me anything else, certainly nothing private or… intimate that you might have disclosed to her in confidence. I promise you. Whatever you have told any counsellor has stayed there in that safe space.'

'You swear?' I whisper.

'Yes.' She takes her hand back.

'But she also told you who I was to Seth? So you'd contacted me to be your debut because of Edinburgh,' I'm trying to piece it all together and she looks away uncomfortably, 'and when Flo realised what you'd inadvertently done, she warned you? That sounds like the sort of thing my sister would do too.' I give a funny little laugh. It sounds weird, slightly disturbed. 'I honestly didn't know he was married.'

'You don't remember speaking to him at that talk of mine you came to?'

'No!' I'm astonished. 'Did I?'

She nods. 'I saw you.'

'I swear I don't remember that at all. You must have felt like you were falling apart.'

She swallows and I can see she's trying to keep a check on her emotions.

'I saw *you*, in my flat, when you were resuscitating him,' I say suddenly. 'I saw how distressed and angry you were when you were trying to get him to breathe.' I wasn't planning to tell her this. I've buried the memory all week, along with several other aspects of that night. 'I'm so sorry for how shocked you must have been. You had every right to be angry. I also understand why you told the police he assaulted me, because I don't believe Seth said that at all; mostly because it never happened. *I* told the police it did so I had the right to remain anonymous. I honestly have no idea why he was half-naked. Charlotte stop! Don't panic – I'm not going to tell anyone you lied to the police, I'd be dropping myself in it too, wouldn't I?' I feel dreadful. She looks as frightened as I imagine I did when Seth burst into the flat almost exactly this time last week.

'Are you going to tell anyone about Flo breaking your patient confidentiality? Is this about the money, because if it is, you can have it all.'

'Of course it's not about the money!' I'm completely bewildered. 'As if I'd ever blackmail you! And there might not even *be* any money: you got all of that – what I just said about the bail, right? I'm telling you I know everything so that we can both… let go of it all? I understand how you're feeling. You're not in this alone.'

She does a strange gulp. 'When you're hypothermic, your heart slows right down and becomes very faint. If you try to resuscitate someone too quickly when they're like that, it can catastrophically alter their heart rhythms…' She starts to tremble violently and I'm worried that people are going to start staring.

'You didn't know any of that when you found him though, did you?' I lower my voice. 'You did your best, Charlotte, and he was alive when he arrived at the hospital, so it wasn't anything you did and it wasn't anything I did either…' I sigh shakily and sit back. I really want a cigarette.

'Do you know that some people also have an extraordinary reaction when they are close to dying from the cold?' she continues. 'They voluntarily remove their clothes. It feels to them as if their skin is burning hot and they strip off. People have been discovered dead in the snow, up mountains, quite naked. They also have an overwhelming compulsion to hide beneath something – to crawl into a small dark space when they are ready to die.'

'Oh!' I gasp aloud. My hand instinctively flies up to cover my mouth. *That's* why he was half-naked? He must have been so frightened.

'I only know this because it's in a forensic pathology book I use for research.' Charlotte fumbles for another tissue. 'I guess because our version of events correlated enough they didn't consider it a possibility. I'm very distressed to have lied and made him into *that* man, but I'm also very glad lots of detail stayed out of the press, things that my children will now never have to read about when they're older, so perhaps the end justified the means. Either way, I'm grateful to you.'

'At least we don't have any more secrets.' I give her a sad half-smile.

'You know what? I'm sorry.' Her chair scrapes back suddenly and she stands up. Her skin has turned pallid, with a slight sheen to it. 'I can't do this, Mia. Maybe it's a good thing that the deal has been taken out of our hands but I should have told you it was off before now. You need to walk away from me.'

I'm completely confused. We've just laid everything bare. I *want* to help her, and Clara and Teddy. 'But, Charlotte…'

'We both need to make a fresh start, to leave behind everything that's happened. Take care of yourself, Mia.' She grabs her coat and bag. 'None of this is your fault, you didn't do anything wrong, please know I mean that sincerely – but I can't see you or speak to you again.'

Before I can say another word, she hurries from the room.

'Charlotte?' I call after her desperately and people around us look over, but she doesn't stop, disappearing up the stairs to the street above.

I feel like a naughty child, deliberately left behind when I don't know what I've done wrong. My eyes fill with tears and as I turn back to the table two older women are already hovering in front of me, clutching trays, ready to swoop in case I decide to leave.

They don't ask me if I'm OK, just watch, beadily, like magpies as I get shakily to my feet and reach for my coat – taking our seats before my back is even turned.

I automatically feel for my phone and purse in my pockets as I make my own way to the stairs. Glancing at the screen I discover I've had two missed calls. One 'No Caller ID' and the other is a London number I don't recognise. There's very little signal down here.

I'm watching Charlotte walking away from me, past the National Gallery towards Piccadilly, when my voicemail finally kicks in:

'Mia, hi. Penny Osbourne. I've just had a call from the OIC – that's the officer in charge of the case – to let me know that you've been NFA'd. They tried to reach you, but couldn't. You'll get a letter in the post explaining your bail has been cancelled and their systems will be updated. But essentially that's it. The police won't be taking any further action. Do call me if you have any questions but in the meantime, I'll—'

'CHARLOTTE!' This time I yell her name at the top of my voice. Lots of people turn round, albeit briefly – it's London after all – and she stops and stares back in surprise, shielding her face from the sun shining right in her eyes, blinding her and making it virtually impossible to see me, as I run eagerly towards her.

CHAPTER TWENTY-ONE

CHARLOTTE

'That's it, brave girl.' Flo hands me some tissues, my eyes streaming, and I wipe my mouth, still bent over. 'Do you want some water?'

I hesitate and my stomach lurches. 'No, I think I'm going to go again.' I brace myself, my mouth opens and I feel my throat rise as my body starts to take over. I wretch so violently it feels like I'm turning inside out as I hang there helplessly before straightening up. 'OK, that's it. I've nothing left. It's not even water coming back up now.'

'Talking of which – here.' Flo passes me a bottle. 'Little sips. You don't want to get dehydrated.' She glances at her watch.

'Just give me a minute.' I hand the bottle back, lean against the wall and close my eyes for a moment trying to steady myself. 'It's my own fault. I haven't eaten anything all day. My nerves are shot to bits.'

'I think we ought to go back out there.'

I nod. 'I know. One second, that's all.' I step out of the toilet cubicle and over to the sink. 'I had a bad dream about Tris last night.' I keep my voice low as I start to wash my hands. 'I couldn't reach him. He was under the surface of shallow water – saying something that I didn't understand. Bubbles were coming up. His eyes were wide. He knew he was dying.' I clear my throat, my voice starting to shake, and straighten up to reach for a paper towel before drying my hands methodically.

'You should have come and got me. That sounds really distressing.' Flo joins me in front of the mirror.

My eyes well up and I blink the tears back furiously before throwing the towel in the small dark hole next to the sink and turning to face her. 'This is all my fault. It's all I can think when everyone tells me how sorry they are for my loss.'

She shakes her head emphatically. 'You were angry with him; you wanted to hurt him. That's normal. You are not to blame for what happened after that.'

'Wanting revenge is one thing, carrying it out is another. The pain I've caused is far worse than the one it was supposed to ease. He's *dead* because of what I did, Flo.'

Flo places her hands on my arms, forcing me to look at her. 'No. That's not true. It was his choice to betray you… time and time again. He lied repeatedly to you – to all of us. We all thought he was a constant, someone who wore his heart on his sleeve and told it like it was. I really respected him for that, but it was all lies. *I* feel extraordinarily let down by him, so I can't imagine what it feels like to be you. It is not your fault he's dead. You really want to blame someone – blame *me*. I should never have told you he was sleeping with Mia. I wasn't in my right mind the day of Mum and Dad's party. If I'd kept quiet about their affair, it might have burnt out and been something you'd never have known about.'

I turn back to the mirror, forcing her to release me, so that I can wipe what's left of the smudged shadows of mascara from under my eyes. 'You couldn't have known what was going to happen. You did what you thought was right at the time.' I let my head hang. 'This is so wrong. I can't do this.'

'Yes, you can,' she says simply. She puts her hand on my shoulder this time. 'You know I've always felt that families keeping secrets from each other is unhealthy and destructive? Well that's a sanctimonious, naïve load of crap. What I thought gave me the right to be an expert on anyone's marriage, never mind the ones closest to me, beggars belief. You need this opportunity to say goodbye to Tris. However it ended, you had two children together, very much born of love. Honour that today, because that beautiful boy and girl are your greatest achievement as a couple and they need you now. You asked them if they wanted to come and they did. Let's help them through this.'

She's right. Clara and Teddy are more important than anything else. I nod, wipe my eyes, smooth my jacket and take a deep breath. They are waiting alongside Mum and Dad in the foyer, holding hands uncertainly. They look so small. I smile at them and hold out *my* hands to them. We will do this together.

We walk into the rapidly filling church. I'm keeping my gaze firmly on them, smiling encouragingly as we walk down the aisle towards Tris, but the flowers I chose from the three of us, now sitting on top of the coffin, are heavily scented white freesias and roses, the same as my wedding bouquet. When I catch the familiar perfume I have always loved, it makes me lift my head. I blink and for a brief moment the hands of a thousand clocks spin backwards in a blur and I see him turning to face me in morning dress, his face full of love. I feel my wedding dress swishing about me, my heart barely containing the joy. I have to close my eyes briefly at the physical pain, blindly letting the children guide me for a second, and when I open them again, he is gone.

*

When the service is over and everyone has left, the children and I have one last moment in the peace of the still church, just the three of us.

'What's going to happen to Daddy now?' Clara asks.

'To Daddy's body, you mean?' I say carefully, 'because everything that made Daddy him, – all of his love, memories and thoughts… his soul… – has already gone to Heaven, hasn't it?'

She nods. 'What's going to happen to his body?'

I take a deep breath. 'Well, because Daddy doesn't need it now – a bit like when a butterfly comes out of a cocoon – Daddy's body will be put into a very warm room and it will turn into soft ashes, like a powder, but it won't hurt him because Daddy isn't there anymore. He's in Heaven.'

'We can't go there because you have to be dead to go to Heaven,' says Teddy.

'That's right, clever boy.'

'Where does Heaven look like?'

'I don't know,' I confess, 'because I've never seen it, but I imagine it's very beautiful, because love is beautiful, isn't it? Come on. Let's go and find the others.'

We reach the door of the church and Flo meets us.

'Now, do you want to go to the pub and have something to eat with everyone else?' I ask the kids, 'or shall we go home? What do you fancy?'

'I'm tired,' Clara says. 'Can we go home and watch a movie?'

'It's my turn to choose,' says Teddy quickly.

'Let's flip a coin when we get back,' Flo suggests. 'Would you like to come in my car with me? Mum's put your seats in it. Do you remember my friend Harry? He watched the fireworks with us. He's going to come with us. Is that all right?'

Clara nods but pulls me down to her eyeline and whispers: 'Are you coming home too, Mummy?'

'I'll come back with Nona and Grandpa after I've said a quick goodbye to everyone at the pub, is that OK?'

She nods.

'I think I might have some Haribos in the car?' Flo frowns as if she's trying to remember. 'Shall we go and see?'

'I want some,' Teddy says immediately. 'Daddy likes Haribos.'

Flo takes their hands. 'Which ones were his favourites? Bye, Mummy! See you in a bit. I like the eggs.' She leads them away gently, and I watch until they're safely in the car, waving, before I go and join Mum and Dad to drive to the crematorium.

*

Moira, Donald and Tris's aunt are the only other people present at the short, private committal. His mother will not look at me as she leaves after the final blessing; she simply acts as if I'm not there, wiping her wetly streaked cheeks as she walks past me. But she's waiting for me by the car.

Shaking with rage in her heavy tweed suit, she's going hunting, for sure. 'How does a healthy man just die?' She stares at me, unblinking, demanding an answer. 'You were there with him at the end? *Just* you, so you tell me! How did my boy die, eh?' She steps forward and I can't be the only one that thinks she's going to hit me, as my father steps between us.

'No,' he says simply. 'It doesn't happen like this. You know how he died. We all do.'

'Once is an accident, twice is surely habit, Charlotte?' Moira ignores him, aiming the comment over Dad's shoulder.

My heart is beating so hard I can hear it in my ears as I simply turn and walk away from them all, forcing myself to ignore the accusations she is continuing to call out behind me. Mum finds me in tears in the garden of tranquillity.

'I know I said I'd come for a quick drink at the wake, but I just want to go back to the kids now. Can you drop me off? It's on the way.'

I expect her to tell me I ought to at least show my face, but she doesn't. 'Of course. Dad and I will host on your behalf and make sure everyone understands, which they will. Don't worry. There's no right or wrong way to do this.'

*

I get back to find the children happily watching *The Aristocats*. I give them a kiss and go upstairs to take my new suit off and hang it up in the wardrobe, changing back into my jeans and a sweatshirt as Flo sticks her head round the door.

'You OK?'

I clear my throat. 'You just missed Moira accuse me outside the crematorium of killing Tris.'

Flo's mouth falls open in horror. 'What?'

'She's certainly upped the blame stakes, that's for sure. I wasn't always the best wife to him. I was often tired, impatient, irritable a lot of the time. I think I was quite a difficult girlfriend to Daniel too… and I should never have sold Tris's book from under him, but to say I literally killed them?' I try to laugh but it sounds slightly hysterical.

'No one seriously believes that, Charlotte, not for a minute. Moira is deranged with a mother's grief. She didn't mean what she said.'

'Yes, she did. Even supposing I was angry enough with him to do it, which I wasn't, as if I'd ever do something like that to Clara and Teddy? Tris was their father! I'd never willingly put my own children through that pain.' I sit down on our bed and start to pull on a pair of socks. 'Plus it's actually *hard* to kill someone.'

Flo crosses her arms and says nothing.

'Especially in an ITU full of people. The police were right outside the door, nurses going in and out all of the time. You can't just slip something into a glass of water, cut tubes or turn off machines. There's always a post-mortem and it would show up.'

'Charlotte—'

My teeth are starting to chatter. 'I'm just saying you'd have to be very subtle to pull it off in those circumstances without getting caught. Something like purposefully pinching the IV tube to block

Lucy Dawson

the fluids, but releasing your grip every time the nurse came to check it. Tris had a cardiac arrest. He was a normal fit and healthy man, but he'd been boozing, had a long lie on the floor, he was dehydrated and hypothermic.

'I've told you about that sort of thing before, haven't I?' I continue desperately. 'It's impossible to shock a flatline, they just do that in TV shows for dramatic effect. It's cardiac compressions, and only then, if you get some rhythm back, can you go for the shock treatment.'

'I know. Nothing breaks like a heart.'

I burst into tears again and she comes over to sit on the bed next to me, holding me while I sob quietly, so the children don't hear. Harry appears at the doorway as I'm blowing my nose, carefully carrying a plate of toast and jam, and a cup of tea, which he puts down on the top of my chest of drawers, disappearing without a word.

'I'm really glad you're giving it another try with him.'

She blushes. 'Me too. Not the queen of self-sabotage anymore, eh?'

So much has changed so very quickly. I take a deep breath and stand up. 'We need to go back downstairs. I want to sit with the kids. Did you see Mia at the church?'

Flo jerks back from me in shock. 'No! Was she there?'

'Probably not if you didn't see her; I didn't look. I invited her—' I feel suddenly tired at Flo's look of astonishment, 'but I didn't expect her to show really. But then again, I also thought she might. It's OK. We've talked about you. It's not an issue. She's not going to say anything.'

'It's "not an issue"?' Flo repeats slowly. 'And you invited her to Tris's funeral?' She shakes her head as if she's not sure where to start.

I walk over to my tea. 'You don't need to say anything. I told you before, I never blamed her for what happened.' The cup is so hot it's burning my skin and I have to set it down again once I've gingerly taken a sip. I have a bit of the toast too, which makes my tummy knot painfully but also makes me realise I am actually hungry. 'That's the point of funerals, isn't it? To mark the point of goodbye – shouldn't she have that opportunity too? Do you think he was meant to be with Mia?' I take another sip of tea and look out of the window. 'He saw her too, that first day I met her. I watched him notice her. I thought it was because she looked like me, but in hindsight, do you think that was the moment he fell in love with her?'

Flo considers her words carefully. 'I think you're completely exhausted and now is maybe not the time to think about any of this.'

'I'm not torturing myself. In some ways it almost makes what I've done with the book easier – my stealing it from Tris, I mean. At least Mia's getting half of everything, which he'd probably want. Although why is it that when he was alive, I was OK with not telling her he'd written the book – like I was protecting her from him – but now he's dead, not coming clean feels like I'm exploiting her? And yet I'm *still* letting it happen. She *still* believes the only reason I contacted her to be my debut was because of Edinburgh.'

'Charlotte, please. Give your poor brain a break from this. Just for today.'

'I think about it all the time,' I confess. 'She ought to know he wrote it.'

Flo sighs deeply. 'I don't agree. This way, Teddy and Clara benefit from the sale of their father's book, exactly as he would want them to. You said Mia is about to fly to LA to meet the producers of the film, there's going to be more press coverage, more roles coming her way. Doors are opening. You've done that for her, no one else. It's right that Mia is being paid for her role in this, because she's doing a job, playing a part, but she doesn't need to know any more than that. Moreover, if you *do* tell her the truth, the only person who will feel better is you.'

I fall silent, my restless thoughts still spinning in endless circles. Round and round…

'I wasn't paying lip service earlier, I am now very much of the opinion that some secrets should be kept,' Flo insists. 'Look at Mum and Dad, what good would it do anyone if they told *their* story now? The people who need to know, do – and that's enough. It's the same with you and the book.'

'If I let this continue, I'll be using her.'

'I wish someone would use me to the tune of at least a million quid.'

I exhale. 'I'm serious. I'm still manipulating Mia now. That's wrong.'

Flo stares at me. 'You're going to tell her, aren't you?'

'It would be the right thing to do.'

'For what it's worth, I think you're making a huge mistake.' She gets up. 'You don't have to decide right now anyway. Just lie down for a minute. The kids are fine downstairs. I'll tell them where you are. Give yourself a moment to just be.'

I move away from the window and do as I'm told, lying down on the bed like a child. She even kisses me on the forehead before leaving the room quietly.

I glance at the space next to me where I am so used to Tris lying. It feels vast today.

'I don't know what to do,' I whisper, closing my eyes.

The front door bell rings suddenly downstairs and I immediately open them again with a jump.

'Charlotte!' Flo yells.

I sigh. 'Coming.' I get up automatically and as I round the corner, looking down the stairs, the person Flo is letting into the hallway glances up at me.

It's Mia.

CHAPTER TWENTY-TWO

MIA

I'm clutching the bouquet so tightly my hand is aching. My sister was right – it was a mistake to come, and all Kirsty was expecting me to do was leave the lilies on the doorstep. She'll be doing her nut in the car right now having watched me ring the bell, walk in and the door close behind me... but as soon as I saw Charlotte through the upstairs window I realised I'm hurting too much *not* to do this.

It's quite a narrow Victorian hallway. Once Charlotte is facing me, we're all uncomfortably close to each other in a triangle, my massive bunch of flowers at the centre. I clear my throat. 'These are for you.' I hold them out to her. 'I was going to come today, but when I arrived at the church it felt really wrong. I didn't want to intrude. Although I wanted to say thank you for thinking of me.'

Florence raises her eyebrows silently and looks down at the floor.

My heart starts to beat faster. 'I didn't actually expect you to be here, in my defence. I was only going to drop them off. It's nice to see you again, Florence.' I turn my head to her and smile politely.

She hesitates. Yes, what is the correct response to that, Florence? 'You too.'

'You're probably wondering how I know where you live – and this is a bit awkward,' I keep watching Florence, 'but my sister told me. True story.' I watch her face redden and I can't deny a part of me feels satisfied. 'We probably don't need to go into that right now though. Maybe it's one of those "least said, soonest mended" things. There was just something I wanted to say quickly, though, if that's OK? I'm not going to make a habit of stopping in.'

'I'm glad you've come, actually.' Charlotte looks at the flowers she's now holding and her voice sounds very odd – breathy. 'I need to talk to you too.'

Florence lifts her head and shoots a look at Charlotte, her eyes wide. I don't miss it.

'That sounds serious. Should I be worried?'

She swallows. 'Mia, I—'

'Mummy, I'm hungry.' A small boy suddenly appears in the doorway to my immediate left, arms hanging heavy and his face mock weary. He looks up in surprise to see a stranger, and I catch my breath. Seth's eyes. They are peas in a pod.

He moves instinctively towards Charlotte and regards me warily. Charlotte registers the reason for my shock immediately, passes the flowers to Florence and picks Teddy up, just about managing to balance him on her tiny hip.

'I'll start tea soon, darling.' She nuzzles his cheek and he leans into her. 'Just give me a minute to finish talking to my friend, and then I'll find you something to keep you going. In fact, maybe Aunty Flo can take you in the kitchen and find you a snack?' She places him down again as a little girl appears in the doorway too. 'Can I have one, Mummy?'

Charlotte smiles tiredly. 'Yes, flappy ears, you can.'

The girl looks pleased and glances at me shyly, it's like being spotted by a fawn – all luminous eyes and long legs – before she escapes off to the kitchen in pursuit of Teddy. As they run away from me it's ridiculous – weird even – but the sudden realisation that I will now never play the role in these children's lives I was on course for, hits me so hard I waver on the spot. I watch them over Charlotte's shoulder moving around a light, bright, cluttered kitchen, bifolds revealing a nice garden beyond. Florence follows them into the kitchen, shutting the door quietly behind them. I can see their shadows moving on the other side of the obscured panes of glass in the stripped pine door.

'Mia, there's something I need to tell you. It's about the book.'

'No!' I say quickly, surprising both her and me. 'Don't.' I correct myself. 'I mean, let's not talk about the book – not today.' I turn quickly and hurry to the front door, fumbling with the door-catch. 'I should go. I left my sister in the car; we need to get back for her kids. Teatime everywhere, right?' I laugh desperately.

'Mia, please,' she steps forward and puts a hand on my arm, 'I really need to—'

'No, you don't!' I shake myself free. 'Please, Charlotte, don't say whatever you think you need to, because you don't.'

Her eyes are wide and frightened. 'What do you?...'

'It won't be long until we get the first payment now,' I continue. 'I'll be in touch so you can tell me which account you want your fifty per cent paid into. Do you need to invoice me? You probably do. Anyway, let me know. I go to LA to start a big acting gig next week, but I'll shout when I'm back. We should talk about the second book soon, I expect? How good is that though, hey? It's been everything you promised me it would be, but it's also really important to me that you, Clara and Teddy are benefitting from all of this, too, given everything that's happened.' *I can't ram it home anymore than this. Please don't tell me...*

She hesitates. 'Didn't you want to say something?'

I shake my head. 'No. Forget it. I've really got to go – sorry.'

'Good luck then,' she says quietly, and I feel sick with relief.

'Thank you, Charlotte.' I almost reach out and hug her, only managing not to right at the last moment. That would be too much.

*

As I clatter down the steps poor Kirsty is pacing up and down outside her car, clutching her phone and looking demented.

'What the hell?' she demands furiously, once we're safely roaring off up the road. 'You were meant to put the flowers on the step and just go. I almost phoned the police! I swear to God, you have some sort of chip missing or something. *You just walked into her house!* What if she'd gone mental and attacked you? You've got to stop being so… impulsive and trusting!'

'I have stopped, I promise.'

'No, you haven't! You just—'

'Kirsty – I didn't write my book. Charlotte did. We just pretended it was me. Whoa – Careful! You nearly took the wing mirror off that Mini!' My sister swerves back and glances at me in shock again, before turning to look at the road in front of us.

'What are you talking about now?' she shouts. 'Why would *she* write your book?'

'Because she's a writer? I'm just the face of it. We were doing a deal together. I obviously didn't know she was married to Seth. I thought she was in the dark about me, too, but now I'm not so sure.'

Kirsty pulls sharply into a space alongside a school, turns the engine off and twists in her seat to face me. '*What?*'

'I think this has all been about her wanting revenge. It dawned on me the other night. I've always been able to hear his voice in the book. I thought it was because they were around each other so much, but it suddenly just clicked. He wrote it, not her. That's why he was so angry with me that night: he thought I'd stolen his book from him and sold it for a fortune. She's been passing off his book as her own.'

Kirsty breathes in sharply. 'To hurt him, or you?'

I shrug. 'Maybe both of us? Perhaps it was just about getting the money. I don't know. I guess it's about the cash *now*. I've been feeling devastated since it dawned on me. I know how ironic this

sounds, but I felt betrayed. I thought I'd have it out with her…
but you know I think she wanted to tell me the truth herself, just
then?' I rest my head back, exhausted. 'She feels really bad about
it, I can tell.'

Kirsty stares at me, her mouth open.

'And as soon as I realised that, I suddenly didn't want her to
say anything!' I laugh. 'You don't need to tell me how messed up
that sounds.' I look back at Kirsty with tears in my eyes. 'I didn't
want to hear her say that she'd only done this to hurt Seth. I need
to feel we've at least achieved something positive… I just saw
his kids and they're beautiful. Similar ages to the boys. Can you
imagine them suddenly being without you, or Bill?'

'Don't,' says Kirsty. 'It's every parent's worst nightmare.'

'Well, not *every* parent, but the good ones… Children don't ask
to be born, do they?' I look out of the window. 'They're completely
innocent in all of this.' I fall silent for a minute. 'I wanted to help
Teddy and Clara. I still want to help them. My agreement with
Charlotte was to split the money 50/50 but I'm going to give it
all to her for the children. I don't want *his* money. That way it can
almost be like they never met me at all.' I blink away the tears.

'But none of this was your fault, Mia.' Kirsty takes my hand.
'You didn't know he was married! You trusted him, that was your
only mistake.' She sighs. 'You just can't take people at face value.'

I laugh, and she frowns in concern. 'What? What's funny?'

'That's the whole reason this happened, because that's *exactly*
what I did.' I take a deep breath. 'Remember last year, when I
was starting to struggle a bit when Hugo and I got engaged and I
was thinking I might want to contact my birth parents after all?'

Kirsty nods, still stroking my hand.

'We were in Edinburgh. Hugo had gone to this stupid talk of
Ava's and I didn't want to. I went off on my own instead and I saw
this woman through the crowd. She was hurrying and I know how
this is going to sound, but she looked like me.' I wipe my eyes.

'I mean, *really* looked like me. She was about forty, right sort of age. I was stunned and I just found myself following her. She was doing an author masterclass, I snuck in and listened to her, she was amazing. I honestly thought I'd found my biological mother, just like that. Fate.' I laugh.

'Oh sweetheart!' Kirsty clutches my hand furiously. 'And she was…'

'Charlotte.' I nod. 'But then afterwards when I went and spoke to her, I asked her if she wrote under a pen name and she said she didn't, so that didn't fit. I knew my birth mother wasn't called Charlotte Graves. I asked her to sign a book for you and her signature didn't look anything like the one I'd seen on the documents Mum showed me either. It wasn't her – obviously. I was heartbroken but I forced myself to smile politely and chat about nothing.' I sigh at the memory. 'I should never have followed her. That way Seth wouldn't have seen me either… because we spoke, apparently. None of this would have happened – the only genuine coincidence was me winding up on her sister's counselling couch. That's how Charlotte found out I was sleeping with her husband.'

'Her sister was your counsellor?' Kirsty is horrified. 'She broke your confidentiality?'

'Yeah, she was at the house just now, actually, which was nice. I saw her collect Charlotte at the hospital the day Seth died.'

Kirsty shakes her head. 'I don't know what to say. I honestly don't know what to say to you.'

I shrug. 'I went looking for a mother, and I ended up taking a father.'

'Oh sweetheart, you didn't take anything! You just wanted to be loved! Isn't that what all of us want?'

I start to cry properly.

'Come on, let's go home.' She starts the car again. 'Mum will be getting worried.'

'Please don't tell her and Dad about the book not really being mine?' I beg. 'Partly because I really do want to help Charlotte and because I don't want them to be disappointed in me. Dad was so proud when I told him. Please, Kirst?'

'I won't say a thing, but they *are* proud of you, we all are. Book or no book.'

I look out of the window, thinking about Charlotte.

'I'm sorry she wasn't your biological mother,' Kirsty says. 'Especially given the actual one was such a disappointment. She didn't deserve a daughter like you, that's for sure. But *we* know how lucky we are.'

'I love you too,' I say quickly, and I do – so much. My family are everything to me.

But imagine if it really had been Charlotte. Millions of people living in the country and we're reunited at a festival in Scotland, of all places... more than an extraordinary coincidence: a second chance.

I wish that had been the story.

A LETTER FROM LUCY

I can't lie, I don't always feel in the right mood to sit down and write fiction that looks at the darker side of life. When I have to engineer it, I listen to a couple of music tracks that remind me of the voices I'm imagining. I pick different ones at the start of every book – a character soundtrack of sorts. I'm never going to be able to hear Mark Ronson (feat Miley Cyrus) *Nothing Breaks Like a Heart* or Sam Smith & Normani *Dancing with a Stranger* ever again without thinking of Charlotte and Mia. Have a listen if you fancy hearing some of the songs I wore out while writing this. I still think they're amazing tracks.

In fact, I had a blast writing this book and I'd love to hear what you think about it. Come and find me on Instagram, Facebook or Twitter, or if you have the time I'd be very grateful for any reviews you'd like to leave.

You can also keep up-to-date with all of my latest releases, by signing up at the following link. Your email address will never be shared, and you can unsubscribe at any time.

www.bookouture.com/lucy-dawson

I have a reader's club you can join too. There's a free short story to download when you sign up via the following link:

www.lucydawsonbooks.com/join-my-book-club

Until the next book though, thanks again for reading *Don't Ever Tell*. I'm very grateful for your time.

With all best wishes,

Lucy x

       📺   www.lucydawsonbooks.com

       📘   lucydawsonbooks

       🐦   @lucydawsonbooks

ACKNOWLEDGEMENTS

My grateful thanks to Laura Bethune, Nathan Johnson, Vanessa Jones, Carla Flexman, Neil White, Steve Cavanagh and Anna Mazolla. All errors are mine and not theirs.

Wanda Whiteley, thank you so much. As ever, you were bang on the money.

Sarah Ballard, Eli Keren and everyone at UA who continue to work so hard on my behalf – thank you.

Kathryn Taussig, Jenny Geras, Kim Nash, Noelle Holten and everyone at Bookouture – I am so grateful for the support you have given me. You've made publishing four books in eighteen months not only do-able but enjoyable. Thank you.

Thank you to the bloggers and authors who give generously of their time in spreading the word. The crime writing community is genuinely fabulous and being part of it is one of the biggest perks of the job.

Finally, thank you to my family and friends for still being there when I eventually put the laptop down and to you, for reading the end result.

Lightning Source UK Ltd.
Milton Keynes UK
UKHW010740220819
348410UK00001B/83/P